Ha...

So far on Kregen I had trod the land of the continents of Segesthes and of Turismond. But the continent of Havilfar was all new and unexplored by me, virgin territory. I fancied I was in for some wild adventures and some seething action in the future, and, as you shall hear, I was not wrong.

There must be absolutely no pining after Delia. I must not think of Vallia, or of Valka, until I was safely out of this mess. I had to do the bidding of the Star Lords, and then get myself home as quickly as possible.

Then I cursed. It was crystal clear why the Star Lords had brought me here.

I had to rescue a slave from these pens.

But which one?

"I shall not forget you, Dray Prescot!"

Manhounds
of
Antares

ALAN BURT AKERS

Illustrated by
JACK GAUGHAN

DAW BOOKS, INC.
DONALD A. WOLLHEIM, PUBLISHER

1301 Avenue of the Americas
New York, N. Y.   10019

Cover art by Jack Gaughan

DEDICATION:

For Deborah-Louise

THE SAGA OF DRAY PRESCOT

The Delian Cycle

FIRST PRINTING, AUGUST 1974

1 2 3 4 5 6 7 8 9

PRINTED IN U.S.A.

TABLE OF CONTENTS

List of Illustrations

A NOTE ON THE HAVILAR CYCLE

With this volume of his Saga, Dray Prescot is launched headlong into a brand-new series of adventures upon the planet of Kregen, that marvelous and beautiful, mystical and terrible world four hundred light-years away beneath the Suns of Scorpio.

Dray Prescot is a man above medium height, with straight brown hair and brown eyes that are level and oddly dominating. His shoulders are immensely wide and there is about him an abrasive honesty and a fearless courage. He moves like a great hunting cat, quiet and deadly. Born in 1775 and learning about life in the inhumanly cruel and harsh conditions of the late eighteenth-century wooden navy, he presents a picture of himself that, the more we learn of him, grows no less enigmatic.

Through the machinations of the Savanti nal Aphrasöe, mortal but superhuman men dedicated to the aid of humanity, and of the Star Lords, he has been taken to Kregen many times. In his early years he rose to become Zorcander among the Clansmen of Segesthes, and Lord of Strombor in Zenicce, and then a member of the mystic and martial Order of Krozairs of Zy. Against all odds Prescot won his way to the attainment of his single highest desire upon Kregen and in that immortal battle at The Dragon's Bones he claimed his Delia, Delia of Delphond, Delia of the Blue Mountains, as his own. And—Delia claimed him, in the face of her father, the dread Emperor of the Empire of Vallia, and before the rolling thunder of Prescot's men and comrades in the acclamations of Hai Jikai.

As Prince Majister, Prescot sailed aboard the Emperor's airboat back to Vondium, capital of Vallia, and his eyes and imagination were filled with the glories to come, for he has no need to tell us that he felt all his dreams had come true. Under his old scarlet and yellow flag, standing proudly at his side, with him sailed Delia, Princess Majestrix.

Thus ends "The Delian Cycle." This volume, *Manhounds of Antares,* opens "The Havilfar Cycle," and, as you will discover in the following pages, a new life does open for Dray Prescot on Kregen beneath the Sons of Scorpio; but that new life is cruelly different from all he expected and dreamed, hurling him into fresh adventure and danger among peoples and places far removed from those he knows and loves.

—Alan Burt Akers

Chapter One

Delia

Delia and I were married.

Delia of Delphond, Delia of the Blue Mountains, Princess Majestrix of Vallia, and I, Dray Prescot, were married.

If that sounds to you like the end of the story, then you are as deceived as I was. Many and many foolish young lovers have imagined, on Kregen no less than on Earth, that in the merry ringing of wedding bells lies the happy end of their adventures.

Oh, I knew the shadowy presence of the Star Lords might again manifest itself in the scarlet and golden shape of a mighty raptor, the Gdoinye, or the Savanti might decide out of their mortal but superhuman wisdom to make use of my services again.

But that was of the future, the might-be. Who reckons of the future when he is in love and newly wedded and all of Kregen glows and beckons before him?

But, just before we could be married, there was one other item of unfinished business. All the way back to the capital I felt strongly that I was moving into a new era of my life. That this was so, although not in the way I expected, you shall hear.

After we had returned from that immortal battle at The Dragon's Bones and life took its new turn, I felt I might be able to relax. The idea that Dray Prescot could ever relax may strike you as strange. But sometimes I can, and occasionally I have been able to throw off the cares of the world for a short time and follow my own inclinations. My relationship with the Emperor would remain on a strange footing, and I know that for all his own intemperate hauteur and pride, he feared me a little, even with armed men of his own choosing about him.

We flew down to land in the square before the Emperor's

palace. So impatient had he been to return that he had driven his airboat ahead of those following. I jumped down onto the hot stones of the square and looked about, surprised at the absence of people where normally one could see chattering citizens, Koters about their business, strings of calsanys, zorca chariots with their tall wheels flickering, all the brilliant hurly-burly of everyday life in Vondium.

A group of men rushed from the open gateways leading into the outer palace courtyards.

They wore garish green and purple rosettes pinned to their buff leather tunics, and flaunting green and purple feathers in their wide-brimmed Vallian hats.

With a curse I ripped out my rapier and dagger and thrust myself forward to stand before Delia.

She pushed me aside in the shoulder, and stepped up to stand boldly alongside me.

"Third party!" she said. "So there are more of them."

"Aye, my love," I said. "And you get back aboard the flier and take off—you and your father."

"If you think just because we are to be married I will meekly take orders from you, Dray Prescot, you hairy great graint, and fly away and leave you in peril—"

"Delia!"

"Come away, daughter! Let the warriors fight—"

"Yes, my father. Here is one warrior who will never run away, and I will never run from his side."

Well, that is my Delia. I had no time to argue with her. The men of the third party who had in secret infiltrated the other political parties of Vallia and sought to overthrow the Emperor rushed down upon me.

With a breath-wasting shout—for I wished to draw all their attention to me—I leaped forward, brandishing my weapons. You who have listened to my story this far will know I ordinarily never shout in action, and as for brandishing weapons, that is a waste of energy. But as I ran headlong at these oncoming killers I knew I must meet them and keep them in play well away from Delia until the remainder of our fliers arrived bringing with them my men of Felschraung and Longuelm, of Strombor, and Delia's Blue Mountain Boys.

Footsteps and the rasp of weapons at my back told me the handful of men aboard our flier had run to join me.

That made the odds a little better, but it was still something like a hundred to twenty.

That we should be thus caught up in this petty struggle

right at the end! We had been victorious and had crushed the third-party conspiracy and now Naghan Furtway, Kov of Falinur, and his nephew Jenbar, who had aspired to Delia's hand, had fled the country. And now this! Truly, I cursed at the stupid and senseless danger my Delia had run into here in the great square outside her own palace.

In a screech of blades the two parties met.

I fought. I had been fighting on and off for many burs past, I had been wounded—slightly, it is true—and now despite all those years of Earthly sailor training, the years with my clansmen of the plains, and as a swifter captain on the Eye of the World, I felt that I was tired.

But while hostile men sought to slay Delia, tiredness in my rapier arm and fatigue in my dagger arm and rubbery feebleness in my legs were sins, all sins, mortal sins!

So I fought and my rapier slashed down faces, and spitted guts, and my main-gauche weaved its silver net of protection, and I held the front cluster of whooping men, racing in for the kill. The crew from the airboat joined in, and, for a space, we halted that fierce onward surge.

But I knew we could not hold out very much longer.

These men attacking us with their flaunting green and purple third-party colors wore in banded rings about their sleeves the colors of yellow and blue.

Now blue is a most unusual color to be found in insignia in Vallia, for blue is the color of the nations of Pandahem, and between Pandahem and Vallia lay an old enmity.

But I knew these colors of blue and yellow belonged to a certain Kov of Zamra, one Ortyg Larghos, a relative of Nath Larghos, who had tried to suborn me into the ranks of the third party, and whose eye I had put out with a stone, and who had now, presumably, run overseas with his accomplices.

I could see Ortyg Larghos leaping about at the rear of his men, urging them on. He was a fat, paunchy man, with a saturnine face in which all the healthy brown hair had fallen away to leave a greasy ring of fuzz around his head and a face as smooth as a loloo's egg.

There was no opportunity for me to bring my great Lohvian longbow into action, which was a pity, for I fancied if I feathered the rast his men might run away. As it was, they looked to be a bunch of mercenary desperadoes, fighting for money. Among them there were Rapas and Ochs, a Brokelsh, even a Womox, but I saw no Chuliks. From this I took heart. It is notorious that the Chuliks, regarding themselves as the most expensive of mercenaries, are choosy as to their employers.

"Hai!" I yelled, and pressed, and flicked crimson drops from my rapier across the faces of a bunch that sought to rush me together. They blinked as the blood splashed them, and in that blinking I spitted them, one, two, three, and the fourth took my dagger through his heart.

A screaming lifted at my back.

Letting the Kov of Zamra go hang I swung about, jumping agilely the while in a frantic zigzag, and stared back at the flier.

A group had brushed past the Emperor's bodyguards, those few men who had descended with us on the bloody ropes from the shattered tower in the circle of The Dragon's Bones, and were carrying him off. I could not see Delia. My heart thumped so that I had to fight for breath.

Not now! Not so close to the end!

The way back lay over spilled blood and cumbering bodies.

At the flier I saw Delia.

She stood with a sword in her hand, a Rapa at her feet coughing his guts out, with his beaked bird's head all twisted askew. She waved the sword at me.

"My father! Dray—they've taken my father!"

"Stay here, Delia!" I yelled it at her with a force that drove her back as she started to run with me. "Go back!" Now I could see, slanting down into the square, the welcome sight of fliers planing in. "Here come Seg and Inch! Get them, my heart, for the sake of your father!"

She knew exactly what I meant.

I did not mean that she would run to the fliers and fetch Seg and Inch and Hap Loder and Varden and Vomanus for the sake of her father the Emperor at all. I meant that she should run there for my sake, for our sakes.

She would have none of it.

I couldn't stop.

The descending fliers had been spotted by the men of Kov Ortyg of Zamra, and they yelled in fear, and scattered, and ran. The group with the Emperor hared off away from the palace, and running with them, angling in from the side, ran Ortyg Larghos himself.

I ran.

That faintness overpowering me must not be allowed to interfere now. I loved Delia and Delia loved me, but if her father died now and my aid proved ineffectual there would be a shadow between us, a shadow never mentioned, never alluded to, but a shadow nevertheless.

The hot stones of the square burned up at me.

I caught them easily enough, for the Emperor was struggling. He was still a powerful man, and well-fed, and filled with the innate majesty of his position, so that he gave them some trouble. I truly believe that this manhandling with its attendant physical exercise changed something about that man, that dread Emperor, the father of Delia. He had never been handled so for years. So that when I caught them and laid about me, he could snatch up a sword and stand at my side.

He was no great shakes as a swordsman, and I had my work cut out to guard him as well as myself, but he kept pressing on, shouting fiercely, through his teeth: "Vallia! Vallia! By the Invisible Twins!" and, when a deflected lunge from me toppled a hapless wight into his path and he could slash down, he yelled: "Opaz the all-glorious! Vallia! Vallia! Drak of Vallia!"

Kov Larghos shrieked at his men.

"Take him, you fools! Cut down the barbarian! Take the Emperor!"

I could understand what Kov Larghos must be thinking. He had been a party to the plots hatched by his relative, Nath Larghos, the Trylon of the Black Mountains, and I guessed Naghan Furtway had promised him the position of Pallan of Vondium itself. Now, with no knowledge of the utter defeat of the third party, he sought to capture the Emperor and use him as a bargaining counter.

"Keep behind me, Majister," I said. "I'll spit you by mistake if you insist on skipping out ahead of me."

I did not speak overpolitely to this emperor.

"This is warm work, Dray Prescot—" He slashed at an Och and the little four-armed halfling interposed his shield and the rapier bounced and clanged. The Och thrust with his lower right arm wielding a spear and I had to skip and slice and jump to avoid the sweep of the sword in his upper right. But he went down, screeching.

"By the Black Chunkrah!" I said. "Emperor, get back or I'll drag you back by your hair!"

"By Vox!" he yelped, swishing his sword about. "I haven't enjoyed myself so much in years!"

He had no idea of the number of times he ought to have been killed. Left to his own devices he would have rolled on the stones of the square with a half dozen rapier thrusts in his belly or his head hanging off by gristle. I beat down a fresh attack and reached out my left hand, thrust the dagger all bloody as it was between my teeth, and took a good grip of the Emperor's hair.

I yanked.

He yelled, as much in pain and injured dignity as fear, and toppled back, whereat I pushed myself in front of him, took the dagger back into my left hand, smashed away a fresh developing attack, and so flung forward with my rapier flickering in and out, very evilly, like the tongues of risslaca.

The Emperor was growing annoyed.

"Just like all my Pallans, Dray Prescot!" he shouted at my back. "Denying me any fun in life."

I had time to yell back, most savagely: "If you think fighting and killing is fun, then you're still a child!"

Ortyg Larghos, Kov of Zamra, had not given up.

He made a last and as he thought final effort to take the Emperor. A solid wedge of his remaining men hurled themselves upon me. I had to use all my skill with the Jiktar and the Hikdar to fend them off. Two Rapas there were, very fierce, with their predatory beaked faces leering down upon me, who hurled themselves forefront of the others. They were not to be dismissed and spitted as easily as those who were coughing their guts out on the dusty stones around the fight.

While engaged with them I saw the Emperor, with his rapier up and out in a most ungainly stance, run at the bunch of men from the side. His face looked then—and Zair forgive me if I felt a tiny spark of joy—very much as my Delia's looked when she stood by me, shoulder to shoulder, against ravening foemen.

Larghos saw his chance. His final chance.

"Take him!" he screeched.

Green and purple feathers bobbed above the Emperor. Yellow and blue arms reached out for him.

I yelled.

The Rapas before me whickered their rapiers about in most professional passes, making me use skill and strength on them, and I could feel my strength slowly seeping away.

Ortyg Larghos was jubilant.

"Stick him, Rapas!" he was yelling.

I fended a thrust on my main-gauche, essayed a pass, took the other rapier rather too low and so had to give and bend to let the blade hiss past my side. I brought my wrist around for the next pass and a steel-tipped clothyard shaft sprouted clear through the Rapa's long roosterish neck. His companion had no time to make a sound as a second arrow feathered itself through his own scrawny neck.

Without turning around I shouted and I leaped for the men surrounding the Emperor.

I shouted just one word: *"Seg!"*

And then followed as marvelous an exhibition of shooting as any man can ever have performed and any man can have had the privilege of witnessing. For as I fought those remaining third-party men in their green and purple, slicing them, spitting them, so Seg shot out anyone who sought to close with me. His arrows sped silently above my shoulders and feathered themselves into the breasts of the men facing me. They could not stand against this whispering death, and they turned, and ran, and they were all dead men, for now the shorter arrows from my clansmen's bows fell among them.

Ortyg Larghos, Kov of Zamra, staggered across the stones of the square to fall at his Emperor's feet. His chest and back sprouted the steel heads and the bright feathers of many arrows.

"You pulled my hair, Dray Prescot."

"Aye," I said viciously. "And I'll pull it again if you rush upon naked steel like that again!"

He lowered his strong square face upon me. "I am the Emperor," he said, but he was not boasting, he was not trying to overawe me. Come to that, he had crawled out of the thicket of dinosaur bones to face my victorious men, and so he could never really boast of being emperor in quite the same way again. He was trying to explain something that saddened him. "I am never allowed to enjoy myself," he said. "Never. It is always inexpedient, bad politics, unsafe."

This was the man who had intemperately ordered my head cut off. I was to marry his daughter, and so that must have made some change in his attitude. I could understand him a little now, and, anyway, some emperors feel that ordering heads cut off is all a part of their function.

I turned away from him, not smiling, letting him see I was not impressed, to greet my men.

Seg had collected arrows from the battlefield as any frugal bowman does, and he and my wild clansmen marched up with all the swing and panache of the immortal fight at The Dragon's Bones still clinging to them. Inch swung his long Saxon ax with an air. Korf Aighos swung his Great Sword of

War of the Blue Mountains and I caught some of the pride
he and his Blue Mountain Boys felt in thus resurrecting
their ancient weapon. Varden stared about with a city-bred
eye.

Hap Loder and Vomanus were talking together, and I
wondered what deviltry they were cooking up. Vomanus was
handling Hap's broadsword, and I hazarded a guess Vomanus
was telling my Zorcander of the longswords of the inner sea,
the Eye of the World.

Delia said: "If you do that again, Dray Prescot, I may be
a widow before I'm married!"

I held her right arm with my left, and turned her, and so,
together, side by side, we walked through the main entranceway of the Emperor's palace in Vondium, capital of Vallia.

"I may do anything for you, Delia," I said. "Anything."

On that beautiful and terrible world of Kregen under Antares there exist a number of forms of contract by which a
man and a woman may agree to marry. When the bokkertu
for our betrothal and marriage was being drawn up Delia
and I, without really having to discuss the matter, instinctively chose that form by which the two, the man and the
woman, are bound the closest together. There were three
separate ceremonies. The first two, the religious and the
secular, were essentially private in character. I will say little
of these, apart from the undeniable fact that I was profoundly moved. They took place a Kregan week—what I
translate out as a sennight, for all that it is six days—after
our arrival back in the capital. We were, after the two ceremonies, man and wife.

The third ceremony, the public festival and procession
about the capital city, pleased me little.

"Oh, Dray, you great grizzly graint! I am supremely fortunate that the people of Vallia love me. And they will love
you, too! So they want to see us happy, they want to see us
drive in procession to all the temples and the holy places and
the various districts of the city. You'll—"

"I'll become used to it all, I suppose. But being a Prince
Majister is something I didn't count on."

"Oh, you'll learn."

After the attempted coup had been put down there was a
considerable amount of clearing up to be done. Kov Furtway
had stirred up as part of his plan one county or province to
attack its neighbor. I was not settled in my mind until I had
had a flier message from Tharu ti Valkanium that my Strom-

nate of Valka was safe. Led by my old freedom fighters they had successfully held off the treacherous attack mounted from the neighboring island to the west, Can-thirda, by its inhabitants, the porcupinelike Qua'voils. Tharu said they'd had to invade after they'd smashed the first attacks, and march to the north to help the colony of Relts there, who had remained loyal to the Emperor. I told the Emperor that Can-thirda should be settled properly, and, to my amazement, he simply said: "Then settle it, Dray, and have done with it."

Later, Delia said: "You silly woflo!" Which is, as we might say on Earth: "You silly goose."

"How so?"

"Why—that is how the great lords manipulate my father. He just assumed since you are now a most powerful and puissant lord in Vallia—the Prince Majister no less!—that you wished to add Can-thirda to your holdings. He has given the island to you."

"Can he do that? I mean, just like that?"

"Why not? He is the Emperor."

"Um," I said, and went off to sort out one or two items that had annoyed me.

Seg Segutorio, than whom no man ever had a finer comrade on two worlds, had been made a Hikdar of the Crimson Bowmen of Loh.

This infuriated me.

I said: "Look, Emperor: who was it stuck loyally by you in the ruins in The Dragon's Bones? Who fought for you? Who feathered those rasts of Kov Zamra's men when they were about to do you a mischief? Seg Segutorio, that's who."

He was slowly coming back to his usual pomp and mystique of being the Emperor, and I knew I must strike quickly before he took once again the full reins into his hands. With the dispatch of his enemies, or their flight abroad, he was now in a stronger position than he had ever been. If he wanted to repudiate all the bargains he had struck with me, he might seek to do so, and slay me, as he had once ordered. From Seg and Inch I knew I could count on absolutely dedicated loyalty. Hap Loder and my clansmen and Gloag with the men of Strombor would have to return home soon, although they were staying on for the great public ceremonies marking my wedding. I was safe for a time. I did not forget the way King Nemo of Tomboram in Pandahem had served me.

I never did trust kings and emperors, and I was not about

to begin now, for all that this emperor was the father of Delia of Delphond.

"What is it you want of me, Dray?"

"Me? It's Seg Segutorio I am talking of! Of your personal bodyguard, the Crimson Bowmen of Loh, half betrayed you, with their Chuktar in the lead. The other half fought to the end and a remnant now serve you—"

"I have sent to Loh for more Bowmen mercenaries."

"Very well and fine. And who is to lead them?"

"I have asked for a certain Chuktar Wong-si-tuogan. I am told he is a most excellent officer."

"Fine, just fine." We were seated in a private chamber of the palace, and the Emperor sipped a purple wine of Wenhartdrin, a small island off the south coast. The Emperor offered me a glass. It was exceedingly good, and I guessed he drank it as much for its quality as through any nationalistic pride. The wines of Jholaix are very hard to excel. "If you believe you are doing the right thing, then so be it. But I would have thought that Seg Segutorio, as a master Bowman, could not be bettered as Chuktar of your Crimson Bowmen of Loh."

The Emperor sipped. On the morrow Delia and I would drive about the city in a gaily decorated zorca chariot, and the bands would play and the flags fly and the twin suns would shed their opaline radiance upon us, and all would be merriment and laughter and joy. This night, sitting closeted with the Emperor, I had the conviction I must saddle a few zhantils before it was too late.

"Rank your Deldars," said the Emperor, referring to an opening move in Jikaida which can be translated out something like our "put your cards on the table," although with the suggestion that this is an opening bet of a protracted bargaining session.

I duly Ranked my Deldars.

"You should forthwith make Seg your personal bodyguard Chuktar. He is intensely loyal, to you and to Delia. You should reward him and Inch—and I suggest you bestow on them the titles and estates of the men who so foully betrayed you. You can have suitable presents made up for others of the men who saved your throne—aye!—and saved your life, too."

"And for yourself?"

"I need nothing beyond Delia. It seems I've acquired Canthirda . . . I shall rename it, for that name has baleful associations to my people of Valka, and it will serve as a useful sister state to Valka."

"Nothing else?"

"We are talking of other people—"

"Your friends."

He sipped more wine, and looked at me. He had mellowed. I'll give the old devil that. He was the most powerful man in this part of Kregen, make no mistake about that. I had a hold on him only through his daughter. For all that I had done for him personally he would discount, put it down to what any person ought to do, must do, to preserve the life of the Emperor. But—he had fleshed out a little, he had lost that abstracted look, as though waiting for the dagger thrust in his back. I had made him far more secure than he had ever been.

"Aye. My friends."

"So they will become powerful. And loyal to you. But I—"

"Do you think I could possibly countenance—let alone take a part in—any plan or plot that would harm you? You are Delia's father. Although," I said, and, Zair forgive me, took a pleasure in the saying, "your wife, Delia's mother, must have been a wonderful person. No, Majister, from me you are safer than if you wore armor even a gros-varter could not penetrate."

I think, looking back, that he half believed me.

Being a prudent man, he would never wholly trust another person. I am prudent, or I think I am, yet I have committed the folly of trusting other people wholly. As you have heard —and if these cassettes last out will hear more—sometimes I have paid for that folly of trust, paid for it in agony and blood and slavery. But I did trust Seg, and Inch, and Gloag, and Varden, and Hap Loder, and having removed valuables from his reach, I trusted Korf Aighos. Trusting these men meant I trusted the men under their command. I had no doubts of Valka.

And, too, now that I knew Vomanus was Delia's half-brother, I could trust Vomanus again, too.

"I believe you, Dray." He had already made up his mind what he would do. "I shall make Seg Segutorio Chuktar of the Crimson Bowmen of Loh. In addition, the estates of Kov Furtway have been confiscated. I shall give them to Seg and create him Kov of Falinur."

"That is indeed munificent—" I began. He held up a hand. "Furthermore, since the long man Inch roused the Blue

Mountains on our behalf, and the Black Mountains are now vacant, by reason of Nath Larghos' treason, I shall give them to Inch and create him Trylon of the Black Mountains."

Now I had to think about this. There are many ranks in the nobility of Vallia which are not at all complicated once one grasps the essential pecking order. A Kov approximates out to a duke, as I have said, and a Strom to a count. Between these there come a number of ranks—some I know I have already mentioned. A Vad, a Trylon. By creating Seg and Inch of unequal ranks, I felt unease.

I said: "I think Kov of the Black Mountains sounds a richer note."

He chuckled and poured wine.

"You will find titles are grabbed after and fought for, Dray. They mean nothing. It is land that counts. Land! Canals, corn, cattle, wine, timber, minerals. Make Inch Kov, if it pleases you."

"It will please Seg." That was true.

Seg and Inch had become firm friends. I own I felt a thump of relief at that.

The Emperor drank and swallowed and wiped his lips. He cocked his head at me. "As for you, Dray Prescot. My poor daughter has caught a tartar in you." He said "clansman," but his meaning was as I have translated it out. "You mentioned Valka and Can-thirda. That fool Kov Larghos of Zamra set himself up as Pallan of Vondium. He is dead. Zamra is yours, and the title of Kov, if you want it, Prince Majister."

The old devil could be sarcastic, too, when he liked.

I thanked him. I did not stutter in surprise this time. I had an eye to the future.

He said: "With all the titles you have collected, Dray Prescot, I think we will need an extra-special sheet of vellum to write them all down on the marriage contract."

Face-to-face, I said: "All I want is to be the husband of Delia."

Then I retired for the night. Tomorrow was the great day.

Chapter Two

Marriage

The great day dawned.

On this day Delia and I would be truly wed.

As I watched Zim and Genodras rise into the Kregan sky over Vondium I found it hard to understand my own feelings. Long and long had I fought and struggled for this day. I had traveled many dwaburs over this world of Kregen. I had fought men, and half-men, half-beasts, and monsters. I had been slave, I had owned vast lands and many men had looked to me as their leader. Much I had seen and done and all of it, really, aimed at this outcome.

There is much I could say of that day.

Some parts of it I remember with the absolute clarity of vision that cherishes every moment; other parts are cast in a vaguer shadow. Here on this Earth the people of China wear white in mourning, whereas my own country chooses to regard white as the color of purity and bridal happiness, of virginity. The Vallians hew to the latter custom, which I think gives brides the opportunity to glow and radiate a special kind of happiness of their wedding day.

When I saw Delia clad in her white gown, with white shoes, a white veil, and—with the happy superstitions that mean everything and nothing on these days—tiny specks of color here and there—a flower posy, a scarlet-edged hem, a yellow curlicue to her wrists—I could only stand like a great buffoon and stare.

They had decked me out in some fantastic rig—all gold lace, brilliants, feathers, silks, and satins—and when I saw myself in a mirror I was shatteringly reminded of that rig I had worn in the opal palace of Zenicce, when the Princess Natema had unavailingly attempted her wiles.

I ripped the lot off.

Memory of Natema, who was now happily married to

Prince Varden, my good comrade, brought back unbidden memories of other great ladies I had known in my career on Kregen. The Princess Susheeng, Sosie na Arkasson, Queen Lilah, Tilda the Beautiful, Viridia the Render, even Katrin Rashumin, who would, as Kovneva of Rahartdrin, be among the brilliant throng at the wedding. I thought of Mayfwy, widow of my oar comrade Zorg of Felteraz, and I sighed, for I dearly wished for Mayfwy and Delia to be friends. I must say that Varden had sent a flier to Zenicce and brought back Princess Natema.

I had greeted her kindly, if feeling a trifle of the strangeness of the situation. She was just as beautiful, and, I knew, just as willful. She was a little more voluptuous, a little more superb in her carriage, for she had had two children. But she and Varden had made a match, and they were happy, at which I was much cheered.

So I ripped off the gaudy clothes that turned me into a popinjay. I wrapped a long length of brilliant scarlet silk about me, and donned the plain buff tunic of a Koter of Vallia, with the wide shoulders and the nipped-in waist and the flared skirt. Long black boots I wore, and a broad-brimmed hat. In the hat I wore the red and white colors of Valka. My sleeves were white silk of Pandahem, for despite the intense rivalry between the islands, Vallia is not foolish enough to refuse to buy best Pandahem silk.

From Valka had come all my notables and those friends at whose side I had fought clearing the island of the aragorn and the slave-masters. They brought with them the superb sword from Aphrasöe that had been Alex Hunter's. This I buckled on to my belt with a thrill I could not deny. With this marvelous Savanti sword I could go up against rapier, long-sword, broadsword, shortsword, with absolute confidence. Even then, in that moment, I admit, like the greedy weapons man I am, I longed for a great Krozair longsword to swing at my side.

But that, like Nath and Zolta, my two oar comrades and ruffianly rascals, could not be.

What they would say—what Mayfwy would say—away there in the Eye of the World when they heard that I had married and they not there to dance at my wedding, I shriveled to think.

There would be much calling on Mother Zinzu the Blessed, that I could be perfectly sure of.

When, in casual conversation, I had mentioned to the Emperor, turning what I said into a light remark, careful not to inflame, that a flier might perhaps be sent to Tomboram, he replied in such furious terms as to dispel the notion. His fury was not directed toward me, for I have cunning of a low kind in this area of elementary conversation-tactics, but against all the nations of the island of Pandahem. I mentioned this to Inch and Seg, for I had in mind asking Tilda the Beautiful and her son, Pando, the Kov of Bormark, to my wedding and, also, if she could be found in time, Viridia the Render. The general opinion was that the thing could not be done.

Only that week news had come in of a vicious raid by ships from Pandahem upon a Vallian overseas colony port. I could imagine the hatreds of the spot; they might be of a different kind, they could not be more intense than those festering in the capital. This saddened me. But I refused to be sad on my wedding day, and so with a last draft of best Jholaix, went down to the waiting zorca chariot.

Delia looked stunningly marvelous—I refuse to attempt any description. We sat in the chariot and Old Starkey the coachman clicked to the eight zorcas, and they leaned into the harness, the tall wheels with their thin spokes spun, reflecting blindingly the opaz brilliance of the twin Suns of Scorpio, and we were off on our wedding procession.

The Crimson Bowmen of Loh with Seg as their new Chuktar rode escort. And—an innovation, a thing I dearly wanted and had spoken hard and short to the Emperor to gain—an honor guard of Valkan Archers rode with us also. I had spoken to Seg about this thing, and we both knew what we knew about bows, but he had agreed, for my sake.

In the procession rode all the nobles of the land high in the Emperor's favor.

There, too, rode Hap Loder and my clansmen. Inch as the new Kov of the Black Mountains rode, talking animatedly with Korf Aighos, and, again, I wondered what the rascally Blue Mountain Boy was hatching.

Between the Korf and Nath the Thief from Zenicce there was little to choose.

I said to Delia, leaning close: "We must keep a sharp eye on the wedding presents, my love. Nath, I am sure, has a lesten-hide bag under his tunic."

Those wedding presents meant a great deal, for it had been through manipulation of them as symbols that Delia had managed to remain so long unwed. Now I had scoured Valka for the best and finest presents the hand and brain of my people could devise. I had brushed aside poor Kov Vektor's presents. The Blue Mountain Boys had them in good keeping, but I scorned to use a beaten rival's gifts. Truly, I had been amazed at the wealth and beauty that had poured from Valka. Ancient treasures had been unearthed from where they had been hidden against the aragorn. Such treasures! Such beauty! And all given freely and with love to Delia.

So we rode in stately procession through the boulevards and avenues of Vondium. The Koters and the Koteras turned out in their thousands to wave and cheer and shout their good wishes. Vondium is not as large nor does it hold as many people as Zenicce, whose population must be a million souls, but I guessed very few people remained indoors on this day of days.

Delia's fingers lay in mine and every now and then she would squeeze my hand. She waved and acknowledged the cheering. Flower petals showered down on us from balconies from which gay shawls and banners and silks streamed. The noise dizzied us with the incessant volleys of good wishes.

Delia said: "I have spoken to Seg, and Inch, and they will free all the slaves in their provinces. It will be hard—"

"Aye, my love, it will be hard. But already my men have been working on Can-thirda. And now Zamra, too, will be cleansed of the evil."

"Oh, yes!"

"Then," I said, with a mischievousness somewhat out of place, perhaps, given the subject and the day, "we will have many more free Koters and Koteras to cheer for us!"

"And aren't they cheering!"

Delia drew back that shimmer of veil from her face. The veil, I knew, had been the gift of her grandmother, laid by in a scented cedar-wood chest against the day when it would frame the glorious face of my beloved. Her eyes regarded her people of Vallia with a warm affection, and her cheeks flushed with a rosy tint that, however naïve it may make me sound, captivated me again. And her hair! That glorious chestnut hair with those outrageous tints of auburn, her hair glowed and shone against the whiteness of the veil.

"You are happy, my Delia?"

"Yes, my Dray, yes. Oh, yes!"

We performed the necessary functions at the sacred places and we did not miss a single fantamyrrh. The people lined the streets and boulevards as we passed at a slow zorca pace.

I saw flowers, and ribbons, flags and banners, many silks and shawls depending from the open balconies. Petals showered upon us in a scented rain. The Suns of Scorpio shone magnificently upon us. Truly, then, as we drove to the acclamations of the multitudes, I had grown into a real Kregan!

At my special request—which Delia, with a regal lift of her chin, had instantly translated into a command—we drove past the Great Northern Cut and past *The Rose of Valka*. There had been wild moments in this inn, and the raftered ceilings had witnessed many a scene of joyful carouse. Even with the crisp and concise stanza form adopted for that song, *The Fetching of Drak na Valka*, it takes a deucedly long time to sing it in its entirety, and usually we sang a shortened version. The old friends of Valka were there, hanging out of the windows, cheering and shouting and waving, and then someone—it was Young Bargom for an ob!—started up the song, and they were singing it out as we drove past. I knew they'd go on singing and drinking all day and all night, for that is the Valkan way.

As was proper we were to finish our promenade of the city by narrow boat.

The water glittered cleanly as we stepped from the zorca carriage and went aboard a narrow boat so bedecked with flowers and colors, with flags and banners, I wondered where we were to sit. The bargemasters had everything organized, and soon Delia and I found ourselves sitting on golden cushions high on a platform in the bows, sumptuously decorated, with a side table bearing tasty snacks, miscils, various wines, gregarians, squishes, and, of course, heaping silver and golden dishes of palines.

No happy function of Kregen is complete without as many palines as may be managed.

The water chuckled past the bows. I knew that water. Sweet is the canalwater of Vallia—sweet and deadly. I felt a comfort to know that through the immersion in the pool of baptism in that far-off River Zelph of Aphrasöe, my Delia was, as I was, assured of a thousand years of life as well as being protected from the fearful effects of the canalwater.

And now it was the turn of the canalfolk to cheer and shout and wave. The Vens and the Venas turned out on their freshly painted narrow boats, lining the banks of the cut as we passed. We had a specially picked body of haulers to draw us, for I had—rudely, viciously, intemperately—refused the Emperor's offer of a gang of his slave haulers. We did not see a single slave that glorious day, and although we knew the poor devils were hidden away in their barracks and bagnios, we could take comfort from our determination to end the evil, once and forever.

All day we traveled about Vondium and as the twin suns sank we saw the monstrous pile of the imperial palace rearing against the last suns-glow and knew we were going home.

"I am so happy, my love, happy and not at all tired," said Delia, and then yawned so hugely her slender white hand looked more slender and moth-white in the dusk than ever.

"Yawning, my Delia, on your wedding day?"

She laughed and I laughed, and we watched as the narrow boat was drawn through the rising portcullis of the palace's water-port. We stepped down from the high platform and the Crimson Bowmen of Loh surrounded us and the Archers of Valka were there, too, and the Pallans, and the nobles and the high Koters, and we went up the marble stairs into the palace.

It had been a perfect day.

A girl's wedding day ought to be, should be—must be— a perfect day.

I was taken off by Seg and Inch and Hap, by Varden and Gloag, by Korf Aighos and Vomanus. We spent some time drinking amicably, but in low key, for none of us subscribed to the barbaric code that demands a groom become stupidly intoxicated on his wedding night. Grooms who do that have scarce love for their new brides.

The room was low-ceilinged and comfortable, with softly upholstered chairs and sturm-wood tables, with Walfarg-weave rugs upon the floor, and with an endless supply of the best of Jholaix and all the other superlative wines of Kregen. Even so, as the Prince Majister, I could order up Kregan tea, than which there is no better drink in two worlds.

Off in a corner I was able to have a few words with Vomanus.

"So you're my brother-in-law now, Vomanus."

He cocked an eye at me, lifting his glass, and drinking. "Half-brother-in-law, Dray."

"Aye. I doubted you, when the racters told me you sought the hand of Delia." I am a man who never apologizes and never begs forgiveness—at least, almost never. Now I said: "Do you forgive me for doubting you, Vomanus?"

He laughed in his careless way and tossed back the wine. He was a rapscallion, careless, lighthearted, but a good comrade.

"There is nothing to forgive. I know how I would feel toward a man who tried to take a girl like Delia from me."

"You are engaged—no, that is not the word—you have a girl of your own?"

"A girl, Dray? Of course not." He yelled for more wine. "I have girls, Dray—hundreds of them!"

Hap Loder came across, bringing more tea for me, and a handful of palines on a golden dish. We talked of the clans and of the new chunkrah herds he had been building up. He was now the power in the Clans of Felschraung and Longuelm, but he had given obi to me and I was his lord and so he would remain faithful to me forever. I knew that he was my friend, and that was more important than mere loyalty.

Tharu of Valkanium and Tom ti Vulheim were there, and I was joyed to see they had brought Erithor of Valkanium. I shouted across: "Erithor! Will you honor us with a song?"

"Right willingly, Strom Drak," he began, bringing his harp forward, and then halting, and, striking a chord, said: "Right willingly, Prince Majister."

"Strom Drak," I said. "Well, it is Strom *Dray*, now, in Valka for me. But the great song will never change."

Others broke in, begging Erithor to sing, for he was a bard renowned throughout all of Vallia. I recalled the song Erithor had been making, after we had cleansed Valka, and the girls of Esser Rarioch, the high fortress overlooking Valkanium, had unavailingly badgered and teased him into revealing its words and melodies. He might sing that song now. If he did, this would be another historical mark to go down beside the other great songs he had made that would live forever.

He saw me looking at him, and lifting his head, he said: "No, Prince Majister. I will sing the marriage song of Prince Dray and Princess Delia only when both are there to hear it together."

Someone—I do not know who it was to this day—roared out: "Then you won't sing it this night, Erithor!"

They all shouted at this, and Erithor struck a chord, and broke into *Naghan the Wily*, which tells how Naghan, a rich and ugly silversmith of Vandayha, was trapped into marriage by the saucy Hefi, daughter of the local bosk herder.

Everyone roared. Kregans have a warped sense of humor, it seems to me, at times.

How wonderful it was to be here, in this comfortable room, drinking and singing with my friends! I am a man who does not make friends easily. I can always rouse men to follow me, men to do as I order, and joy in the doing of it . . . but friendship. That, to me, is a rare and precious thing I seek without even acknowledging I seek it, except in moments of weakness like this.

Seg's Thelda would be busily clucking about Delia now, and knowing Thelda, I knew she would be full of her own importance as a married woman with a fine young son— called Dray—and with all the good will in the world exasperating by her own importance and knowledge of the marriage state.

It was time I rescued Delia.

I stood up.

Everyone fell silent.

Erithor had been singing on—the time passes incredibly quickly when a skald of such power sings—and now he finished up an episode from *The Canticles of the Rose City* wherein the half-man, half-god Drak sought for his divine mistress through perils that made the listeners grip the edges of their chairs. The thrumming strings fell silent.

I cleared my throat.

"I thank you all, my friends. I cannot say more."

I believe they understood.

They escorted me up the marble stairs where the torchlight threw orange and ruby colors across the walls and the tapestries and the silks, where the shadows all fled from us.

Delia was waiting.

Thelda bobbed her head and Seg put his arm around her and everyone carried out the prescribed gestures and spoke the words that would ensure long and happy life to Delia and me. Then, already laughing and singing and feeling thirsty again, they all trooped downstairs and left Delia and me alone.

The bedchamber was hung with costly tapestries and tall candles burned unwaveringly. Refreshments had been tastefully laid out on a side table. Delia sat up in the bed with that outrageous hair combed out by Thelda gleaming upon her shoulders. I confess I was gawping at her.

"Oh, Dray! You look as though you've eaten too much bosk and taylyne soup!"

"Delia—" I whispered. "I—"

I took an unsteady step forward. I felt my sword swinging at my side, that wonderful Savanti sword, and I reached down to take it out and throw it upon the table, out of the way—

and so, with the sword in my hand, I saw the tapestries at the side of the bed rustle. There was no wind in the bed-chamber.

They must have waited until they heard everyone else depart, and only Delia's voice—and then my voice. That had been the signal.

Six of them there were.

Six men clad all in black with black face-masks and hoods, and wielding daggers.

They leaped for the bed in so silent and feral a charge from their concealed passage behind the arras that almost they slew my Delia before I could reach them.

With a cry so bestial, so vile, so vicious, so horrible they flinched back from me, I hurled myself full upon them.

Their six daggers could not meet that brand.

The Savanti sword is a terrible weapon of destruction.

Had they been wearing plate armor and wielding Krozair longswords I do not think they would have stood before me.

So furious, so ugly, so absolutely destructive was my attack that I had slashed down the first two, driven the sword through the guts of the third, and turned to strike at the fourth before they could swivel their advance to face—instead of the beautiful girl in the bed—me.

"Dray!" said Delia.

She did not scream.

In a lithe smother of naked flashing legs and yards and yards of white lace she was out of the bed, snatching up a fallen dagger, hurling herself upon the sixth man. He stood, horrified. I chopped the fourth, caught the fifth through an eye—the mask could not hope to halt the marvelous alloy-steel of the Savanti blade—and swung about to see Delia stepping back from her man.

The six would-be assassins lay sprawled on the priceless Walfarg-weave rugs.

"Oh, Dray!" said Delia, dropping the bloody dagger and running to me, her arms outstretched. "They might have slain you!"

"Not with you to protect me, my Delia," I said, and I laughed, and caught her up close to me, breast to breast, and so gazed down upon her glorious face upturned to my ugly old figurehead. "Sink me! I feel sorry for the poor fools!"

Later I carried the six out to the door and dumping them in the passage roared for the guard and half a dozen Crimson Bowmen appeared. The Hikdar wanted to rouse the palace, but I said: "Not so, good Fenrak." He was a loyal Bowman who had fought with us at The Dragon's Bones and had been promoted, to his joy. "This is my wedding night!"

He shook his head.

"I will see to this offal, my Prince. And in the morning, then . . ." He started his men into action. He was a rough tough Bowman of Loh, and thus dear to me. "I wish you all joy, my Prince, and eternal happiness to the Princess Majestrix."

"Thank you, Fenrak. There is wine for you and your men—drink well tonight, my friend."

As they carted the black-clad assassins off I went back to Delia and closed the door on the outside world.

I must admit, knowing what I do of Kregen, that this was a typical ending to a wedding day. It had roused the blood, though, set a sparkle into Delia's eyes, a rose in her cheeks. How she had fought for me, like a zhantil for her cubs!

In the morning—and I a married man!—we made inquiries. The story was simple and pathetic. The would-be assassins, being dead, could not tell us what we wanted to know, but one of them was recognized by Vomanus as being a retainer of the Kov of Falinur, who had fled. This had been his last throw. This is what I believed at the time. Then, the truth did not matter; later I was to wish I had prosecuted more earnest inquiries, for what Vomanus told us was correct. What he could not then know was that this assassin had left the employ of Naghan Furtway, Kov of Falinur.

When we talked of this, and used the name, Thelda pushed up very wroth, her face flushed. "I am the Kovneva of Falinur! And my husband Seg is the Kov! Do not speak of the Kov of Falinur as a traitor!"

Delia soothed her down. Being a Kovneva was greatly to Thelda's liking, although Seg had laughed and said that being a Kov would not drive his shafts any the straighter when he was hunting in his hills of Erthyrdrin.

Naghan Furtway had been stripped of his titles and estates. Henceforth I knew we must think of him as Furtway, and he would seek to injure us in some way. And this was the man, together with his nephew Jenbar, whom I had rescued from the icy Mountains of the North at the behest of the Star Lords!

I will not go into details of my life after that in Vondium, the capital city of Vallia. That life was remarkable in its activity, for I had much to do, and in its uneventfulness. I took the palace architect, one Largan the Rule, and we went ferreting about in the secret passages. I have mentioned the usual custom in great palaces of having secondary passageways between the walls. These I inspected, and found many fresh alleyways of which even Largan the Rule had no knowledge, and so had those that would be weak spots bricked up.

It seems I had the knack of poking my beaked nose into all the places I was able to investigate and find some way of improving what went on. High on my list of priorities was organizing the canals better, in such a way that arguments over rights-of-way need not take place at crossings. Until a great program of canal building could be undertaken to create overways and underways on the cuts, I instituted a country-wardens service, which provided for families of men and women to live near the crossings and superintend the traffic.

As was to be expected I spent a great deal of time at the dockyards and slipways making myself thoroughly familiar with the great race-built galleons of Vallia. I looked into their artillery, the catapults, the varters, and the gros-varters which Vallia herself had developed.

As for the Vallian Air Service, a body of fliers I had always held in the highest respect, we discovered that Naghan Furtway had contrived through his contacts to disperse the Air Service during the time of his abortive coup. I met again Chuktar Farris, the Lord of Vomansoir, who aboard *Lorenztone* had plucked Delia and me from midair where we flew astride Umgar Stro's giant coal-black impiter. I thought I detected about his exquisite politeness an edged air of pleasure, as though his love for Delia found equal pleasure that she had at last married the great ruffianly barbarian she had chosen—against all common sense.

"We searched for you, Prince Majister, and found instead the Kov of Falinur and his Kovneva."

I saw Delia smile at this, and had to chuckle myself.

How high and mighty we all were with our titles these days, and then we had been a draggle-tailed bunch running and hiding across the Hostile Territories!

I asked after Tele Karkis, the young Hikdar of the Air Service, and Farris frowned and said: "He left the Air Service. He—disappointed us in that. I have not seen or heard of him for a long time."

Naghan Vanki, he of the sarcastic tongue and the silver and black outfit—an approximation to Racter colors, those—

was still active, although away in Evir in the north at the time.

My sojourn in Vallia had already given me a feeling that blue was the color of Pandahem and therefore of an enemy. I was able to instantly quell this irrational feeling my own way by thinking of Tilda of the Many Veils, and her son young Pando—a right little limb of Satan if ever there was one. But, still, it was strange to see the Vallian Air Service men clad in their smart dark blue, with the short orange capes. The blue was so dark as almost to be black, and I guessed had been given that blue tinge to take away the odd dusty shabby look unrelieved black gives.

Delia and I flew a considerable amount of the time on our journeys to the Blue Mountains and to Delphond. Court officials worried over this, for the airboats were always giving trouble and were not to be relied upon. We visited Inch in the Black Mountains, and soon found he had palled up with the Blue Mountain Boys, and he and Korf Aighos, who ran the place from that eerie and cloud-capped mountain city of High Zorcady, were hatching plans that would further unite in friendship the whole mountain area. We flew all over Vallia. We went up to Falinur where Seg had betaken himself, with Thelda, to take charge. Seg had chosen an ord-Kiktar to run the Crimson Bowmen of Loh in his stead when he was away on his estates. This man, a veteran, intensely loyal, was called Dag Dagutorio—I believe I have not mentioned the system in Erthyrdrin over names and what the *torio* means, but that must wait for now—and I saw the Emperor felt more at ease when Dag was around and Seg was away up in Falinur. That must have been the motive of the munificent gift of a Kovnate to Seg.

An ord-Jiktar meant Dag had risen eight stages in the rank structure as a Jiktar. Two more and then he might become a Chuktar. I doubted if the Emperor would employ two Chuktars to command his Crimson Bowmen; and I surmised that Seg would be not too unhappy to let the job go to Dag.

Certainly, I had insisted that a Chuktar be appointed to command the new Vallian Imperial Honor Guard of Valkan Archers. The Emperor had smiled at this, and said: "Then, since you love Valka so much, son-in-law, and since you insist on creating the Valkan Archers as a bodyguard, you may pay the Chuktar his wages. For me, I can only pay a Jiktar."

I fumed, but I paid.

Anyway, what was mere money? Valka, Can-thirda, and Zamra brought in immense amounts. And Delia's Delphond and the Blue Mountains brought in more. We could have employed an army of Chuktars.

One man of the court surrounding the Emperor I should mention at this time: the Wizard of Loh, whom men called Deb-so-Parang. I spoke with him a number of times, and told him of Lu-si-Yuong, the Wizard of Loh to Queen Lilah of Hiclantung. Deb-so-Parang nodded, and stroked his beard —like all Wizards of Loh he was strong on the artifices of his craft, but I could not underestimate their powers—and said that he was not acquainted with him personally, although since the fall of the Empire of Loh the Wizards, by the seven arcades, had spread all over Kregen. He was a pleasant old buffer and, a mark against him, he had not forewarned the Emperor of the plot against his life and his throne.

I had, of course, questioned the Todalpheme in Vondium, who monitored the tides, about Aphrasöe. All they could say was for me to ask the Emperor. This I did and he said, simply enough, that when Delia had been crippled from her fall from a zorca he had heard the Todalpheme of Hamal—where the Vallians bought their airboats—knew of a mysterious place where cures might be affected, miracle cures.

So now I knew.

I think you will not be surprised when I say that I did not, as I most certainly would have done a few seasons ago, immediately call for a flier and take off for Hamal. I had become so much more settled than I ever had been before I did not recognize myself as the same man who had swung a great Krozair longsword and set off across the Hostile Territories on foot to reach my Delia, the man who had vowed that nothing and no one would stand in his way. It had always been Delia first and then the quest for the Savanti of Aphrasöe, those mortal but superhuman men who had thrown me out of paradise.

But, for me, Vallia and Valka and my Delia were paradise. Paradise enough.

So I stored the information away and went busily about my business. We honeymooned on Valka, my marvelous island with its wealth and its beauty, and we sang songs in the high hall of Esser Rarioch and we had a tremendous time. We traveled to Strombor. My emotions when once again I beheld the enclave city of Zenicce and strode the opal palace and thought of all the things that had happened there—they defy description. And Gloag, who had become grand chamberlain and the strong right hand to Great-Aunt Shusha—who still lived—could not do enough for us. We rode out onto the Great Plains of Segesthes and I caroused once more with my clansmen, and they roared out the great Jikai for Delia and me. Oh, yes, I lived very high off the vosk in those rousing days!

So much, I had. So great a wealth of everything that when I said to Delia I wanted to go to Zamra and sort out some problems arising out of the freeing of the slaves, and she said, "I think, dear heart, I will wait another week before I know," my heart leaped and I consigned everything else to the Ice Floes of Sicce. There are stories on Kregen as well as on Earth wherein a man does not know his wife is expecting a baby until she tells him. It is a poor husband who is not at once aware of the possibility of a child by reason of nature's interruption, and proof positive is what is awaited.

The proof came.

"You will wish to be with your own people, Delia. Thelda will be useful, although I fear a sore trial to you. And there is Aunt Katri. We leave for Vondium at once."

Aunt Katri was the Emperor's sister, childless now, her offspring having perished one way and another, and she was a kind and warmhearted soul. And, in Vondium, there would be the greatest doctors of the land with their acupuncture needles at the ready. I would call in Nath the Needle, for I had a high regard for that particular doctor.

So, in the fullness of time, Delia bore twins.

A boy and a girl.

The boy was to be Drak.

The girl was to be Lela.

She was named for Delia's mother.

I walked about like a loon. Any onker had a brain twice as big as mine in those days, and nothing in two worlds held more foolish pride. How could an ugly lump like me produce two such marvelous children? Delia, of course, with her superlative beauty, was solely responsible for the babies' gloriousness. The twinned principle is strong on Kregen, by reason of the twin suns in the sky. Very early on, on Kregen, twins were regarded as lucky and means were devised of keeping both children alive and well, where here on Earth twins were regarded as bad luck, and very often would be killed off—or one of them. Twins! A boy and a girl! By Zair, but I was a lucky fellow!

A summit of happiness had been reached.

Further problems arose in Zamra, and Delia was nursing well and everything was fine and wonderful in the palace of Vondium, and at last she said to me: "You great onker, Dray! I know the slave problem on Zamra is worrying you. You'll have to go there. I shall be perfectly all right, here in my father's palace."

"Tell Thelda to get Seg down here, and I shall send for Inch. Then I will go to Zamra."

So it was done, and I bid them Rembree and took off.

I called at Valka first, and then flew north. We touched down on a small island for the night and I wandered about the camp, restless, fretful, feeling the hilt of the Savanti sword swinging at my hip. I was a great man, now. A Prince Majister, married to the most beautiful and glorious girl in two worlds. I owned vast tracts of land. Money by the sackful was mine. And I was the father of two perfect children.

Pride, pride!

The blue glow grew swiftly, treacherously—and I all unprepared. I stared in a horror made all the more horrible by my complete unpreparedness. I felt the blue radiance calling me and the gigantic outlines of the Scorpion beckoned and enfolded me and then I was lying on harsh and stinking dirt, stark naked, with the smell and groan of slaves all about me, and a harsh boot kicking me in the ribs, and a voice snarling:

"Get up, rast! Get up, you stinking cramph!"

Chapter Three

The Scorpion sets a task to my hands

I was naked.

I was unarmed.

I was a slave in a slave bagnio.

My only hope was that I was still on Kregen.

You may judge of the shock of this transition when I tell you I did not instantly grab that cruel kicking boot and topple the fellow down and twist his neck.

I lay there, choking with the horror of it, shaking, feeling waves of nausea rush and flutter over me as though, once again, I sped down the great glacier of the Mountains of the North. But this transition into another part of Kregen struck home with shrewder intensity. I had waited while Delia had been delivered of our children, and I had wanted to suffer along with her, uselessly, of course, for the techniques of acupuncture ensured the birth should be painless. She had smiled up at me and reached out her arms to me, and I leaned down and kissed her dear face, and together we joyed in an experience that she alone had to bear, and I alone had to wait in useless suffering.

The boot smashed into my ribs again.

"Get up, you stinking yetch!"

Perhaps I had been feeling that this was my punishment for being so high and mighty, for letting Delia bear our children—although, Zair knew, I had done everything a mere man can do on these occasions—perhaps the pride that comes before a fall had humbled me. But that second series of savage kicks made me take stock of my new situation.

I had been a slave before. I had been dumped down unarmed and naked before on Kregen. I knew the Star Lords had picked me out once again to perform some task for them, and if this task bore any resemblance to those that had gone before I must sort myself out quickly.

The boot felt warm and slick in my hands.

I pulled.

The slave-master fell.

I took his throat in my hands and choked him a bit, and leaned over him and snarled into his ear: "Kick me again, rast, and your neck will snap." Then I threw him from me.

I stood up.

Around me the groan and moan of naked slaves ceased.

They stood cramped up in a small chamber hewn from soft rock, crumbling, with the ceiling threatening to fall at any moment. Condensation on the walls and drops of niter glittered in the radiance of the twin suns pouring in the barred opening to the cave.

The slave-master scrabbled up.

He tried to lash me with the whip.

I caught the lash and pulled and took the slave-master again by the throat and lifted him up.

"I told you, kleesh—" I began.

A little Fristle female, all furry and curved, with her tail lashing in frenzy, caught my arm.

"Do not kill him, dom! They will be cruel to us all if he is found dead."

Well, I had no love for Fristles, those cat-faced half-men I had known before. But I remembered Sheemiff of the warrens of Magdag, and so I did not break the slave-master's neck. I choked him a little and then threw him against the wall. He fell and lay limply.

A big barky Brokelsh shouldered up, angry.

"Now we are in trouble!" All the slaves were naked. There were about a dozen of them. The Brokelsh started off for a black hole in the back wall. "I'm off."

The other slaves ran after him, including the little Fristle woman, who chittered in her fear as she ran.

I went over to the barred opening. The bars were solid logs of lenk. Outside I could see a clearing with papishin-leaved huts, a backing of jungle unfamiliar to me, and guards patrolling with ready weapons. There were some unusual circumstances about the slave compound, something I couldn't then put my finger on. I shook the lenk logs in fruitless anger, raging against the fate that dragged me from Vallia and Delia and hurled me contemptuously somewhere else on Kregen, summarily bidden to do the dictates of the Star Lords.

A sound at the back of the cave brought me around, snarl-

ing. Being weaponless I lifted my hands in the discipline of
unarmed combat of the Krozairs of Zy. Any man without a
weapon on Kregen is at a disadvantage, but the Krozairs of
Zy as part of their mystic devotions practice their own brand
of hand-fighting, and very deadly it is, to be sure.

"Come away, dom," said the girl who faced me.

She was young, filthy, dirty with long and tangled black
hair. Her face showed the gaunt look of the half-starved, but
her body was firm and supple, and she looked fierce and
wild.

"Why do the guards come here alone?" I pointed to the
unconscious slave-master.

She shrugged her dirt-caked shoulders.

"He wanted pleasure, and would clear all but one out of
here for that, into the other cells and passages."

I did not need to be told that this girl was the one the
slave-master sought.

She nodded. "I am Tulema. But come away, quickly—"
She pointed into the clearing. A couple of guards were walking toward the barred opening. They could not see into the
cell, or so I fancied, but very quickly they would, and then
there would be trouble. I nodded and followed Tulema.

There must be absolutely no pining after Delia. I must not
think of Vallia, or of Valka, until I was safely out of this
mess. I had to do the bidding of the Star Lords, and then
get myself back home as quickly as may be.

Then I cursed.

It was crystal clear why the Star Lords had brought me
here.

I had to rescue a slave from these pens.

There had been at least a dozen in this cell when I arrived.
Now they had hurried out. I followed after Tulema, ducking
my head beneath the rocky overhang, and found myself in
a corridor that led to a maze of passageways and so on to
a wider cave in which hundreds of slaves sat and squatted or
paced about.

Which one was I expected to rescue?

The Fristle woman, the Brokelsh, and now Tulema—from
these three I must find out who had been in that cell when
the slave-master was knocked unconscious. I must not let
them out of my sight.

I did notice, looking about the vast prison-cave, that there
were a large number of halflings here. In general, on Kregen,
there are to be found usually far more human beings than

halflings, and the halflings, too, are not just one race but many. Here, the balance was quite otherwise.

A sudden commotion went up and then all the slaves were racing down toward a large opening cut in the cave. Tulema looked at me, shouted, "Feeding time!" and was off.

Perforce, I ran after her.

High in the rocky ceiling wide crystal facets showed the gleam of fire. I knew that crystal. It comes from Loh—exactly where is a closely guarded secret—and on it a fire may be kindled and it will not crack or distort. It is much used for holding heat and light above ceilings. . . . I was to find that this crystal did *not* come from Loh, and thereby was cheap enough to light slave quarters—but I run ahead of my story.

That crystal is known as fireglass.

So it was that plenty of light in the cave allowed me to keep the supple form of Tulema in sight. Through the opening the cave passage debouched into a series of openings, each one walled off from its neighbor. Each cell was strongly barred off from the clearing, also. The slaves ran past these cells and on into another spacious cave where food had been left spread out over the floor.

The scene that followed, given the circumstances, should not have sickened me. The slaves fell on the food with cries and fought and struggled over the choicest portions. Coarse stuff, it was, plentiful, belly-filling. A kind of maize grows on Kregen, dilse, that can be mixed with milk and water and pounded, salted, and served up in a variety of ways. It is cheap where it grows freely, for it needs little cultivation. Great tureens of dilse stood about, the carrying poles all carefully removed from the handles of the tureens. It steamed. Also there was a little Kregan bread—those long fluffy rolls, although this stuff was stale and hard—sacks of onions, a few rounds of cheese, and what was clearly a single vosk cut into portions and cooked. By the time Tulema and I reached the feeding cave all the vosk was claimed, the bread was vanishing, the onions were rolling about with frantic figures in pursuit of them, but there was plenty of dilse for those unable to secure the better food, those too weak and feeble to fight for it.

Now I understood why Tulema's face showed a thinness her body did not reveal. That is the blight of dilse.

A large and somewhat ferocious Rapa was striding past me. He held a thick rasher of vosk, a piece of bread, and no less than four onions. He knocked an Och away, who attempted with one of his four arms to steal the vosk rasher. The Och tumbled against the wall, screeching. Tulema shrank back.

I said to the Rapa: "I would be obliged if you would share that vosk rasher, and a piece of bread, and half the onions with this girl, here."

The Rapas are notorious in their treatment of women. Once my Delia had been threatened with the horrible fate of being tossed naked into the Rapa court. The Rapa leered.

"You may go to the Ice Floes of Sicce," he said, and went to push past.

Well—maybe I was some kind of Prince Majister—but here and now I was slave in a slave pen. I knew slave manners. I hit the Rapa in the guts and took the vosk, the bread, and two of the onions. The other two rolled over the floor and were instantly pounced on by an old Fristle woman.

The Rapa tried to straighten up, hissing, his beaked face vicious, his crest swelling. But I hit him again, with my free hand, and turned to Tulema.

"Eat."

"But—you—"

"I am not hungry."

That was true. Only moments ago I had risen from the campfire, replete with the finest delicacies Valka could offer.

She fell on the food ravenously.

If you were not strong and determined and ruthless here you would not die of starvation, for you could eat dilse, but you would slowly decline. Maybe, I thought even then, there was purpose in this. I had some inkling of slave-masters' ways.

We walked away and I waited for Tulema to finish eating. Then I said: "Tulema. Listen closely. I want to know the names and conditions of all the people who were with us in the cell when—" I hesitated. I could hardly say to her, "When I arrived," for that would demand explanations I would not give, and if given, would not be believed. I finished: "When the slave-master was knocked down."

The food inside her warmed her. She did not giggle— slaves only laugh and sing when something special happens, like the master falling down and breaking his neck—but she let me know she thought my remark highly apposite.

"I think I can remember. But why?"

Instinctively I had to quell my instant rush of bad language, my browbeating intolerance of any who would question an order. I said: "Does anyone escape from here, Tulema?"

"We believe so—we hope so—but I am frightened to go—"

That did make some kind of sense, but it was a tortuous thread. Tulema told me something of herself, and thereby something also of where we were. She came from a seaside town called Pellow, and she sounded sad when she told me of her home in Herrelldrin. She had every right to be sad. We were on the island of Faol, and she shivered as she told me. The island lay off the coast of Havilfar.

Havilfar!

So far on Kregen I had trod the land of the continents of Segesthes and of Turismond. I had touched at Erthyrdrin, in the continent of Loh. But the continent of Havilfar was all new and unexplored by me, virgin territory. I fancied I was in for some wild adventures and some seething action in the future, and, as you shall hear, I was not wrong.

After the meal a sudden shrilling of a stentor's horn made everyone jump and then rush madly for the exits. I stumbled along after Tulema, trying to keep her in sight in the frenzied rushing to and fro of slaves. Screams and cries rang out, people shouted for friends, and I saw the way the slaves kept darting frightened glances back, into the dimmer recesses of the caves.

We all pushed up against the lenk-wood bars.

I blinked against the glare of the twin suns and looked out. I knew we were in the southern hemisphere of Kregen now, and therefore the suns would cross the sky to the northward, but just where we were off Havilfar in relation to the equator I could not say. I guessed we were nearer that imaginary line than I had been in Vallia, nearer, even, than I had been in Pandahem. For the northern sweep of Havilfar rises out of the southern ocean east of southern Loh, below the rain forests of Chem. I fancied Inch's Ng'groga would not be too far away, down to the southwest.

In the clearing cut from the jungle I saw guards strutting, banging their whips against gaitered legs, swaggering in their tunics of forest green. Among them a number of well-dressed men and women moved as though on a shopping expedition.

I say as though on a shopping expedition, but then I thought that was what they were doing—shopping for slaves. In that I was wrong.

A group advanced to the cage where we stood and Tulema shrank back. Other slaves with us pushed forward boldly. Tulema held my arm. Without any sense of rancor I guessed she saw in me a meal ticket and did not wish to lose me. My sentiments were not to lose her, for she could tell me of the people in the cell when I arrived.

In the mob of slaves pressing up against the bars one man stood out. He was dark-haired, and his hair was cropped. He looked lithe and bronzed and fit. He had about him an alertness, an air of competence, and I saw the way he stood, loosely and limberly. The people with him pressed against the lenk-wood bars.

"A very fine bunch at the moment, Notor,"* a guard was saying to one of the customers. The guard I categorized in a moment: hard, arrogant, whip-wielding, a true slave-master, toadying now to the highborn of the land.

The man he had addressed as "Notor" also merited little attention, being fleshy, bulkily built, with a dark beard and moustaches. His eyes were like those of a leem. He wore a fine tunic of some fancy pale lavender silk, and boots, and at his side swung a sword. He carried a kerchief drenched in perfume. The party with him, other nobles and their ladies, were likewise attired in silks and satins against the heat. They were a chattering, laughing, carefree group of people—and my heart hardened against them, for all I had been as happy and carefree in what, although it was but a bur or so ago, now seemed another world.

"Yes, Nalgre," said the lord. "I think so. What do you advise for this season? A dozen? Would that be enough for us?" He sniggered. "We are passable shots, Nalgre."

"The finest shots, Notor Renka," quoth Nalgre the slave-master. "I believe, with all due deference, you could easily accommodate a full score."

Tulema tugged me back again.

"Do not press against the bars so, Dray!" I had told her my name, Dray Prescot, without so much as a Koter for title. I had had my fill of titles for the moment.

I shook her hand off, for I wanted to learn as much as might be of the situation in which I had been placed, a problem to solve and someone to save—someone, I had no idea who.

At that instant, when I was about to press forward and so join the mob, slightly separated from the others, clustered

*Notor: Lord. Prescot has used *notor* a number of times previously in his narrative and I have amended it to *lord*. I feel, though, that *notor* is peculiar to Havilfar and so have used it throughout as Prescot does.   A.B.A.

around the lithe dark-haired man, I saw beyond the bars a man I knew. He walked with the notables and laughed and glanced over the slaves, and waved a scented handkerchief airily.

The man was Berran, Vadvar of Rifuji, a noble of Vallia who had been a secret member of the third party, and who had led his men to the aid of Naghan Furtway to fight at The Dragon's Bones. I had thought him dead. Now he was here. I wondered how many others of the leaders of the abortive coup had fled to Havilfar.

Feeling it was prudent not to be recognized I stepped back away from the bars. I must have stepped smartly, for Tulema let out a squeal, and I realized I had trodden on her toes. I do not apologize, so I said: "Who is that man with the dark hair and handsome face? A slave who looks unlike a slave?"

She recovered quickly. From the corner of my eye I could see the Notor Renka and his party, and with them Berran, moving away with the slave-master, so that danger had passed.

"He is a guide. They are brave men—I wish—" She swallowed. Her face wore a drawn look of misery. "I am frightened to go with them. I can offer nothing—but everyone says they can save us."

Chapter Four

Manhunters of Faol

A few quick questions established just what was going on here on the island of Faol.

Slaves were taken from the cell and, now that I understood, I was not surprised to see the willingness with which they went. They tried to hide that eagerness, they tried to dissimulate, but for all that they fairly skipped out of the cell. They were not happy merely because they were being let out of a cell. Their joy ran in deeper channels.

The man Tulema had called a guide went with them, and I could see him trying to hush his companions, and for a space they would slouch along like dejected slaves, only to go pushing on toward the slave barracks at the far end of the clearing. Guards surrounded them, harsh, vicious men in the leaf-green tunics, with whips and swords and spears.

The notables who had done their shopping had gone.

They were not here on Faol buying slaves.

They were on holiday.

They might even—and I hoped Zair might have mercy on them for so abusing a great word—they might say they were on a Jikai.

For these slaves would be hunted.

They were quarry.

On the morrow, given clothes and a knife apiece, they would be let loose in the jungles of Faol, and then the nobles and their ladies, dressed up in fancy hunting clothes, would take after them. Oh, it would be great sport. They'd hunt the slaves right across the island, making great sport of it all, shouting "Hai, Jikai!" like as not.

I felt sick.

That human men and women could so debase themselves frightened me. No wonder the men of Aphrasöe so passionately wished to cleanse the planet Kregen, to give it honor and dignity, to remove forever the stain of slavery.

One tiny spark of hope there was, one ray of hope in all this morass of horror and ugliness.

That hope made the slaves walk out so eagerly on what would be a dreadful chase through the jungles, hunted and slain for sport.

For the guards had no way of knowing that the young men the slaves called guides would lead the hunted creatures to safety.

Tulema told me.

"The guides are very brave men, Dray! They can find their way through the jungles, and they can lead the people out to safety! And then, they come back here, through the tunnels in the rock, at the back of the caves, they return to lead out more slaves to freedom!"

"They are brave, Tulema," I said.

"Oh, yes! They take who they can, but they are promised rewards for their help, and I cannot reward anyone, for my parents are dead and I was a dancer in a dopa den, and I am afraid . . ."

A thought occurred to me.

"Why does not everyone escape out through the tunnels in the caves?"

She shook her head. "The ways are terrible and fraught with danger. The shafts are steep. The stone crumbles. Men can slide down, no one can climb up."

Well, I could be sure that slaves had tried to get out that way, and had failed. Slaves do many things to escape. The fear of death will not stop them, only failure of a scheme will hold them back from escape.

An old crone wandered across the cell, sweeping with a rustly broom of twigs, cleaning up. Everyone moved out of her way. She was not a human being, and here I saw for the first time a member of the race of Miglish, the Miglas, who inhabit a large and important island off Havilfar.

"Get out of the way, you onker!" said one of the slaves, pushing the crone. She spat back at him and waved her broom, her long tangled hair about her face.

"May Migshaanu the All-Glorious turn your bones to jelly and your teeth black in your mouth and may she strike you with the pestilence and your eyes dribble down your cheeks, you cowardly nulsh!"

The Miglish crone waved her broom, whose stiff twigs were

no more wildly tangled than her dark hair. The slave fell
back, but still he mocked, and, indeed, the Migla looked a
strange and unwholesome sight. She wore a gray slave breechclout and a gray sacking garment. Her words tumbled out in
a torrent. Tulema pulled me back, saying, "She is an evil
old witch, Dray!"

The Migla swiped her broom at the dusty floor and tottered
across to the lenk-wood bars where a guard in the leaf-green
opened the narrow, barred door for her. She went out, still
complaining, her thin bent back hard and angular beneath
the sackcloth. She was evidently a tame slave and employed
to clean up. Truth to tell, cleaning up was always necessary
in these slave pens of Faol.

The slave who had pushed her spat on the floor.

He was a fine upstanding young man, with a limber body
on which the muscles showed long and supple, clear evidence
that he could fight his way to the choicest parts of vosk, the
fattest and juiciest onions, the best knuckle of bread. Tulema
glanced at him, and away. He stared boldly at her, and walked
over, moving with an arrogant lilt to him, a cock of the chin.

"I have not seen you before, shishi," he said, and he smiled
with the wide meaning smile of a young man who imagines
he knows all there is to know of the world and its wicked
ways.

Shishi is a word I do not much care for. It carries certain
connotations when spoken in that way by a man to a girl,
and is far from respectful. It had been used by various men
to Delia when we were in captivity and most of the men who
had so spoken to her were dead. I started to say something,
in my usual intemperate way, but Tulema put a quick hand
on my arm and spoke loudly over my words.

"There are many slaves here, dom. It is no wonder you
have not seen me." And then, with meaning, she added:
"Why have you not gone with a guide to freedom? You are
a strong man—"

"Yes, I am strong."

And, there and then, to my amazement, he started in on a
series of calisthenic exercises, bulging his muscles, striking
poses, making his body an exhibition of muscular strength.

I did not laugh, for, as you know, I do not laugh often.
Although, looking back, I see I seemed to do nothing else
but laugh during that wonderful time in Vondium when
Delia and I were first married.

"This man is a Khamorro of the land of Herrell," Tulema

whispered to me, her eyes wide and fearful. "They know a very terrible means of breaking men's bones. Do not, Dray, I beg you, even think of fighting him."

"Do not be frightened of him," I said.

"You do not understand! I do not know what kham he may have reached, but if you touch him he will kill you."

About to make some noncommittally brave and no doubt foolish reply, I stopped my wagging tongue. A girl had walked into our cell and approached the bars, and stood staring out in hopeless longing upon the mingled opaline rays of the twin suns. There can be no shame about nakedness among slaves, for between us we did not own so much as a pocket kerchief to cover ourselves, but this girl's stance, the way her arm reached up to clasp a lenken bar, the long line of her body, moved me. Her hair waved in a bright and genuine golden color about her shoulders, and her face, pallid and clear, revealed a beauty that seemed to light up the dank dark cave-cell.

I fancied I remembered the glorious golden hair shining as she ran from the cell on my arrival, when I had thrown the whip-wielding slave-master.

The Khamorro, after taking my measure, as he must have supposed, and seeing that hesitation on my part, thereafter ignored me and fell into conversation with Tulema. I looked at them both and, for the sake of an honor that has often been a sore trial to me, as you know, vowed that if he troubled her I would break his neck for him, despite his secret knowledge.

If I simply walked up to the golden-haired girl and began to talk to her, she might think my intentions were the same as the Khamorro's toward Tulema. I was saved a solution to that dilemma by the entry of another girl, beautiful and lithe, but with a yellow hair that in its dustiness and lack of shine could in nowise compare with the golden glory of the first girl, who stood now so sadly at the lenken bars.

"A princess!" said this second girl, in a high and mocking voice. "The proud Lilah says she is a princess! Is not this a great joke?"

Slaves can relish a joke, if it suits their somber moods, as well as anyone else. And, too, most of these slaves knew that with the help of the guides they would win free of the chase and so escape with their lives and liberty. So they were in nowise as downcast a mood as are slaves who see before them only another day's toil as hard and agonizing as today's, and after that another, and another, and the only surcease in death.

The beautiful girl with the golden hair did not turn around. She spoke in a low musical voice that gave full expression to the beauty of language universal Kregish undeniably possesses.

"I am a princess, Tosie, in all truth. But what good that will do me I cannot say."

"You cunning liar!" This Tosie was furious, now, her head thrown back, her hands on hips, her whole stance indicative of intense personal anger and frustration. "You promise the guides much money and great rewards if they will guide you out, pretending to be a princess. Well, then!" Tosie's face took on a triumphant look as she screamed: "If you are the Princess Lilah, then I am the Queen Tosie! You should bow and scrape to me! I'll promise the guides anything to take me away from this awful place!"

Tosie was no queen, that appeared certain. But if this Lilah was a princess, then she was the one the Star Lords wished me to rescue. What their ends might be I did not know, but the rescue of this glorious Princess Lilah was a task to which they had set my hands. I would not fail them; I must not, for until I had completed their mission I would not be allowed to return to Vallia and my Delia, my Delia of Delphond.

"It is because I am Princess of Hyrklana that I may not do as you intend, Tosie. I can only offer rewards to the guides when I return home to my father's palace."

"And I shall offer rewards, too! Money! Lands! Zorcas! Totrixes! Women—and money again! Whatever you offer I will double. If you think you will escape and leave me here to be hunted, alone and without a guide, you think wrongly!"

A blast on the stentors' horns cut into the argument. The sound was different from the call that had driven everyone in such great panic out of the feeding hall and into the cells to crowd up against the lenken bars. The slaves began that surging movement, shouting and pushing, and all rushed off toward the feeding cave. By this time I fancied a juicy chunk of vosk would not come amiss, so I started off, too.

I looked back.

Tosie, who called herself a queen and was probably a dancing girl in a dopa den like Tulema, had gone. Tulema herself was just running out, assisted by the Khamorro. I would find her again, if necessary, but now, with the knowledge that it was the Princess Lilah I must rescue, I could let Tulema go.

Lilah turned listlessly from the bars.

"Come, Princess," I said. "If you would eat we must hurry to the feeding cave."

She looked at me.

Her eyes were blue, and though I could guess they would normally be bright and clear and frank, now they were clouded with suspicion.

Before she could say what so clearly lay in her mind, I said swiftly, "There will be a struggle for the food, Princess. We must hurry."

She stood there, drooping and defenseless, and the thought occurred to me that if ever my Delia found herself in this position again—which Zair forbid!—there would be a man ready to protect her without thought of reward.

"You—call me *princess*—"

"I see you are. Now, come."

She went with me through the barred cells and passage-ways and so into the feeding cave. We were too late. Most of the other slaves had already taken what they could snatch and the remainder were clustered about the dilse tureens.

My instincts were to knock down the nearest person eating a hunk of vosk and chewing on onions and snatch the food away. Perhaps I was growing weak and feeble, but I did not. I said, "We must eat dilse today, Princess. At the next feeding time you must run very swiftly."

She made a small dismissive gesture with her hand. I noticed her fingers, very long and slender, and I tried to imagine them plugging into the heaped food on the floor and bunching into tiny fists to strike away those who would snatch the food first. She would not starve, but she would grow lean of face and listless on dilse.

We were fed at regular intervals, I guessed every five burs or so—something like three and a half hours—and the reason for this lavish expenditure of food was quite clear. Whoever owned this island of Faol, where slaves were run and hunted as quarry, had to please his customers; and these came from many islands and lands even from beyond Havil-far, so the slaves must be well fed and active to furnish good sport.

I would relish a short interview with this fellow.

At the next feeding call, when the stentor horns boomed and clamored through the passageways and cells cut in the rocks, I grabbed Lilah's hand and fairly dragged her along. Many slaves clustered about the entrance to the feeding hall, of course, just before they guessed the call would come, and these rushed in first. I plowed my way through them and halfway to the mess of food let Lilah go and lunged on.

How had my pride been humbled!

Here I was, a naked slave grubbing and fighting for food scattered on a filthy floor, when only a day ago I had eaten all the delicacies my heart could desire—and then I shut all self-pity from my mind. I hardened—and I am only too prone to being a soft man in many things, as you know.

Lilah accepted the food. She might have thought to stand on her dignity, but when she saw the dripping hunk of vosk I snatched up, and felt the firm lusciousness of the onions, smelled the cheese—it was a dreadful smell, in truth, but it was food—she could not hold back. She ate with a strange pathetic mixture of ravenous hunger and a finicky set of table manners. I just wolfed the stuff down.

And then, again, that clamoring of stentor horns broke out afresh and with wild cries all the slaves ran out of the feeding cave to press themselves against the lenken bars.

But I had not quite finished the chunk of hard bread, for in my lazy, wealthy way back in Vallia I had grown used to the finest food, and so was slow with this lenklike loaf.

Lilah said, "Dray—we must run! It is the call for the jiklos! Hurry!"

She might know what in hell a jiklo was, I did not, and I wanted to finish this confounded chunk of iron-hard bread. Lilah was terrified. She did not catch my arm, as Tulema would have done, to drag me away. She started for the exit, and turned, her golden hair swirling, and cried, "Hurry, Dray! Hurry!"

Chewing on the bread I walked after her.

Truly, pride is a foolish item in a man's baggage!

I heard the jiklos, then.

I heard an eerie, spine-chilling, frightful, and obscene hissing and howling, a scrabbling of claws, the rush of bodies. Lilah screamed and ran. I turned to look back.

A glimpse, I had, a glimpse back through a freshly opened entrance to the cave. Ruby light spilled out from the space beyond.

Through that bloody radiance dreadful forms ran on all fours over the filthy floor. I saw matted hair crested into upswept combs, and trailing out to the rear. I saw flashing

"The manhound threw himself against those bars, slavering."

eyes. Teeth glinted like rows of daggers. Hands and feet pounded the dust and filth of the floor. Red tongues lolled. The jiklos howled at sight of me—and then Lilah was there, pulling me on. We stumbled back through the entrance to the feeding cave and iron bars clashed down, almost crushing us.

The leading jiklo threw himself against those bars, slavering. His eyes regarded me with the utmost malevolence.

I looked at him.

And I saw what he was.

I felt the sick nausea welling up.

So I first made the acquaintance of the Manhounds of Antares.

Chapter Five

Manhounds

"But they're *men*!"

I have seen many and many a sight that might drive any normal man insane. I have never considered myself a normal man, and for that hubris I have suffered. But I do believe that the Manhounds of Antares made as strong an impression of decadence and evil and horror upon me as anything I have seen on Earth or on Kregen.

They were men.

But they ran on all fours. Their faces were human faces. But they had fierce sharply serrated teeth, they had pricked ears, pointed and mobile, they had squashed pug noses that could wrinkle up and sniff and follow a scent that might baffle bloodhounds. They had the bodies of men. But their hands padded against the ground, and their rear legs were shorter and thicker than those of a man who walks upright. Their nails were sharp hard claws, glinting evilly. Their hair was brushed and combed upward into a cock-fighting crest, and streamed out in a loose mane, like that of a horse, from the stiff crest.

They wore brave red jackets, cut like a dog's jacket. They wore gray breechclouts. Around their necks were strapped leather collars, studded with metals.

They were hunting dogs.

But they were men.

The Manhounds of Antares, the jiklos of Faol.

Pressed up against the lenken bars Lilah still held my arm. She had not shrunk from touching me, from pulling me away. Just beyond her I could see Tulema and the Khamorro. Now I understood a little why Tulema, for all the promises of the guides, hung back from escaping, was so terrified of the manhunt.

47

"Yes, Dray Prescot," said Princess Lilah of Hyrklana. "They are men."

Men. They were not halflings, even, men-beasts for beast-men with a weird mutation of head or body to mark them out from true men—and who, on Kregen, is to say who is a true man and who is not? Gloag was a man for all his bristle-hide and bullet-head. Inch, too, was a man. But these —things? These Manhounds of Scorpio? Were they truly men?

The answer could not be denied.

Some agency had so guided their development, over the seasons, as to transform them from ordinary men into jiklos. I could with revulsion imagine some of the training. They must have been strapped into iron cages from birth, made to walk always on all fours, taught to run and hunt, and by evolving senses regained man's lost capacities of smell and hearing. They might be unable to stand upright at all, now.

And the final blasphemy, at least in my eyes, was to dress them in red coats, to sully the image I held of my own old scarlet, the scarlet of Strombor!

Shadows moved in the jungle clearing beyond the bars. The slaves huddled, waiting to be picked as quarry. Tulema hung back and the Khamorro, arguing with her, at last slapped her across the face and pushed her back. He moved toward the bars with arrogance, and other slaves shrank back from him.

Lilah said, "Here they come now. . . ."

Into the cleared area before the barred rows of cages, rather like a shopping arcade, stepped Nalgre, the slave-master, with his guards, and his customers. I ignored all that, started to push my way toward the Khamorro. Tulema was sobbing, now. She had lost this Khamorro and she must have assumed she had already lost me, absorbed as I had been with Lilah. Tulema could not know that it was by the Star Lords' command that I must rescue Lilah.

"No, Dray Prescot," said Lilah. I recognized the tone. She was a princess, I felt no doubt. "You will be killed."

Again she put her hand on my arm. I could feel the soft-ness of it, and yet the firmness, too, as she gripped me.

What might have happened then, Zair knows, for a Fristle nearby, whose fur was much bedraggled, said quickly, "Here is Nath the Guide."

The guide pushed through to the bars, and I left off trying to reach the Khamorro. This guide was much like the first one I had seen, lithe, well built, fleet of limb, as I judged, with a handsome head and a mass of dark hair. Nath the Guide. . . .

Well, there are many Naths on Kregen.

Around him perhaps a dozen people clustered. They were eager. They had been able to arrange deals with the guide to be taken out. And all the time Lilah's hand gripped my arm.

Nalgre the slave-master cracked his whip. The customers with him jumped, and then laughed, and pointed out to one another choice specimens of slaves within the cages. It was all a part of the show Nalgre put on.

These nobles and wealthy men and women who hunted human beings for sport were little different from the bunch I had seen before. A quick check showed me that Berran was not with them. The Notor who, by his appearance and gestures, considered himself the most important personage there was a heavily built man, with brown hair, a face pudgy from too many inspections of the bottoms of glasses, too many vosk-pies, and smothered in a mass of jewels and silks and feathers.

He was pointing now and Nalgre was nodding.

Nath the Guide whispered: "It will be all right. He will choose us. Now remember! Act as slaves, for the sake of Hito the Hunter!"

This Notor fancied himself as a great jikai, it was clear, for the guards swung open the lenken-barred gate and began to herd out more than a dozen of the slaves. One fragile Xaffer was rejected, and I guessed the poor devil had been subsisting on dilse and nothing else for too long. In the heat and dust of the compound, with the smells of sweat and fear all about us, we were prodded out. Lilah clung to me. I caught a glimpse of Tulema hanging back, her face agonized, tear-streaked, and then the lenken bars smashed shut against the slaves who remained unselected.

"We're in for it now, Lilah," I said. "We'll soon be free."

"I pray it be so, Dray Prescot."

With guards around us, their spears everywhere ready to prod mercilessly, we were taken through the clearing to the slave barracks. Here we would be prepared for the next day's hunt.

You will already have realized that the Dray Prescot who walked so docilely with the slaves, prodded by spears, was a very different person from the Dray Prescot who had so witlessly and violently resisted any slave attempt upon him—

as when, for instance, I was captured and flung down before the Princess Natema, and had thrown Galna at her, for good measure. I was trying to calculate out if escaping now, this instant, would serve our ends better than waiting. Once I had taken this lovely girl Princess Lilah of Hyrklana back home, I would then strike at once for Vallia. I did not wish to make a leem's-nest of it.

I have been hunted as quarry for sport since that occasion on Faol—notably by the debased Ry-ufraisors, who sacrifice to the green sun, calling Genodras by the name of Ry-ufraison. That was many seasons later, of course—many years ago, now, too—and I wander in my tale. It is worth note that here on Faol I found the people referring to the red and green suns, the Suns of Scorpio, not as Zim and Genodras but as Far and Havil.

While I had no doubts that I could survive in the jungle, and this without boasting, which is a fool's trade, I had doubts about Lilah. Nath the Guide told us we would be given clothes, and boots, and a knife apiece. Also food. Almost decided in my mind to consign these trinkets to the Ice Floes of Sicce and make a break for it right away, I witnessed an event that changed my mind.

The arrogant Khamorro would have nothing of waiting. He had chosen his time, and now, by Morro the Muscle, he would break a few backbones and escape into the jungles. His name was Lart. I had had trouble with a Lart very early on during my second visit to Kregen, and so I watched with great care.

Lart the Khamorro flexed his muscles in the slave barracks. Other men walked small when a Khamorro passed. We were given fresh food, although the promised clothes were denied us, and the food was good—thick vosk and taylyne soup, beef roasted to a prime, fresh roandals, the break of Kregen in long loaves and done in the bols fashion as well, and, lastly, palines.

We were packed off to the first floor of the building, leaving the hard-packed earth below empty. By leaning out over the sturm-wood balustrade we could see the guards patrolling down there. One test of the walls showed they would resist bare hands. The only way out was down the stairs, past the guards, and through the doors.

Lart the Khamorro flexed his muscles and started down the stairs.

Three guards stood up, alert, and their spears twitched down into line.

"Get back, cramph!"

Lart laughed. He jeered at them.

"If we kill you, rast, the cost of your worthless hide will be deductible." One of the guards, with a thin black goatee, swung his spear so that the point glittered in the light falling through the windows at his back. "But I would willingly pay that to degut you!"

Lart laughed again and then he moved and that guard lay on the ground with a broken neck.

The other two cursed and swiveled their spears. Lart the Khamorro swerved very lithely and ducked and another guard was caught and, for an instant, held in a terrible grip. He catapulted over Lart's back and when he hit the ground his little round helmet rolled away from what was left of his skull.

The third guard shouted, high and filled with terror.

"Hai! Guards! A madman is loose!"

"The fools!" whispered Lilah, at my side. "Don't they know he is a Khamorro?"

"Evidently not, Lilah." I watched, fascinated. I saw how Lart worked, the smooth play of his muscles, the cunning tricks of body-contact, all the skills I had absorbed under the pitiless tuition of the Krozairs of Zy were here being put into action, under my nose, and me skulking on a stair!

But I knew what I was doing.

The main doors were fast bolted by a massive beam of lenk.

Lart rushed for them and began to lift the beam. The third guard, still yelling, made the mistake of trying to thrust his spear into Lart's back. The muscles rippled on that sinewy back. Lart slid the spear—and that was neatly done, by Zair!—and cut the guard under the chin with the edge of his palm. The guard choked and writhed and died. The trick was an old one but reliable if you were quick enough to hit the target.

Again Lart began to lift the lenken beam that took two men to place. He got one end up and was about to slide it down when with a rush and a volley of oaths three more guards raced into the dirt-floored chamber. Up on the stairs we all yelled in warning.

If Lilah expected me to run down to help Lart, she was mistaken. Anyway, I had the hunch that if I did so a haze of blue radiance would engulf me, and a giant scorpion would enfold me in its pincers and I would be flung—where? Back to Earth, probably. Then I would have to languish how many years before the Star Lords once more thought to employ me about their mysterious business on Kregen?

For the sake of Delia, not for Lilah, I remained where I was.

Anyway, even as Lart, in a sudden and destructive flurry of blows, chops, stabs of finger and knuckle, body-swerves and cunning lifts and back-breaking holds, disposed of the three guards, what I knew must happen came to pass with the furious advent of a Deldar. He came in through the side door, waving his sword, and with him came three crossbowmen.

"You stupid, dopa-sodden cramphs!" The Deldar was bellowing. "Have you no sense in your onker-thick skulls?"

I perfectly agreed with him.

"Feather me this rast!" screamed the Deldar. The three crossbows leveled.

Even then, even then Lart the Khamorro with his marvelous skills in unarmed combat almost got them. He dodged the first bolt, almost missed the second, taking it high in his left shoulder. But this slowed him a fraction, jerking him off balance, and he took the last quarrel clear through his belly.

He coughed and doubled up.

Still, he moved on, lifting his hands. And now, because he was mortally wounded, he moved slowly enough for that cunning hand-pattern to be clearly visible. I recalled the burs of training spent with the Krozairs on the island of Zy in the Eye of the World. My body responded to the remembered thump and smash of fist, and hand-edge, and knuckle, the way Zinki could always throw me until I learned the secret ways of counterbalance, and weight-shift, the poise, the blows, the whole mystic art of body-fighting I had learned as I had learned how to wield a Krozair longsword. Well, give me a sword anytime, but without a metal weapon—or a wooden one, come to that—a man may do terrible damage with his bare hands.

But Lart had been slowed too much.

The guard Deldar could bring his sword down in a vicious blow and so finish Lart the Khamorro.

Lilah gasped and turned away.

I admit, I felt queasy about leaving a fellow human being to fight alone, like that. But—and however brutal and selfish this sounds, I do not care—what was Lart to me beside my mission for the Star Lords that must not fail, my concern for Lilah—my love for Delia, my Delia of the Blue Mountains?

"The stupid rancid-brained onkers!" the Deldar was shouting. He kicked Lart's dead body. "They didn't know to keep away from a Khamorro. You!" He swung violently on his three crossbowmen. "Never get within reach of a Khamorro! Never! It is certain death." He fumed on, and as the bodies were cleared away he shouted up at us, gawping from the balustrade. "Get back up there and rest! Aye, rest! Tomorrow you run and will need all your strength. And if any cramph among you wants to break out of the door—he'll taste my steel!"

There was one furious Deldar. No doubt, Lart would be deductible.

There were palliasses and thin blankets, and before we went to sleep, Lilah said, "Lart fought well, Dray. He was very skilled, a high kham, I have no doubt. And he was very brave."

"Aye, Lilah," I said, turning over and pulling the blanket up. "Very brave and very stupid."

Chapter Six

How Nath the Guide aided us

The morning broke fresh and glorious with the twin Suns
of Scorpio bursting up over the jungle levels and casting
down their streaming mingled jade and ruby light. The air
smelled clean and invigorating, and however dank it might
become in the jungle, as we ate a huge breakfast I own we
slaves felt happier than any of us had any right to be.

Lilah had told me that she had been on a visit of state
with an uncle to a neighboring country of Havilfar when her
airboat had been attacked and captured. She called the fliers
vollers, and when I mentioned that they always seemed to
be breaking down, she turned a puzzled frown my way, and
said, "Not reliable, Dray? You do an injustice to the voller
builders! Why, our vollers can outfly the fastest saddle-birds
in all Havilfar!"

I let the matter go, but I did not forget it.

She was not completely sure how she had come to be
brought to Faol. She knew the island, of course, off northern
Havilfar; and she had heard casual tales of great hunts to
be had there. She had no idea that this Jikai was the hunting
of people, and she had met the jiklos with utter horror.

Like all the continents and the nine islands of Kregen—
with the exception of Vallia—Havilfar is divided up into
different countries. I set myself to learn their geography and
histories, as well as Lilah could inform me, and when it is
necessary for you to know any part of these, then that is
when I shall introduce it.

In the circle of vaol-paol all things may come to pass.

Nath the Guide winked at us as we shuffled outside and
into the cleared area before the slave barracks. Waiting for
us and backed by a strong guard contingent stood Nalgre
and his customers. Today the great hunters were dressed in
leathers, with tall boots, wide hats, and a massive armory

54

hung about them. The chief weapon of the hunt would be
the crossbow. As always, I studied the weapons of those who
were my foemen and who sought to slay me.

The fashion in swords here was for the short straight blade,
perhaps not quite as robust a brand as the shortswords of
my clansmen, but a useful and all-purpose cut-and-thrust
weapon that would do its work efficiently and without fuss.
The crossbows were beautiful artifacts, the wood a close-
grained hurm—a close relative of the ubiquitous sturm-wood
—and the butts and stocks shone in the mingled rays of the
suns. The bows themselves were of tempered steel. Most of
these crossbows were spanned by cranequins, one or two by
goat's-foot lever. I did not see a single windlass. The bolts
were fletched in leather. In addition these infamous hunters
had loaded themselves with various bloodthirsty weapons. It
infuriated me to see, for instance, a plump and laughing
woman, her hair looped up in a net of priceless pearls, leaning on her crossbow and talking to her companion, who kept
digging the point of his vosk-spear into the ground. They all
looked a little self-conscious in their hunting leathers and
they handled their weapons rather as tourists handle imple-
ments with which they are not totally familiar.

All this spending of money and time and effort—to hunt
a raggle-tail bunch of half-naked slaves through the jungles!

Half-naked: we were issued with gray slave breechclouts
which we put on, out there, on the ground, in sight of everyone. Lilah acted as though the hunters did not exist.

I waited for the clothes and the knives, but Nath the Guide
whispered fiercely and at his words I forbore to inquire,
sensing a part of the secret the guides kept against the manhunters of Faol.

In this little group of slaves—sixteen of us—only Lilah and
I and two others, a man and woman, were humans. All the
rest were halflings. I couldn't equate Nath as a slave. Despite
the air of docility and fear he assumed there was about him
the unmistakable sense of the free man, the man who fought
against odds, and expected to win.

This fine morning Nalgre had his little pet with him.

He clicked his fingers and a jiklo ran across the clearing
toward him, tongue lolling, eyes bright, frisking about him.
I watched, sickened. This jiklo was a woman. She panted
about her master on all fours, pricking her ears, emitting little
gobbles of pleasure at his notice of her, and at the dribble of
ground vosk he let fall, which she lapped up greedily. She

wore a red bolero jacket, and a gray breechclout, and she ran on all fours, and she was a Manhound of Antares, and she was a woman.

The studs and plaques on her leather collar were all of gold. Her brown hair frizzed up into that angry matted crest, and blonde streamers of hair fell back in a tail from the central mass. Her naked rump frisked about Nalgre, and had a tail sprouted there, I suppose, one might have accepted the picture more.

Lilah's supple figure quivered at sight of the jiklo, then she controlled herself. The halflings were whispering to one another, and a couple of Fristles unashamedly clasped each other in their furry arms.

I had no doubt why Nalgre played with his pet before us. "Look," he was saying. "This is a manhound. These are the creatures who will chase you and hunt you and pull you down."

The jiklo trotted over to us. The halflings went rigid with fear. I looked down as the red bolero swung past. The thing emitted little gasps and wheezes, and the pug nose wrinkled up. The thing was smelling us! She was taking our scent!

"Get away, you filthy kleesh!" snarled the human man, a husky youngster called Naghan, who came, so he said, from Hamal itself. He told us this with pride. The girl with him screamed as the jiklo's tongue, all lolling and wet and red, rasped down her naked calf. Naghan kicked out and then he, too, screamed and writhed as a guard lashed his back with a cunning whipblow called the rattler.

"Stay in line there, you rasts!" shouted Nalgre.

He turned and spoke quietly to his customers the hunters, and then they glanced swiftly and at an angle beneath their hands at the suns, to tell the time, and then all turned and walked off out of the clearing, back to their comfortable Jikai villas to await the time to be off.

The time for the slaves to leave was now.

With the whips cracking about our heads, and words of advice from Nalgre, we set off. His advice amounted to: "Run and run, cramphs. If you do not afford good sport and are taken without a good chase, you will be more sorry than you may imagine!" He snickered as he said this, and fondled the female jiklo, who crooned in pleasure at the touch of her master's hand.

We set off due east.

The jungle closed above our heads and strange noises rose

from the depths of the greenery. The brilliant light of the
twin suns muted to a long lazy green-gold radiance, and
here and there mingled shafts of ruby and jade struck down
through interstices in the leafy cover. The trail was hard-
packed for the first dwabur. Five miles was a fair distance
to travel, and when we came out to a little clearing the slaves
were happy to flop down, panting, to rest.

Nath the Guide crossed to a heap of lichened stones and
lifted one to the side. I looked over his shoulder.

In the hollow between the stones lay clothing, food—and
knives! Also there were clumsy-looking shoes.

The halflings pounced on the shoes first.

Well, that made sense. I have been accustomed all my
life to going barefoot, and I had walked across the Hostile
Territories, and the Owlarh Waste without footwear. The
journey across the Klackadrin, too, was not without a lively
memory or two, and then I had been barefoot.

I said I did not want a pair of shoes.

At this Nath the Guide protested, saying I would slow the
others up. They were putting on the clothes, simple gray
tunics and floppy hats, and Lilah, too, implored me to don
a pair of shoes. In the end I did so, to quiet her noise.

We ate and rested and then set off again.

"When will they catch up with us, Nath?"

"Not until the suns have passed the zenith." He chuckled.
"And if we press on boldly they may never catch up with us
at all. There are secret ways."

He kept us going east. The jungle looked like many another
jungle through which I have traveled, with trees and growths
familiar to Earth as well as Kregen. Lilah was holding up
well. If we could keep going and get well ahead, we might
clear right out for good.

Toward early evening we left the edge of the jungle, which
had thinned considerably, and came to an immense ravine
cut through the earth athwart our path. A light rope bridge
hung above the abyss. We crossed, not without a deal of
swaying about and a few screams, and after we had reached
the other side Naghan from Hamal said: "Let us destroy the
bridge."

That seemed a sensible idea.

"No," said Nath the Guide. "If the bridge is gone the Jikai
will surely know which way we have gone."

Well, that seemed sensible, too.

In the end, bowing to Nath's superior knowledge of the problems of the manhunters, we left the bridge intact.

For a space I walked along with Nath, while Lilah walked with Naghan and his girl, Sosie. The guide intrigued me. I questioned him, casually, about his life.

"We are of Faol, too," he said. "I live in a village on the southern shore, and the young men are dedicated to helping the slaves. The manhunters are very terrible masters."

I congratulated him, thinking of the dangers he and his comrades faced. "I think," he said to me, glancing sideways as we walked, "you have been on many great Jikais yourself."

"Aye," I said, thinking of the great days when my clansmen had hunted across the Great Plains of Segesthes. "But I have never hunted humans for sport."

"Humans?" He looked at me oddly. "But only Naghan and Sosie, Lilah, and yourself are humans."

The Fristle man was at that moment helping the Fristle woman along, putting his furry arm about her waist and half carrying her. I was about to make what I considered a fitting reply when Nath broke away from me, looking up, shouting a warning.

"Vollers! Quick! Into the bushes—and remain still, for the sake of Hito the Hunter!"

From the shelter of the bushes we looked up, as a flier passed overhead, traveling slowly due east. Well, that answered one question I had intended to put to Nath—how the manhunters would know in which direction we had gone. He had been right about the bridge.

When the voller had gone we stood up, breathing our relief, and set off again. The country was opening out now. From the edge of the jungle beyond the ravine at our back the sky filled with the quick darting shapes of flying foxes, hereabouts called inklevols, black against the dying suns-glow.

Nath the Guide pointed ahead across the open land, dotted here and there with clumps of trees, gently rolling and gradually undulating away to a distant horizon.

"Tomorrow we cross the plain and then—"

"Then we are free!" exclaimed a Brokelsh, rubbing his black bristle body-hair in his excitement.

We made our little camp in a hollow, surrounded by trees, in the bend of a small river. Nath showed the usual skills of the hunter in preparing a smokeless fire and of shielding the flame-glare by a palisade of twisted rushes. The knives he had provided were poor things, it was true, but they did enable us to cut wood and leaves and so fabricate a softer bed than the ground. We ate and drank water from the stream, and Nath had been able to provide a little wine for us. Truth to tell, freedom was the wine we all craved.

We sat for a short space, talking, Nath and I. I had said to Naghan earlier: "Sosie and Lilah will sleep side by side, and you and I will sleep outside them." And he had replied: "It is a good plan."

Now I said to Nath: "And is manhunting the chief occupation of the high ones of Faol?"

"Yes. It is their ruling passion. Nobles come from all over Havilfar, and the lands beyond, to go on a Faol Jikai."

He sounded proud of that, which was strange, but he added: "They bring in money, which helps my people, and we arrange for the escape of the slaves."

"The hunters did not reach us, as you suggested they might."

"No. Tomorrow will be a day of careful marching."

I was itching to ask about Lilah who, as a princess, would in the societies I had previously known on Kregen be far more valuable as a subject for ransom than as a subject for a hunt. I put the point to Nath the Guide, who yawned, and said carelessly: "Oh, there are many girls who claim to be princesses and queens, and, mayhap, some of them are. But then—if a customer knew he was hunting a princess, and with all that would follow at the end of the hunt, think how much more the pleasure!"

"I see," I said.

It did make sense, of a kind that sickened me anew. I rolled over and pushed up against Lilah where she lay asleep, one arm outflung across Sosie, and so let my eyelids close.

Tomorrow we would cross the plain and reach safety and then I could deliver the Princess Lilah of Hyrklana to her friends and take off for Vallia. As sleep overcame me, I wondered vaguely if I might not prosecute two of my obsessions on Kregen as I was so near Havilfar. For on Havilfar lived the scarlet-robed Todalpheme who had taken Delia to Aphrasöe and who might therefore tell me where that marvelous Swinging City was situated on the face of Kregen. And the other obsession was to discover more of the fliers, the vollers, and their manufacture.

So I slept and with the first rays of Far and Havil striking low over the plain I awoke, sat up and rubbed my eyes, and reached for the cheap knife and stood up—and Nath the Guide was gone.

Chapter Seven

Princess Lilah of Hyrklana rides a fluttrell

In a babblement and confusion the slaves ran about looking for Nath the Guide. They shouted along the stream and broke through thickets, and looked behind clumps of rocks. I studied where the guide had slept. His gear still lay where he had left it—blanket, shoes, knife, a leaf with a few palines—and as he had slept a little apart from us whatever had taken him in the night had rested content with the one meal.

Lilah shivered. "Poor Nath!"

"Leem, by Hanitcha the Harrower!" Naghan said fiercely.

"We are on our own now." The squat-bodied Brokelsh rubbed his black body hairs as he spoke. "We had best move now!"

"We will eat first," I said. "And then we will march."

I did not anticipate an argument, and broke bread and gave some to Sosie and Lilah. We shared out what we had. In truth, it was little enough, and I fancied I must hunt our meat before the suns sank beyond the western horizon. "Also," I said, "we will set watches through the night."

I took up the knife left by Nath. It was of the same cheap manufacture as our own, but it was steel, for which I was thankful. His shoes, too, would be useful. Like ours they were cheap, crudely made from a single piece of cattle hide, pierced for thongs all around and then drawn up on a slip-string, like moccasins. There hung about them an odd little odor, as though they had not been perfectly cured.

We set off, striking due east by the suns, walking smartly.

After a time, thinking to put a little heart into the slaves, for they were mightily downcast by the savage and inexplicable disappearance of Nath the Guide, I struck up a song. I took the first one that jumped into my head. It was *Morgash and Sinkle*, all about a man and a maid and the laughable

61

plight of their marriage, and was known all over Kregen. These Havilfarese knew the song, and some of them joined in with me, and so, singing, we marched on across the undulating ground.

I kept that old warrior's eye of mine well open.

This night, I vowed, we would not sprawl out and sleep like a bunch of schoolchildren on an outing; we would march on by stages under the light of Kregen's moons. She of the Veils and the Twins would be up early, and the maiden with the many Smiles would follow later, to make the land almost as bright as an Earth day.

Despite the horror I knew slavered at our heels, the march would have been pleasant had I been in certain company. Had Seg Segutorio been with me, or Inch of Ng'groga, or Gloag, Hap Loder, Varden, or Vomanus—Delia—well, I was not foolish enough to wish my Delia here in this situation. But she would have responded with her marvelous spirit and enjoyment of life, her brave smile and her untiring love. This Princess Lilah was a fine girl, but I could understand the air of strain, her distrait appearance of barely suppressed terror. I wondered how that other Lilah, that Queen Lilah of Hiclantung, the notorious Queen of Pain, was faring now.

And so, marching across that gardenlike plain, I fell to maundering in my thoughts about Nath and Zolta—and Zorg, my oar comrade, who was now dead. I missed my two rascals, Nath and Zolta. I remembered many a fine carouse and singing session we had indulged ourselves in, back in Sanurkazz. There was Pur Zenkiren, too, Grand Archbold elect of the Krozairs of Zy. One day the great summons would come and I must return to the Eye of the World so that all the forces of the Zairians of the southern shore might go up against the Grodnim of the hostile northern shore of the inner sea.

That day would come.

If Nath and Zolta were with me now—there'd be some wild goings-on, by Zim-Zair!

Twice during that long march we saw fliers crisscrossing above. We hid. I felt an invisible net was closing about us.

Some of the shoes we wore were thinner in the sole than others, and a Relt, one of those more gentle cousins of the ferocious Rapas, soon complained that his bare foot was hurting. We inspected the hole, and pursed our lips, and I gave him one of Nath the Guide's shoes. The other shoe went in similar fashion to Sosie. We slogged on. In my usual fashion

—a cross laid on me I do not seem able to be free of—I had taken charge of this little fugitive band in the absence of the guide. They looked to me—Zair knows why people always look to me in moments of crisis—and so I had to respond with due propriety. I told them when to rest, and I caught one of the little six-legged rabbitlike animals of the plains called xikks and we cooked and ate the poor creature. Presently I roused them and we set off again, and now, ahead of us and spreading to encompass both north and south, a massive and darkly brooding forest spread its waiting wings.

Everyone looked ahead, pointing and chattering.

A harsh and demoniac croaking blattered down from above. I looked up.

Up there, circling in wide planing hunting circles, rising and falling on the air, flew a giant scarlet and golden-feathered hunting bird. A magnificent raptor, the Gdoinye, the messenger and spy of the Star Lords, who had snatched me from Vallia and dumped me down in a stinking slave pen.

I shook my fist.

The raptor circled, its head cocked and no doubt one beady eye regarding us and relaying what it saw back to its masters, the Everoinye. I wondered, for a moment, if the blue radiance would engulf me—but the raptor emitted another raucous squawk and flew off. I did not see the white dove of the Savanti.

"What in the name of the Twins was that?" said Lilah.

"A bird," I said. "Had I a bow—"

"You would not shoot so wonderful a creature, surely?" said Sosie, shocked.

I knew what I knew, and so I did not reply.

I looked back.

Dark against the ground the dreadful shapes of jiklos pressed hard on our trail.

At once all was confusion and the slaves began a mad run for the forest. I kept close to Lilah. One of my shoes loosened, the slipstring slipping, and I kicked the thing off. I could run more fleetly in my bare feet than clogged down with these clumsy shoes, and so I loosened the other and kicked off, too. We all ran.

We neared the trees, and I could see rocks and gullies in which the trees grew at crazy angles.

Lilah was panting and gasping, her golden hair blowing. I picked her up and ran.

Naghan had picked up Sosie, too, as the Fristle man had

picked up the Fristle woman. We were all hunted slaves, no longer simply men or halflings.

I flung a glance back.

The manhounds were terribly close. Beyond them rode zorca-mounted hunters, yelling, waving their weapons, having a fine old time. I ran.

We plunged into the first outlying trees and I picked a gully and ran up it, dodging tree branches, hurdling fallen trunks. Naghan, carrying Sosie, ran with me. We plunged on into the thicker trees, clambering over rocky patches, diving into underbrush, scratched and torn, plunging on and on.

Of course, my every instinct impelled me to dump Lilah down and, knives in fists, turn and battle these filthy manhounds, these high and mighty hunters. But I quelled that primeval instinct. My mission was to rescue Lilah, not to get myself killed in however enjoyable a way slaying manhounds and devilish hunters astride their zorcas.

Now we could hear the high excited keening of the jiklos. They were men! Men! Yet they were more fiercely predatory hunters than any bloodhound, any wersting, and to fall into their clutches would mean a hideous death.

We struggled and scrambled on, and came to a wall of rock.

"Put me down, Dray. We must climb."

"Get started, Lilah. When you are at the top, I will follow."

Sosie was already climbing, and Naghan following. Of the others I could see or hear nothing.

Lilah sprang at the rocks, began to haul herself up by ridge and crevice, her long golden hair very bright in the waning light of the twin suns.

I waited.

After what seemed a very long time I heard Lilah call, and about to wheel about and follow her, I caught the feral movement in the greenery opposite, the dagger-bright flash of jagged teeth.

A manhound sprang out from the trees, hurtled straight toward me.

And then—something for which I had not been prepared, the jiklo shouted to me, shouted words of a thick local language that, through the gene-manipulative pill of Maspero's in far Aphrasöe, I was able to understand.

The manhound spoke in a thick rasping whine, a hoarse and bloodthirsty howl.

"You are done for, you two-legged yetch!"

He bounded straight for me. The long mane streamed back from the central crest. His nails glittered. His eyes were bloodshot. And his teeth—could they ever have been the teeth of normal man? Sharp and jagged, serrated, as he opened his mouth to snarl at me those teeth looked like the teeth of risslaca honed to rip hot flesh and blood!

I poised, let fly one of my knives.

He tried to duck, but he was not quick enough.

The knife buried itself in one eye.

The jiklo let out an insane scream.

He was bounding into the air, rearing, his face a demoniac mask of hate and blood-lust. He pawed up at the knife hilt. He twisted, he toppled, he fell.

There was no time to recover the knife.

Up those rocks I went like a grundal.

From the open space the fresh sounds of a second jiklo struck over the slobbering shrieking of the first. Lilah screamed something incoherent. If that had been my Delia up there she wouldn't have been screaming, telling me something I already knew; my Delia would have been hurling rocks down to protect the back of her man.

Without looking back I lashed out with my foot and felt my heel jar into something hairy and hard, and the howling changed key into a yowling. I scrambled up the last few yards of the rock face and swung about at the top, on all fours like a damned jiklo myself, and so peered over the lip.

The bounding demoniac shapes of more manhounds ferreted through the trees and sprang into the space before the rocks.

"Sink me!" I said. I stood up and grabbed Lilah's wrist. "The rock won't stop them. By the Black Chunkrah, woman, stop that blabbering and run!"

Oh, yes, I, Dray Prescot, ran.

We fled through the rock gullies with the overhanging trees making the way alternately dark and light, shot through with the last rays of the sinking suns, so that all the world turned an angry viridian blood color, most unsettling.

Farther on I caught up with Naghan and Sosie, who ran, gasping and panting, in a way distressing to me.

We paused for a quick breather and in that space of hard-drawn breaths we heard the click and patter of jiklo claws following us. Sosie screamed again, and Naghan clapped a hand across her face—but gently.

"If we split up we will stand a better chance," said Naghan, the young man who claimed with so much pride to come from Hamal.

"Agreed," I said. Then: "I wish you well, Naghan, and you, Sosie. May Zair go with you."

Of course they had no idea what or who Zair was, that was quite clear, but they understood, and commended me to the care of Opaz.

"Remberee!" we shouted, and then ran as fast as we might over the rocks and splinters up separate gullies.

After only a short time I hoisted Lilah to my shoulder and was able to progress at a faster rate. Only a short time after that we heard the most horrendous screams and shrieks, the snuffling howling of jiklos, the blood-crazed shrieking, and we knew that Naghan and Sosie would never return home to Hamal.

There was nothing I could do about that, and I thrust all thoughts of the despicable way I had been acting lately out of my mind. I had to free this Princess Lilah, otherwise the Star Lords would hurl me back to Earth.

This I knew.

She of the Veils rose into the sky and very quickly the Twins added their combined pink light so that we could press on without fear of falling into a crevasse or pitching over the precipice of a river bank. The trees thinned away and we had to decelerate our rapid onward march as the land trended downward. We skidded and rolled in a great sliding whoosh down a sheer scree-clad slope—highly dangerous, is scree, to one without experience—and at the bottom we found rocky inclines which led us out onto the hard banks of a river. Perforce, we had to turn south and follow the river, seeing its waters slide and gleam below us in the encompassing pink light. Occasional rocks and falls interrupted the river's flow, but I made Lilah walk on all night, with stops to rest now and then, and in the end carried her, fast asleep on my shoulder.

There was no question of my being tired.

By morning the river banks had sunk to a nice level meadowlike embankment. Through the early morning mists I could see the supple sheen and glide of the river, smooth and unmarred, and presently, after a little rise and a few gorselike bushes, we came to the sea.

The sea.

Well, I wondered if that harsh interdiction of the Star

Lords against my venturing out onto the sea still prevented me from doing what I had for so long missed.

As to that, ever since my cruel transition here to the manhounds' island of Faol I had not been acting as Dray Prescot would ordinarily act, and I had rationalized that out. I was most dissatisfied.

Lilah let out a cry of joy.

"Look, Dray! Across the strait! The White Rock of Gilmoy!"

I looked across the sea. Over there the dark bar of land penned in a strait which was, so I judged, in flood. Standing proudly forth, like a sentinel finger, was a tremendous pillar of rock on that opposite shore, white and blinding on its eastern edge where the light struck it, shadowed on the west.

"You know where we are, Lilah?"

"Yes! That white rock is famed throughout Havilfar. It stands on the northern shore of Gilmoy and I have flown over it many times. I had no idea Faol was close." She shivered at this.

"Then we must find a boat."

The notion struck my fancy. The Star Lords had forbidden me to journey by sea; they had also bidden me rescue Princess Lilah, and to do that I must take to a boat. Now let the Star Lords unravel that knot—I cared not a fig for them. We walked along the beach. I could see no boats at once, and in that I felt disappointment.

A house, set back against the line of gorse-covered hills backing the beach, showed a thread of smoke from its chimney. In a pen at the side two dozen or so flying beasts flapped their wings and shrilled. They were sitting on lenken bars into which their claws sank, and they were chained by iron. They looked to be not as large as the impiters, those coal-black flying animals of The Stratemsk, but larger than the corths. Their coloring varied, tending generally to a beige-white and a velvet-green, and their heads were marked by large vanes after the fashion of pteranodons. They looked to be nasty brutes, well enough. Lilah took an eager step forward.

"Fluttrells!" she exclaimed. "We are in luck, Dray. The wind-eaters will carry us swiftly over the strait to Gilmoy, and from thence home to Hyrklana!"

Before I could answer the door of the house burst open and a ragged mob of men wielding weapons sprang out. They did not stop or pause in their rush but came on with an intent

I have fronted many times. The pen was to hand. There was only one thing I could do. I grabbed Lilah and fairly ran her across to the sturm-wood bars of the pen. I selected the nearest fluttrell, and gave it a great thumping flat-handed smack around its snouted face to tell it who was master—I had no shame in this brutalization, for death ran very close to our heels—and hoisted Lilah onto the bird's back.

"Can you fly one without stirrup, clerketer, rein?"

"I am perfectly at home in or on anything that flies in the air."

The feel of the flying beast between her legs had changed Lilah—either that, or she was scenting her homeland. She looked at me with a triumphant expression.

"Mount up, Dray! Let us be off!"

"Not so, Princess." Swiftly I released the locks of the chains holding the fluttrell. "You must fly for your home. If I take off with you these men will follow and we will surely be caught. You must go—I will hold them off until you are well clear."

"But, Dray! They will slay you!"

"I do not think so, Lilah."

I gave the fluttrell an almighty thwack and with a bad-tempered squawk it fluttered its wings and rose into the air. Lilah had to cling to its neck, ducking her head beneath the great balancing vane. She looked down on me. I snatched up a length of timber from the pen and with this cocked in my fists—and my fists spread in the old Krozair longsword way as I had done aboard Viridia the Render's flagship when I fought her Womoxes—I awaited the onslaught of the men from the house.

"You will be slain, Dray Prescot!" she called down.

"You are safe, Lilah! Now go!"

She kicked the sides of the magnificent flying animal. "I shall not forget you, Dray Prescot!" And then, faintly as she rose into the limpid morning sky: "Remberee, Dray Prescot!"

I admit it now—I can look back and see and understand my feelings then—I welcomed the coming fight. I had run and crawled and pulled my forelock long enough. These men might be justified in their instant attack upon us—although I doubted that—but they would rue the day they tangled with me.

No doubt the Star Lords thought that a good joke, too.

As I held that length of lumber prepared to show these

yokels a little sword-practice, I felt, suddenly, treacherously, the shifting sensations and the blue radiance close about me, and I could no longer feel the wooden longsword—and I was slipping and sliding into the radiant blue void.

Chapter Eight

Prey of the Manhounds of Antares

The stink of slaves lay in my nostrils with that thick choking odor so familiar to me.

A voice said: "I can guide you out, Golan, by Hito the Hunter! But you must run——"

"I can run, Anko! And I will reward you, liberally, magnificently! I am a Pallan——"

"And me! And me!" other voices lifted, beseeching, begging, pleading to be led to freedom.

I opened my eyes.

I had failed the Star Lords.

The brazen notes of a stentor's horn filled the caves and passageways and like swirling weeds at the turn of the tide all the slaves raced madly off to the feeding hall. I stood up. By the Black Chunkrah! I'd go down to the feeding cave and take my food if I had to snatch it from all the Khamorros in Havilfar and all the guides in Faol!

So the Princess Lilah of Hyrklana with the golden hair and the beautiful form had not been the one I had been sent here to rescue.

There was but one thing I could do.

I must find the correct slave to be rescued and take him or her out to safety. Guide or no guide.

Down in the feeding cave I saw a lithe and limber young man with dark hair, very alert in carriage now he was alone with only slaves about him, talking earnestly with a bulky man who had once been plump. His face, much sunken in, still contained traces of the habitual power of command he had once wielded. This was Golan, and he had been a Pallan, and had been betrayed, and so sold into slavery and found himself dispatched to Faol, where slaves brought a high price.

Golan?

I lifted my chunk of vosk—a Rapa who had thought to dispute with me its possession lay on the floor unconscious— and shook it at the rocky ceiling. "You stupid Star Lords!" I said, but I did not speak aloud, for I did not wish to attract unwelcome attention to myself, and although insanity was common enough among slaves, it was still regarded with a leery suspicion. "Idiot Everoinye! How am I supposed to know whom to rescue out of this mad crowd?"

I received no answer, and expected none, and so sank my teeth into the vosk and stared sullenly at my fellow slaves.

My beard had grown and my hair, too, making me look even more wild and uncouth and slavelike. All the same, Tulema recognized me instantly.

"Dray! I thought—how did you—? Have you crawled back through the caves?"

"No, Tulema. I didn't go." Then, to allay her suspicions, I said: "Here, finish this vosk for me. I am heartily sick of this place, for I thought I was safely away, and then I was not."

Instead of saying, as one would, "Tell me about it," she seized the remaining chunk of vosk with my teethmarks sharp upon it and wolfed it down. No one, it was clear, had been looking out for Tulema.

Could my target be this girl, with her lithe body and dark hair, all matted with dirt, her savage ways, this girl who had been a dancer in a dopa den? I did not think so. It was, in truth and given the circumstances of my return, far more likely to be this Golan, who had been a Pallan. A Pallan, as you know, is a minister of state, a high official, and if he had been disgraced and sold as a slave, it might be my duty to return him and thus affect some great design in the political structure of Kregen. Lacking any other clues, I decided it must be Golan.

Of one thing I could be sure. If it was not Golan then I would be seized by the blue radiance and hurled back into the slave pens tunneled into the caves.

Then again—if it came to the worst, I might not be. I might be flung back to the Earth of my birth.

"Listen, Tulema. I mean to go again and this time I mean to break through to freedom. Will you come with me?"

"I dare not, Dray! You know why—the manhounds . . ."

"They are most fearsome beasts—no—fearsome men. But I will look out for you."

As you will instantly perceive, I was trying to copper-bottom my bet. If by chance Golan was not the target, and Tulema was, then I would be safe.

"You will, Dray! I think—I believe—"

Then this rough tough dancing girl from a dopa den turned away, and I saw her smooth shoulder with the dirt marks upon it quivering as she sobbed.

I felt pity for her—of course I did. But she was just one in exactly the same situation as all of us. I started to work at once. I took her shaking shoulder, and shook it, and her, so that she quivered, and I said: "This Golan, who was once a Pallan. Was he there when you and I first met?"

"Yes, he was." She sniffed and sniveled, and I brushed the tears from her eyes.

"There is no need for tears, Tulema. We will go out together from here, you and I, in safety."

She eyed me from under her long lashes where the teardrops trembled. "Lart the Khamorro. Did he?"

About to say, "He is dead," I paused. I lied. I said: "I do not know, Tulema. I told you, I was thrown back unwanted."

"Oh."

That evening after the meal I fixed up with Anko the Guide that he would include me in his party. He looked at me with approval.

"You look as though you can run."

"Oh, yes," I said. "I can run."

The tame slaves were let in and they swept out the refuse and muck. Most of them were sly, inventive, cunning creatures. The old Miglish woman whacked her broom about crossly, swearing at everyone in her vile way, threatening them with all manner of horrendous fates at the hands of Migshaanu the All-Glorious. Tulema squeaked and caught my arm and we moved into another cave.

I kept my eyes open for any other Khamorros. They would be useful on the hunt if only they would learn to rein and bridle their arrogance and contempt for other people.

The following sequence of events was much the same as before. Nalgre came with his whip and his customers and guards, and the bunch of slaves who clustered most urgently against the lenken bars were chosen. Anko the Guide gathered his little group about him—fourteen of us—and the barred gates were open.

I looked about for Tulema.

She was not visible.

Golan was about to be herded through. I seized him by

the arm intending to haul him back and go find Tulema, for I did not wish to split my options, but a hefty guard seized Golan by the other arm and pulled.

Golan yelled.

"Let me go! Let me go, you hairy yetch!"

The guard hit me and I put my hand up and another guard hit me, and Golan was gone and two guards lay on the floor, unconscious, and then I was bundled out with the rest. At once I shoved my way into the middle of the crowd of slaves blinking in the sunshine. Tulema would have to take her chances, now, and I must not miss Golan. She had evidently allowed her fears to overwhelm her at the end. Anko the Guide looked at me in some surprise as I shuffled along with the slaves.

Nalgre and his guards were dragging out the two unconscious guards in their leaf-green tunics—their helmets had rolled and were instantly snatched back into the crowd of slaves, as is the slave way with all unattached objects—and were yelling and banging their whips and looking for whoever had done this heinous crime.

"You are not a Khamorro," said Anko the Guide.

"No. And look downcast, slave."

He gulped. "Yes. Yes, that is right."

We were taken to the slave barracks, where all went as before, except that there was no pathetic brave and foolish Lart the Khamorro to throw away his life so uselessly.

In the slave barracks this time there were two other parties of slaves ready for the great Jikai. We had some conversation, but I knew none of them, and now was more convinced than ever that Golan was my man.

Next morning Nalgre, with his admiring customers in attendance, went through his little routine with his pet jiklo. The female creature frisked about, lolling her red tongue, rubbing her flanks against his legs, sniffing us. Then we set out through the jungle. The other two parties went north and east. We struck south. As Anko said: "We do not wish to draw too many hunters down upon us, no, by Hito the Hunter. We cross the great plain, and then we will be safe across the river."

This Anko was much like Nath, and I hoped no untoward accident would befall him, also. He found his cache of clothes and food and shoes and knives, and cheerful at the prospect of liberty before us, we set off. The jungle was left far in the rear and we tramped across a wide plain where

"Nalgre went through his routine with his pet jiklo."

palies and that deerlike animal of such grace and beauty, the lople, ran and grazed in herds. We might run across leem here, too, and I kept my hand on the hilt of the cheap knife Anko had passed out from the cache.

The palies were the easiest to catch of the plains deer, and we caught, cooked, and ate one before settling down for the night. I own I felt the tiredness on me. I had suggested we march on by the light of She of the Veils, but Anko had laughed and said the high and mighty hunters did not relish hunting by night. He added, losing his smile: "They like to see their quarry."

Faol, as I was to learn, is mostly jungle in its northern half, nearer the equator, but a shift in the land height and the more southerly aspect give this part of the island a more open terrain. The plain over which we now trod curved around to merge with that over which I had marched previously, right across to the river. Now I felt an unease I put into words to Anko the Guide before sleep.

"We are exposed here, Anko. Would not the jungle have afforded us more cover?"

"There is some truth in what you say. But to the north the chances of complete escape are more limited."

Well, he ought to know. Once more I was struck by the bravery and self-sacrifice of the guides. Anko told me a little more of their philosophy, which was not based, as I had thought, on the twin-principle so common on Kregen, in which the Invisible Twins and Opaz figure so prominently. The guides came from a people of Faol who believed in absolute evil as a principle of life, unarguable and factual, and they were therefore dedicated in opposition to this force. He would not speak of the manhounds. I took this as a wise precaution, for the fears that had destroyed the courage of Tulema were rife among all the slaves. Only the presence of a guide gave them the courage to run. When a bunch of slaves were chosen to be hunted without having arranged for a guide to be among them their chances were nil. Luckily, so Anko said, the guides usually contrived to be with a party due to be hunted.

When I said to him, "And what do you guides seek in this work?" some of my old uncouth sailor ways slipped out. But he smiled.

"For every successful party guided to safety, we receive great honor in our own land, which is on the southern coast. Our young men regard this as a duty laid on them for the honor of their forefathers. Also, the more runs a young man makes, the prettier are the girls from whom he may choose his bride."

You couldn't argue with that.

Yes, he had heard that the Kov of Faol's name was Encar Capela, that his greatest pride was his packs of manhounds, but beyond that he knew nothing of him.

We slept.

In the morning, Anko the Guide was gone.

Zair forgive me if I had slept too long or too heavily.

There were tracks in the short grass of the plains, and blood spots, and signs of a struggle. I could not tell the others with me of Nath the Guide's disappearance, but here the tragedy was too obvious and too unnerving for them to take much in except for the need of instant flight.

It seemed clear to me, then, that the guides were being murdered. Someone had discovered the work they were doing. Probably Nalgre, with that confounded female jiklo of his, had been told by one of the tame slaves—and I instantly suspected that the old Miglish witch was the one. She nauseated me, I confess, with her twisted face like a gnome's, all bulbous hooked nose and rubbery thin lips, and bright agate eyes that saw so much, and her foully breathing mouth that told the secrets of the slaves and the guides.

Perhaps, just perhaps, I thought, if Golan was not the right target and I was thrown back into the slave pens I would take the old crone and shake the truth out of her.

The horror of it made me angry. The guides, fine upstanding young men, were risking everything to bring the slaves to safety, and the dark and devious ways of spies were bringing them to their deaths.

Golan wanted to run with the others. I managed to hang on to him and convince him he should eat something. Then, munching roast paly, we set off marching after the others.

We were on our own now. If we went due south we should reach the land of the guides, where we might look for shelter. I angled our march, striking a little to the west in the southerly direction, and soon we were able to see the other fugitives as dots, jerkily rising and falling over the small undulations of the plain away on our left front.

There was in me no desire to sing, and I kept a weather eye cocked aloft for Gdoinye or flier. A voller arrived first and the damned thorn-ivy bush into which I pitched Golan and myself was deucedly hard and prickly and sharp. We cursed as we crawled out. That was only the first. All morning as Far and Havil wheeled across the sky in their mingled lights, we had to dive and burrow our way into bush or crevice or rock shadow.

Golan had completely accepted me as his mentor, and, in truth, he was almost witless with fear. We pressed on and I made him keep up a good pace. From a thicket I cut a stout cudgel for him and a length that might serve as a wooden longsword. I swung it about. Wood it might be, it still felt good in my fists.

Maintaining a straight line of direction is often difficult, although to me, an old sailorman, navigation is an old habit and I knew we had not circled around when I heard the voices off to our left. I said to Golan, viciously: "Keep quiet!"

He did not say a word. His big, fallen-in face showed the horrors that rode him.

We crept forward carefully.

Through a screen of bushes I looked down and saw half a dozen of our fellow-fugitives running and stumbling, falling and picking themselves up, to run wildly on again. Then I saw the reason for that mindless fear.

Bounding in long loping leaps after the slaves raced the outriders of a pack of manhounds. I have seen the work of William Blake, here on Earth, and muchly admired it. And who is there who does not inwardly shiver at the terrifying images of "Tyger, tyger burning bright!"?

There is a picture by William Blake, a print, now, I believe, in the Tate Gallery in London, depicting Nebuchadnezzar. The king of Babylon was stricken, and became as an animal, and crawled away into exile. Blake's picture shows him crawling, with long beard, and hairs, as it were, growing into eagle's feathers. There is on his face a look of such inward horror, and pain, despair, and terrifying madness as would drive pity into the heart of any man.

There is about the picture much orange and brown and somber ocher. There is a static quality about it.

For all that the Manhounds of Antares are vicious and filled with a febrile energy, slavering, quick, and deadly, there is about them, too, something of that awful quality of un-comprehending doom.

So they ran and howled and the thick saliva slobbered from their mouths from which the red tongues lolled.

I saw the leader leap full upon the back of the last struggling fugitive.

The wretch emitted a despairing shriek and fell. He was a Rapa. And then a strange thing happened. The manhound did not kill him, for all their fangs can rip the reeking flesh from their living victims. He lifted the Rapa up in his arms, squatting back, and so waited.

His companions poured on in wild hue and cry.

A bunch of zorca riders galloped up—and the manhound released the Rapa, who shrieked and fled.

And now I saw the great Jikai.

The zorca hunters emitted wild whoops and spurred their mounts, and charged after the crazily running Rapa. He ran and ran, in a dead straight line, without the wit to dodge, although I do not think that would have done him the slightest good. The crossbows winked in the streaming mingled light of the Suns of Scorpio. The bolts loosed. The hunters were poor shots. Many missed. Three or four bolts struck the Rapa, all aquiver, and he stumbled, fell, and then tried to struggle on.

Their crossbows discharged, the zorca riders bore on. They hefted their spears and they cast and only one pierced the Rapa. This was clumsy butchery. The hunters unsheathed their swords, and now they reined in around the Rapa and I saw the blades rising and falling.

Golan was being sick.

"Keep quiet, calsany!" I said.

I took notice of the youth who had flung the only spear to strike. He had a rosy laughing face, very merry, and he was now red with exertion. But his face was no redder than the sword he waved wildly above his head and with a shrill yell plunged downward yet again.

"Well done, Ortyg! Well done!" his companions called.

Then—I went stiff with rage and passion.

For these miserable cramphs, these misbegotten of Grodno, shouted out the words, the great words, "Hai! Jikai!"

Almost, I rose up and flung myself upon them.

But Golan, who once had been a Pallan, was being sick in the grass, and the Star Lords had commanded me to rescue him.

I watched, trembling, hating the poltroon I had become, as the zorca riders spurred away. The flanks of the zorcas showed the blood-red weals. Spurs and zorcas are not a fit combination for a true rider!

A single manhound, sniffing after the rest, trailed up toward us.

Maybe he caught our scent on a vagrant breeze; maybe he was the rogue of the pack. But he came straight for us, head down, rump high, his hair blowing in a mane behind him, his crested topknot stiff and arrogant, his jagged teeth exposed.

Golan's sick spasm had passed. The other fugitives were almost out of sight beyond a grassy clump, the manhounds well up to them, and the great and puissant hunters spurring madly after. One turned, and shouted, and I guessed he was calling the manhound who doggedly climbed toward us. This man, in his leaf-green tunic and small round helmet, was a guard, probably the packmaster, in charge of the jiklos.

Then I had to concentrate on the manhound. He was a big fellow, very vicious, and had he possessed a tail it would have been lashing angrily. He had seen us now and he let out a slavering screech and charged for us.

For just an instant I saw the guard wheel his zorca, and then I leaped up, the wooden longsword cocked in that special Krozair grip. The manhound leaped. I saw his teeth, jagged and sharp, the saliva flecking from his thin lips, and his eyes all bloodshot and mad with hunting lust.

His clawed hands reached for my throat, and his teeth sought to rip out my jugular, for with the intelligence I knew these fearsome beasts still retained, he had recognized I was not a meek victim, but stood there with a club to meet him and bash out his brains.

In that he was mistaken.

This length of wood cut from a thicket was no clumsy bludgeon. It stood in lieu of a deadly Krozair longsword, second only to the great Savanti sword itself.

I took my grips, brought the wood around and back, and so, with a chopped "Hai," drove the splintered end full in the manhound's savage face. He tried to swerve, but he was too slow. He bundled over, screeching, splinters mantling his cheeks and one eye gone and then—and only then—did I bring the wooden longsword down in a blow that caved in his rib cage. Two more blows finished him.

The soft plop of zorca hooves on the grass brought me around.

The guard was a fool.

The first rule of a crossbowman is always: "Reload!"

He came at me with his sword.

He was angry, annoyed that a valuable jiklo had been

slain, and he did not even have the same sense as that jiklo to recognize I was not an ordinary fugitive slave run as quarry.

He slashed violently down and I slid the blow and smashed him across the thigh—a favorite stroke, that, with the Krozair longsword—and had the weapon been edged steel he would have been less one leg. As it was he screamed in pain and I was able to reach up, inside the curve of the zorca's neck, and take him and so hold him and drag him down. When I stood up, grasping the zorca's reins, Golan staggered across.

"By Opaz! I have never seen the like."

"Mount up, Pallan, and let us ride. Otherwise you will not have the chance to see the like again."

And so, mounted up, forward and aft, and damned close together, too, on so short-coupled a mount as a zorca, we rode hard for the south.

Chapter Nine

The fears of Tulema, dancing girl from a dopa pen

The Pallan Golan was not the man the Star Lords wished me to rescue from the Manhunters of Faol.

Once more I found myself hurled disdainfully back to the slave pens cut from the rocks fronting the jungles, once more the stink of slaves filled my nostrils, and the stentors' brazen notes called us all to push and herd like vosks to the feeding cave. I had taken Golan safely through to a village where the headman, who knew nothing of the guides and so convinced me we had strayed from our course, promised to care for the Pallan. We had passed over a wide river by means of a raft I had fashioned, and we learned we were in another country on the southern shore. Clearly the villages and land from which the guides came lay farther to the east. The headman of the village knew little of what went on in what he called North Faol. The Trylon of South Faol had long ago refused to bend the knee to the Kov of Faol, and the headman kept himself aloof from what went on across the river.

After a good meal and a bit of a sing-song with the girls of the village dancing in the firelight—for I had foolishly thought my mission for the Star Lords accomplished—I was whipped up by the blue radiance and . . . well, here I was again, and all to do over.

If you think I was growing mightily annoyed by this time—you are right.

Although enough time had elapsed for my hair and beard and moustache to grow somewhat shaggy, still Tulema recognized me.

This time my original excuse would not satisfy her, and so before she could follow on her first quick exclamation of surprise, I said: "Yes, Tulema. I have come back. Like the guides, I feel it important to do so. Perhaps this time you will come out with me."

"Oh, Dray—the manhounds!"

"I am here, am I not? And I have been out—*there*!"

She was still as absolutely terrified as ever.

Something would have to be done about Tulema. I knew the person I was supposed to rescue was still in the caves. Unless, of course, he or she had been killed and the Star Lords were punishing me for failing. I would not contemplate that. Some of the original group in the pen when I had first arrived here had gone out; some were left. I could not explain to Tulema, but I managed to get her to identify them for me. I still could not bring myself to believe that Tulema herself was the right one. I had had experience then of the way in which the Star Lords worked. I did not know what their plans for Kregen were, but I had previously rescued people for them who I could see would be important in the scheme of things. Much as I respected the tough hardness of Tulema, and her pitiful fears of the jiklos, I could not envision her as a mover of politics, a maker of nations.

"There is Latimer," said Tulema. "He is frightened to go."

I grunted. "Suppose he is picked to go, anyway, without a guide? What then?"

"Don't say it, Dray!"

Latimer turned as I approached. We had just eaten, but there had come no stentor call to parade before the bars of our cages. He was a middle-aged man, say a hundred and fifty or so, still virile, with dark hair and a broken nose and eyes that did not quite meet mine when we talked. He showed by his rib cage—or rather by its absence against his skin—that he could fight well enough to secure good food. In conversation I learned he was a shipping merchant of Hamal. Only after a little cross-purpose talk was it borne in on me that he was a voller shipping man, and not a galleon owner, as I had imagined. At once I decided this must be the man I sought. Vollers were important. Latimer was a voller owner. Ergo, the Star Lords wanted him out in the world again so that some great scheme to do with the Havilfar fliers might come to fruition.

How snobbish all this sounds! How stupid, that I should seek out people I thought important by what they did! Tulema I intended to persuade to come with me; if she would not, I could not find it in my heart to force her. Only if this Latimer were not the one, would I force her.

We went out, we struck westward, I rescued Latimer— again the guide disappeared and again I vowed to try to get to the bottom of that mystery—and saw the voller magnate safe, and again I was tossed back in a radiance of blue fire into the slave pens.

Tulema said: "You have come back, Dray."

I was so desperate that I had to make an effort to be polite to her. She had to be the one. And she was frightened to go. Well, there was a cure for that.

More slaves had been brought in, a consignment from the mainland had evidently arrived, and the pens and caves were full again. To be safe, I said to Tulema: "Are there any slaves still here who were with us when—?"

She shook her head. "No, Dray. They are all gone."

"Except you."

"Yes. And you!"

"Oh. Me." At the stentors' call I smashed my way through the crowds of newcomers and took two heaping helpings of the best. I wanted Tulema fit and well for the break, and she had been eating dilse for a long time.

There seemed to me a need to keep a record. I ticked off all the people as Tulema recited their names. "And Tosie? She went out?"

"Yes. Right after that Lilah who put on such airs."

"I hope she is safe."

"Oh, she'll be safe. Anyone like her who pretends to be a queen will be safe, no matter what."

Yes, I thought, more cheerfully, yes, Tulema must be the one. There was a rough fire about her, practically obliterated in these conditions by her uncontrollable fears of the jiklos. She had heard too many stories of what the manhounds did to pretty girls.

The old Miglish crone began her eternal sweeping-up and Tulema shuddered and drew me away. I thought the dark thoughts I had thought when I'd seen the blood spots near Anko the Guide's blankets . . . but I was going out and Tulema was the one, so—did it matter?

Of course it mattered.

I took the Miglish woman by the shoulder and I could feel the narrowness of her, the bony hardness. She tried to twist away, leering up at me with her pouched eyes, her witch-face hideous, like a rubber mask melted in the fire. She revolted me, this halfling monstrosity.

"Do you betray the guides, Migla?"

She cackled, trying to hit me with her broom.

"I betray nothing! By Migshaanu the All-Glorious, may your eyes dribble out and your guts cave in—"

"Enough of that, crone!" I snarled. "Remember: if any guides are betrayed, you will be flayed and your skin hung up for all to see!"

Of course, I could not prove anything, and she would not be frightened into revealing her guilt. She might have nothing to do with the tragedy, but she was an old witch, and hideous, that was plain to see, as Tulema said, with a shiver.

I remembered what Nath the Guide had said about human beings, and I could see a point. There were no Chuliks among the slaves, as I have remarked; they are a very fearsome race of half-men, half-beasts. But something about this old Migla made all my Homo sapiens ancestry rise up in revulsion.

In that foul nose of hers black hairs sprouted. She always kept herself tightly covered up by her gray slave blanket and the breechclout was capacious and droopy enough to conceal her legs down to her knees. Her calves were always smothered in filth. Her hair remained a wild and tangled mass of knots and mud and caked filth. Truly, she was an abomination.

But, for all that, I could not prove she was the traitor.

Last time, when I had rescued Latimer to no avail, I had kept awake most of the night and still the guide had disappeared. I had not seen or heard it done. As usual, the guide had slept a little apart from the rest of us, to be on guard. This time, I vowed, I would afford him the protection he tried to give us.

The reason for this stealthy betrayal seemed obvious enough to me. Surely, by this time, even Nalgre, the slave-master, must have noticed how willing the slaves were to be run, to be sent out to a hideous death. This would please Nalgre and his master, the Kov of Faol. They would wish to maintain this satisfactory state of things, and continue the guides in their desperate undertakings. I wondered, not without a shiver of anger, what the guides' yillages were making of the non-return of their fine young men. Truly, the ways of man and man are mysterious and barbarous beyond belief.

In addition, these thoughts also showed me that the old Migla witch, if she had been truly to blame, had no further need of betrayal. Once Nalgre caught wind of the conspiracy to free the slaves, then he would take up the savage and sorry business from there.

With all the numbers of fresh slaves within the barred caves cut into the rock I could not easily find a guide. Most of the slaves pushed and shoved, seeking better sleeping places, arguing, fighting, the girls looking for protectors, and everyone racing whooping like mad people when the stentors' horns blew for feeding time. Tulema had to be built up in strength before I could risk taking her out to be hunted. While there was a ready supply of slaves, Nalgre could not care how many managed not to be selected for a Jikai; so long as there were enough for his customers and they were kept happy, then Nalgre would not worry over the few slaves who were never picked.

I did see one incident that indicated how he solved the problem if it became too acute.

An old slave—it may have been the same Xaffer, or another, for they are a strange and remote race of halflings—was dragged out, screaming, and lashed to a wooden stake. He was flogged to death there. Tulema stared dry-eyed, hard and contemptuous, seeing in the fate of the Xaffer the possibility of her own ending.

"That is what happens to skulkers who are too old for the hunt," said Tulema. "If they are not employed as tame slaves to clean and cook like the old Miglish witch and her friends."

"That will happen to you, then, Tulema, if you can eat only dilse."

"Better, perhaps, ol' snake, than the manhounds."

I shook my head. "You are coming out as soon as you are fit and strong, Tulema. There is no argument. But the guides are few."

"They know when there are customers. Who can blame them if they do not wish to spend time they need not, in here, with us slaves?"

So there was time for Tulema to eat well and to shed that half-starved look on her face that came from dilse, and for her supple body to be genuinely lithe and firm again, on good food. A day came when the stentors' horns blared out in the call that summoned the manhounds, and drove us slaves to the lenken bars, to be selected for the great Jikai. I looked at Tulema. As always, she shrank back, but she was as fit and well as she might ever be in this dreadful place, and I could not wait any longer.

Out on the compound splashed with its jade and ruby light stood Nalgre, with his whip and his guards, talking in his important, belly-thrusting, strutting way with a group of customers. I recognized one man there; he was the heavily built Notor with the pudgy face from too many vosk-pies who had led the hunt when Lilah and I had escaped. Nalgre was speaking to him.

"Indeed, it is strange, Notor Trelth."

"And you have no explanation, Nalgre? A long way, we went, a very long way, and a scuffle in rocks and trees. I looked for a kill on the plains."

"Why not try the jungles this time, Notor Trelth?" Nalgre spoke with quickness, eagerness, anxious to please.

"Yes. I will give it thought," said this high-and-mighty Notor Trelth.

Tulema whispered: "There is a guide here, Dray—"

"Good." At once I looked about for the lithe young man with the dark hair who was risking his life for us. I saw him with a group and pushed my way across with Tulema. Whether the guide might be persuaded to take us or not, he would listen to me when I told him the disastrous news.

Chapter Ten

Of the two faces
of Hito the Hunter

Of course the guide would not believe me. He scoffed. His name was Inachos and he was as young and athletic as the other guides. Also he was a little impatient.

There had been no time to tell him in the barred caves, for the guards had thrust through and taken out the slaves Notor Trelth selected, and in the resultant confusion Tulema and I had been pushed out with the rest. There were eighteen of us, this time, a large party, and only when we had settled down for the night in the slave barracks had I been afforded the opportunity of talking privately with Inachos.

"What you are saying is lunacy. By Hito the Hunter! No guide would be taken unawares."

"So I had thought. But it has happened, three times to my certain knowledge."

"And you have told no one else?"

"To alarm the slaves would not have been wise. Their fate rests in the hands of the guides. You must take the news back to your villages and warn them."

He looked at me, his head on one side, looking very alert and handsome. "I cannot believe what you say. But a warning must be taken, just in case."

"I shall stay awake all night," I said.

"If it pleases you."

A cocky youngster, I thought to myself, one who believes no secret party of assassins can creep upon him in the pink moonlight.

Inachos the Guide must act his part as a cowed slave the next morning as we went through those ghastly preliminaries Nalgre the slave-master carried out with such relish. With Tulema near me, generally held by my left hand, I kept very close to Inachos. If he refused to take me seriously, I knew that tonight his eyes would be opened.

87

Nalgre approached us and Inachos stiffened up, but the slave-master flicked his whip lightly over me—I bore it! I, Dray Prescot, bore it!—and then turned away as Notor Trelth called. Inachos relaxed, breathing hard through pinched nostrils, looking frustrated. I felt sorry for him.

Very soon thereafter we were trotting away. Inachos said we could strike north through the jungle and find the coast easily where we might pick up a vessel from the island of Outer Faol whose people, simple fishermen, he called them, would call for the sake of the alligators in the mud-swamps. Faol was not really close enough to the equator or well-watered enough to possess a really dense rain forest. The jungle was capable of being traversed by many trails, although, of course, not being a pleasant place. I thought of what had previously been said about the northern jungle offering no real safety, but Inachos knew his business, and fisherfolk and a boat so close to hand sounded more tempting than another long slog over the plains.

Just over half a dwabur along the trail through the dim green and russet twilight of the forest Inachos halted us to produce his cache of clothing, food, and knives. I put the shoes on, with a grimace, and took the cheap knife with the thought that around me there was literally a forest of wooden longswords.

The longswords existed literally within the tree branches, as the greatest statues of two worlds already existed within the stones from which they were carved.

From my previous experience I did not believe the hunters would tackle us before the next day. That night Inachos found a comfortable dell by a small and somewhat marshy stream and we set up camp. He handed us the wine and my fellow slaves upended the leather bottles with great gusto. Tulema was exhausted. She sat with her back against the bole of a tree, licking the last of the paline juice from her fingers. I took a wine bottle over and she drank greedily. Inachos called: "Have some wine yourself, Dray Prescot. You will have need of it."

"I like wine," I said casually. "But I prefer tea."

"Drink," he said.

Tulema had left a few dregs swilling in the leather bag, but to please Inachos, for he had risked much stowing the wine away in the cache, I lifted the leather and drank what there was and went on drinking thereafter, miming. Inachos chuckled.

"Tomorrow we will be through the jungle. We will find a boat. And tonight, nothing will disturb our rest."

We took precautions against the nocturnal denizens of the jungle. There are but a few snakes on Kregen, and these poor and miserable of spirit—with the exception of a breed of horrors of which I will speak later—but there were other perils and we twined vines about ourselves on the branches of trees, and rammed hard and thorny spikes in the wood to make a palisade. Already the slaves were yawning. Tulema was fast asleep. I fancied a conversation with Inachos, but he grunted and took himself off to a branch lower than those on which we slaves perched, saying that we must rise early.

A Gon moaned uneasily in his sleep. His chalk-white hair glowed an eerie color in the light of the Maiden with the Many Smiles striking pallidly through the leaves. Even in the warrens of Magdag the Gons had been able to shave that white hair of which they are so ashamed. I kept my weather eye open for Inachos, who lay, a darker blot, against his tree lower down.

My eyes closed.

How long I sat there, wedged against a branch springing from the main trunk I do not know. I remember I recollected there was some powerful and compelling reason why I must keep awake this night. I had slept well on those other nights when we slaves had been run as quarry for sport, and the last time, with the voller merchant, Latimer, I had kept awake most of the night, or so I believed. I opened my eyes, blearily, gummily. I looked down.

Inachos no longer sat in his tree perch.

Instantly I was wide awake.

I picked out his form, creeping down the tree, going carefully, and as he went dropping dark drops down onto the wood from a wooden vial he had unstoppered, a wooden vial I had taken to be a stick. He was going carefully so as to make the dark drops splatter effectively, and so as not to lose his hand- and foothold; he was not, I judged, going carefully so as not to awaken the slaves.

Quietly—and when I wish to be quiet it takes a very sharp ear indeed to hear me—I unlashed the vines and crept down the tree after him. He jumped very lithely to the packed leaf-droppings of the forest floor and ran swiftly along the trail ahead. Quietly, I followed.

After a few moments we reached a clearing, and on the brink I paused. Inachos stood in the center of the clearing, bathed in the radiant pink light of the Maiden with the Many Smiles, with She of the Veils adding her own luster to the scene. He reached up his arms.

Silently, a flier ghosted down into the clearing.

No further evidence was needed.

The man in the flier had no need to lean out and shout cheerfully to Inachos: "Ho, there, Inachos. By Hito the Hunter! I shall sink much wine this night."

And Inachos the Guide had no need to reply: "And I, also! This work makes a man thirsty! The yetches stink so!"

No, there was no need for them to say these words to convince me, to make me see what a credulous fool I had been.

Everything fell into place.

With a shout full of bestial hatred I charged into the clearing, bounded across the open space, struck Inachos senseless with a smashing blow to the nape of his neck, and reached in my hands and hauled his companion all tumbling onto the jungle floor.

Even then, I swear, I did not mean both of them to die, for I wished to question them. But Inachos must have had a weak skull, or my blow must have been too hasty and impetuous. As for the flier pilot who had come to pick the guide up—when I turned him over I saw the hilt of his knife thrusting up from his chest. As he tumbled out of the flier the knife had sliced whicker-sharp between his ribs. I wrenched it out with a foul Makki-Grodno oath.

What a credulous idiot I had been!

The guides were not being murdered by assassins sent by Nalgre. Oh, no! Nalgre hired the guides. They came into the caves and told the slaves they would take them out to safety, and the poor deluded fools went out, gaily, expectantly, filled with hope. They thought they were being taken to safety, and then, every first night, the guide would disappear and the slaves were on their own. They would be ripe fodder for the great Jikai! How much more cunning this system was to get the slaves out and running. Without hope, they might run, but they would not give sport.

The quarry were given a reason to run by the guides. They thought that with a whole day's start they stood a chance. And, too, I saw another sound reason for this dastardly plot. The different parties of slaves could be channeled into different parts of the island. Then different hunts would not become entangled and Nalgre would not have to face irate customers whose quarry had been snapped up by neighboring hunters.

And—that doughy-faced Notor Trelth had agreed to hunt through the jungle and the guide, Inachos, had directed us northward so as to keep within the confines of the jungle!

The more I considered the foul scheme the more I saw its elegance and simplicity—and its horror.

Maybe there were no real rear entrances to the caves.

Certainly, the manhounds had entrances there, to herd the slaves out for selection. All the time I thus reviewed the diabolical schemes of the Kov of Faol and his slave-master, Nalgre, I paced back and forth in the moonlight.

Then I went back to the tree where my companions slept and tried to rouse them.

Every last one was fast asleep in a drugged stupor.

That provided the last evidence. The wine so thoughtfully provided by the guides, which they did not drink through care for their charges, was drugged. The guides simply got up and walked away and were picked up by flier.

If I bashed a length of timber against the tree in my anger, I feel that needs no explanation.

In the end I had to unlash all the slaves, every one, and Tulema first, and carry them, snoring, over to the airboat. The flier would just take all the eighteen of us, although we were jammed in—no novelty to slaves accustomed to being jammed in hard together in barred prisons.

Delia had given me instructions in the management of airboats. I took the flier up quickly, savagely, sped low over the jungle in the streaming light from the moons of Kregen.

The flight had to be undertaken right away; it would have been madness to have waited until the morning. Come the morning, though—and here I believe my lips ricked back over my teeth in a most ungentlemanly fashion—the great hunters on their manhunt would find no quarry for the manhounds to drag down, for them to loose at with their gleaming beautiful crossbows, for them to chop down with sword and spear.

When, at last, Zim and Genodras—or, as here in Havilfar, Far and Havil—dawned over the jungle levels I brought the airboat down into a cleft in the trees. Below, a river ran, a broad sluggish ocher-colored river, with mud-banks and the scaled and agile forms of water-risslaca active about their own form of hunting. At least, much as I was wary of risslaca and with horrific memories of the Phokaym, they, at least, hunted for food.

I took the airboat low along the dun water and at last found what I sought, a place where the banks had eroded and fallen and the jungle had voraciously grown over the tumbled earth and so created a roofed space beneath. Management of the voller was a tricky business, but I got her neatly inserted under the overarching leaves. She was a craft built along somewhat different lines from those I had been accustomed to in Vallia and Zenicce, being altogether sturdier of construction, with lenken planking and bronze supports, although still of that swift and beautiful leaf-shape.

The Gon rolled over, snorting, and pushed into Lenki, a Brokelsh whose black bristles were the thickest I had seen on one of his kind, and Lenki snorted in his turn, and turned over, and struck a Fristle, and so, with much groaning and blowing and yawning, the whole pack of slaves woke up.

Leaving them to sort themselves out I swung down beneath the trees to the water's edge.

Certainly there is much beauty in the greenery of Kregen. A profusion of gorgeous flowers was opening to the first rays of the twin suns, and I stood on the ledge of soggy earth watching as moon-blooms opened wide their second, outer, ring of petals, and as scarlet and indigo and yellow and orange flowers of a myriad convoluted shapes prepared themselves for the day. A swim, which I would sorely have welcomed, filthy as I was, was not to be recommended. Many risslaca had woken up and were prowling. I scooped a handful of the water and splashed my face and body and heard a harsh and malevolent croaking in the air above my head.

I looked up.

The Gdoinye hung there, his pinions beating against the dawn breeze down the river, his head cocked. In the streaming mingled light of the suns he looked glorious, shining, refulgent. I shook my fist at him.

"You are an idiot, Dray Prescot!"

"You told me that before, on a beach in Valka!"

"An onker of onkers, Dray Prescot, a get-onker!"

"So I know!" I shouted back as the accipiter swung there, squawking hoarsely at me. Without a thought I knew those in the airboat could not be a witness to this astounding confrontation.

"You will be allowed a little more time to play your games. We trust they amuse you. There is yet time."

"Time for what? I play no games with you. Why do you force me against my wishes—"

But, with a hoarse cry, the raptor interrupted.

"We do what we do for reasons beyond your understanding, Dray Prescot. When you grow up, you may then grow a brain to comprehend the simple facts of life on this planet. Now you are as a suckling baby, as your antics here in Faol have shown."

"Antics!" I roared. "Antics! I've been trying to do what I thought was right—and no damned help from you! How do I know who—"

"When you reach Yaman you may discover answers you will never find in Aphrasöe."

"I didn't ask to be brought to Kregen! But now that I'm here I have found my own destiny! If you want my help you'll have to—"

But the Gdoinye had heard enough of my puling roaring, for he winged up and away, a golden and scarlet messenger of glory, from a bunch of Star Lords I'd as lief squeeze between my fingers and let drip through in a red mush. He soared up, shining in the mingled light of the twin suns.

His last harsh cry streamed down with that opaline light.

"You are a fool, Dray Prescot!"

Then he was a mere black dot against the suns-glow.

I cursed.

Oh, I cursed!

But, of course, there was nothing for me to do but go back and do as the Star Lords ordered and get Tulema out to a place of safety. After that . . . and then I knew that after that, before I could investigate the scarlet-roped Todalpheme, before I could spend pleasant days discovering more about the vollers, before, even, I could return to Vallia and Delia, I would have to return to the barred slave pens of Faol and warn the slaves. I would have to defeat the Kov of Faol and Nalgre and put paid to this foul and despicable game they played with their two-faced treacherous guides.

When I turned back to the cleft in the river bank with its camouflage of trees the slaves were out of the airboat and clamoring their wonder like a pack of jackdaws. Of them all, apart from Tulema and myself, only one was a human being, the rest being halflings of one sort and another. This young man, who had fed himself well in the caves, kept much to himself and spoke little. He said his name was Nath, but I did not believe him. He had red hair, and so might be a Lohvian. When a Brokelsh had pressed him, this Nath had said he came from Thothangir, and, again, I did not believe him.

This Nath na Thothangir walked toward me swinging one of the guide's swords. I eyed him meanly.

"Where are we, Dray Prescot? How did we come here?"

I gathered the rest of the slaves about and told them what had happened. They were, as was to be expected, exceedingly enraged, and a Relt, ordinarily one of the kindest of peoples, began threatening to have the guides tossed into a neighbor's pit back home. The neighbor, he informed us, was a Rapa of some wealth and power. We all agreed. The guides deserved such a terrible fate, for their duplicity and heartlessness as much as for their cruelty.

After that, with a flier at their disposal, the slaves began a volatile and acrimonious wrangling as to our destination.

I said to Tulema: "Where in all of Kregen do you wish to go, Tulema? Where is your home?"

She laughed, and the tears stood in her eyes.

"I have no home since I was abducted from Herrell, and I have no wish to return there. Where you go, Dray Prescot, there will I go, also!"

Chapter Eleven

"Where you go, Dray Prescot, there will I go also!"

This was a right leem's-nest.

I stood gawping at Tulema who had once been of Herrell. She said it again, stamping her foot.

"Where you go, Dray Prescot, there will I go, also!"

She meant it, that was perfectly plain.

She could not go with me, that, too, was perfectly plain.

What had the Gdoinye meant, that I was playing games here in Faol, that my antics amused them? If I was to rescue Tulema for the Star Lords' devious purposes, did that mean I had to take her back to Vallia?

What, then, would Delia say?

As to that, I had no doubts. No other woman in two worlds means anything beside Delia. But I still had a duty to perform, and Tulema, because of that—and because she was young and frightened and alone—must be cared for.

Deciding that the most prudent course was to say nothing more of our destination to her—and seeing that that, too, was the cowardly way and thereby, as may surprise you, feeling a gust of amusement rather than of anger—I set about sorting out the halflings. They had to be told what I intended to do. If left to themselves they would have begun fighting bitterly over the different places they insisted on reaching immediately.

The only justification I can offer for my decision was that these halflings, escaped slaves, did not have the Star Lords breathing down their necks.

Those that had had necks, that was.

Sammly, from distant Quennohch, for instance, only with extreme kindness could be said to have a neck, his head, as it did, sprouting from between his two upper limbs. But he was a good-hearted fellow, and said he wouldn't mind being set down somewhere convenient in Havilfar. He could work his passage home aboard any of the regular voller lines. His left center limb scratched at his carapace as he spoke.

"Does anyone," I said over the hubbub, and quieting them by the rasp in my voice, "know the way to Hyrklana?"

"I do," said the youth who said he was Nath na Thothangir.

"Then that is where we shall fly." I silenced the immediate babble of protest. "If anyone wishes to alight earlier, they will of course be allowed to do so."

By Zim-Zair, I said to myself, with another uncharacteristic chuckle, I was running a coach service!

Tulema grabbed hold of me and started in slapping. I fended her off, astonished.

"What, Tulema? What the blue blazes is the matter with you?"

"The matter, indeed! I know! You lust after that yellow-haired Lilah, that calls herself a princess!"

"By the Black Chunkrah! What other friends do we have in Havilfar if you won't damn well go home?"

Also, although I did not tell her so, I wanted to make sure Lilah had indeed reached safety.

None of them seemed to consider my warning about the guides; they refused to face up to the fact that those people they had seen leave the slave pens in such high hopes were all dead. Tulema simply assumed that Lilah was free. I devoutly hoped that was so, remembering those vicious men and the pen of fluttrells waiting to be mounted and sent in whooping pursuit of the golden-haired princess.

Without arguing further I went up to the flier and we ate what little food there was and drank from the river and then I shouted: "I am leaving now. All aboard who's coming aboard." That was enough to make them pack themselves in as best they might. They settled down with a considerable amount of flutter and argument as I inched the voller out over the river, turned her, and sent her streaking skyward.

The direction we needed to travel was southeast, according to this Nath na Thothangir, who sat up at the controls with me. We had to strike due east for some way before risking turning south. We had no wish to fly directly over the slave pens, for we knew other fliers would rise to challenge us.

"Hyrklana is on the east coast of Havilfar. It is a large and powerful kingdom." Nath spoke with a bitterness in his voice I had no explanation for, and I had no inclination to find the reasons. Then, with a fleeting sideways look at me, he said: "That dopa-den dancing girl. She mentioned a name—"

About to snub him for speaking in such a way about Tulema, for I did not miss the scorn in his voice, I paused for two reasons. One was that I was surprised he should reach the same conclusions about Tulema as myself; the other that, after a pause, as it were, to gather his breath, he went on: "She mentioned the name of the Princess Lilah."

"And if she did?"

"You know her? That is why you wish to travel to Hyrklana?"

"Perhaps."

I did not believe in giving away information.

"You will be sorry if you venture into Hyrklana uninvited. As in Hamal, the arenas there are ever hungry for fresh fodder."

"As to that, we shall see what we shall see."

And with that pompous reply this redheaded young man who claimed he was Nath na Thothangir had to rest content.

We crossed a stretch of sea and left Faol to our rear, at which, I confess, I felt much relief. New land spread out before us, and this youth Nath told me it was Hennardrin. We turned and flew south, along the coastline. Presently, with much of the day gone, and a smooth eight-point turn to starboard we flew over the White Rock of Gilmoy. So, if Lilah had not been caught this was the way she would have flown.

We went on and Nath began to fidget as our southerly course swung us inland. Below unrolled a massive forest, with clearings here and there in which towns had been built. No one so far wished to get off this aerial excursion. We were all hungry and thirsty by now, and so I said we would descend and hunt for our supper.

One of the halflings pushed his way through the jumbled passengers at my back and, puffing a little, smoothed down the yellow fur around his eyes and mouth and polished up the laypom-colored fur beneath his chin.

"If you will continue for another four or five dwaburs, on this course," he said in his smooth honeylike voice, "you will come to a fine city built by a great orange river. That is Ordsmot. There, I believe, you will find all the food and wine you may require. You see," he finished, and I detected a huge relief and happiness in him, "I am Dorval Aymlo of Ordsmot."

Over the chorus of voices declaring that this was splendid news, I considered. This Dorval Aymlo was a member of the halfling race sometimes called Lamniarese—the Lamnias—of whom at that time I knew little. You must understand that, in accordance with my original plan, although surrounded by many different kinds of half-men I introduce them to you only when they come upon the stage of my story. I believed this Aymlo of Ordsmot to speak the truth. *Ord,* as you know, is the Kregish for "eight," and a *smot* is a large town, large enough, at times, to be considered as a city. I guessed why it had been given the name of "Eight-town"—it would be divided up into eight sections, each occupied by a different race.

"Done," I said. "And many thanks to you, Horter Aymlo."

Horter is, of course, the Havilfar equivalent to the Vallian Koter, or Mister.

The airboat sped onward in the gathering darkness with only two of the lesser moons hurtling close by above.

We had traveled a considerable distance since leaving Faol —thanks be!—and I fancied this voller was a far speedier craft than any I had flown in before. Also, I had the hunch that the confounded thing would not break down as frequently as those the Havilfarese sold to Vallia and Zenicce and their other overseas customers.

Tulema was looking ahead and she saw the great bend of the river, shining faintly in the growing light of the Maiden with the Many Smiles rising away to our left, and she cried out in delight. A mass of twinkling lights in an immense circle, crisscrossed by the four main boulevards in a huge wagon-wheel demarcating the eight precincts, showed us without mistake where lay Ordsmot upon the orange river. I sent the airboat slanting down to an enclave near the river at Aymlo's directions. The lights spread out around us. The dark masses of trees rushed past and I slowed our descent. Buildings flashed past beneath.

"There!" said Dorval Aymlo, pointing over my shoulder. "Where that tower rises, beside those warehouses and the beautiful godown!"

By his words and his tone of voice I knew he was pointing to his home.

We landed in a courtyard with buildings on three sides and the river on the fourth. Doors opened and lights flared. The Maiden with the Many Smiles was hidden for a space by buildings and trees, and it was unusually dark upon Kregen where we were in Aymlo's home in Ordsmot.

He cried out in a great voice: "It is me! Dorval Aymlo! I am home, my children! *I am home!*"

I know how I felt, and I am sure that everyone aboard felt just the same. How we longed to be able to shout the same words, filled with joy and happiness!

I climbed out and Aymlo, who would have alighted next, was pushed aside by Tulema. She hated to let me out of her sight. I stood on the hard-packed earth of the courtyard and I smelled the wonderful sweet scent of the night flowers, and I saw the people from the house running toward us, bearing torches that flared their glowing hair upon the night.

"It is me, Dorval Aymlo!" the Lamnia called again.

He started to run forward.

The youth Nath, who said he was from Thothangir, stood at my side. In his hand the guide sword gleamed from the torchlight. I had kept the other sword. Nath swore.

"The old fool! Cannot he see they bear weapons!"

Truly, in the torchlight the flicker of spears showed bright in the forefront of those men toward whom Dorval Aymlo ran with his arms up, crying aloud in his joy.

And a voice lifted, a harsh, brutal voice.

"Aye! We know you are Dorval Aymlo! This house and this business are yours no longer! Know that I am Rafer Aymlo, your nephew, and these are my men, and this house and this business is mine! And know, also, old fool, that you and all those with you are dead, dead, dead!"

Chapter Twelve

How Dorval Amylo the merchant of Ordsmot came home

Even as Dorval Aymlo shouted in a high and shocked scream of utter disbelief and despair, I jumped forward, the sword low. This was no business of mine. But the old Lamnia had been so happy—he had been so overjoyed and he was a kindly old soul—and now, this!

So I jumped forward, like a headstrong fool, and Nath of Thothangir leaped at my side, his red hair black in the torchlight.

Aymlo screeched and stumbled and fell—and that for a surety saved his life, for the spear thrust passed above his prostrate body. In a twinkling I had thrust in my turn, and recovered from the lunge, and taken the next spear and so, twisting, hacked down the furry face of the Lamnia attacking me.

Nath fought with a series of clever but overly vigorous cut and thrusts. I smashed into the other Lamnias, for I knew that they would in truth kill us all if they were not stopped, and that would not please the Star Lords. Among the Lamnias were Rapas and humans and these fought, on the whole, with more skill and viciousness than the Lamniarese, which was only natural. Very quickly I found three Rapas at my side wielding fallen spears, and these were released slaves, my fellows. We fought and for a space the compound resounded to the shrill of battling men, the slide and scrape of steel, the shrieks of the wounded, and the bubbling groans of the dying.

The very savagery of the ex-slaves' rush, the sudden reversal of their own weapons, the blood spouting from gaping wounds, unnerved our opponents. One of our Brokelsh was down, with a spear in his guts, but that was the extent of our casualties. Our opponents fled. Dorval Aymlo stood up, holding his hands in the air in horror. The Maiden with the Many

Smiles floated serenely above the rooftops with their notched outlines and upflung gable ends, and her pink radiance streamed out upon that scene of destruction.

"By Opaz the All-Merciful!" exclaimed Aymlo, scarcely able to speak. "What devil's work is this?"

A Rapa laughed nastily, wiping his spear on the clothing of a dead Rapa he had slain. "It is very simple, old fool. This bastard nephew of yours stole your house and your góods and he would have slain you to keep them!"

"Well," said Dorval Aymlo, in a voice of pain, "the deed has brought him nothing but sorrow. For, see, here lies the body of Rafer Aymlo, all dead and bloody."

And, indeed, there lay the nephew, with the laypom-colored fur beneath his chin dabbled with blood and bisected by a great swiping gash. I knew that was not my handiwork. The redheaded youth who said he was Nath of Thothangir was more than a little of a hacker with a sword.

We all went into the great house, on the alert, and found a frenzied attempt on the part of female Lamnias to pack up the stolen wealth of Dorval Aymlo and to depart. We stopped them. Aymlo wanted nothing of revenge. We discovered his wife and six children, still alive, penned in a filthy basement, and we released them to hysterical scenes of sobbing and laughter, to which we slaves left them and so found ourselves food and drink. The business as merchant carried on by Dorval Aymlo was extensive and he was a relatively wealthy halfling. His nephew had trapped him and sold him into slavery, and he had wound up on Faol, sport for the great Jikai. Now he was home, and he could not do enough for us.

The next day we had to consider what to do. From Ordsmot many of the released slaves could find their way home to various parts of Havilfar, and Aymlo was only too happy to give them, freely and without interest or thought of return, sufficient gold to get them comfortably home, broad gold deldys, the Havilfar coin corresponding to the Vallian talen.

Aymlo's next-door neighbor, and others, crowded in to congratulate him, for he was a kindly man and well thought of. Among those whom the news brought hurrying to Aymlo's house was a man. He was, in the Kregan way, tall and well built, with a handsome open face with a fine pair of black moustaches, and it would be difficult to say how old he was between, say twenty and a hundred-and-twenty—as is the Kregan way.

His name was Tom Dorand ti Ordsmot, and he took an instant shine to Tulema. This Dorand did a considerable business with Aymlo, and all the time, between congratulating the old Lamnia on his remarkable escape and bargaining over new deals, his bold eyes kept straying toward Tulema. She knew, at once. She did all the things that, I suppose, most women have done since the very first Delia of Kregen captivated the very first Drak of Kregen, many thousands of years ago, as the old legends have it, when Kregen itself first emerged from the sea-cloud to receive the light of Zim and Genodras and be blessed by the dance of the seven moons.

She was talking to me, most animatedly, and she kept tossing her hair back and laughing, and arching her back the better to reach for a glass of wine, or a miscil, or stretch for the platter of palines on the sturm-wood table. We had all been through the baths of nine, and were sweet and clean, and, truly, Tulema looked very desirable, with the lamplight shining on her hair and sparkling in her eyes. I often think that the light from a samphron-oil lamp is particularly kind to a woman.

I felt a great relief, and took myself off, and let Dame Nature, who operates as successfully on Kregen as she does on this Earth, get to work.

Come to that, I took the trouble—which was no real trouble and was, in any case, a duty of friendship—to find out what I could of this Tom Dorand. He was a solid upstanding citizen of Ordsmot, respected in all the eight precincts. He carried on a lighter business, ferrying goods up and down the orange river from Ordsmot, the entrepôt hereabouts. Between them, he and Aymlo had a good thing going with regular contracts.

With all the halflings rescued from the manhunters taken care of, with Tulema almost certainly off my hands, there remained only Nath.

"I care not where I go, Dray Prescot. Do not worry your head about me, although I give you thanks for my life."

"As to that," I said, "so be it."

Later Tulema spoke to me. She was very serious. Her dark eyes regarded me solemnly.

"You may think it strange, Dray. But I have not been a

dancing girl in a dopa pen for nothing. I know men. I know your heart is somewhere I can never reach."

It may have been flowery—Kregans love a fine phrase—but it was true.

"I hope you will be happy, Tulema. Tom is a fine man." She flushed at that. "Oh, so you noticed!"

I didn't chuckle, but my lips ricked up a trifle.

"I did not wish to hurt you," she went on. "But I am hard enough in this world to know a chance when one comes my way. You do not love me—and—" here she flared up, and spoke with a great show of bravura contempt—"and I do not love you! I shall marry Tom. I think, though, I shall choose a lesser contract, just to be safe. I shall be happy. He owns many lighters, and will soon go into the voller business. And Dorval Aymlo is rich and is our friend."

"May Opaz bless you, Tulema."

It seemed to me, then, that I had fulfilled the wishes of the Star Lords. I tried to imagine how a lighter owner, and a man who might go into the voller business, might have some effect on Kregen that had drawn him to the attention of the Star Lords. I knew they did nothing without good cause. They had wanted Tulema rescued—and she now was engaged to marry Tom Dorand ti Ordsmot and no doubt they would have children, possibly twins, and it would be these children in whose interest the Star Lords operated. I guessed the Star Lords worked with an eye cocked very far into the future.

My task appeared, as I say, to be finished. Truly, I was a simple onker in those far-off days!

Prevailed on to remain as a guest with Dorval Aymlo, and then specifically invited to the coming nuptials, I agreed to wait twelve days, two Kregen weeks. Then—Vallia!

Halfway through the first week, dressed up in a fine dark red tunic, with white trousers, and a turban of white silk upon my head—very fashionable gear in Ordsmot, then, the turban—I wandered about the town. One could walk quite freely in any of the eight precincts, only taking a little care not to be too far from the area of one's own race by night-fall—and then only if none of the greater moons were in the sky—for skirmishes and clashes between the races were relatively rare. There was no Chulik sector, and I saw none of those fierce yellow-skinned tusked halflings in Ordsmot at that time.

Coming in one evening I was halted by Aymlo, who was in a high old state of excitement. He was dressed up in the

most profuse and lavish clothes, with jewels smothering his
turban, and a golden belt, and curled slippers of foofray
satin. The house blazed with many lights and the expenditure
of samphron oil must have been prodigious. "Dray!" he said,
clutching me by the arm, his yellow fur glowing. "Dray—the
Vad of Tungar visits me!"

I congratulated him.

Tungar, I knew, was a large and prosperous province of
the country whose boundaries ran ward and ward with those
of Ordsmot. Ordsmot, of course, was a free city, with her
own elected council and Kodifex, chosen by rote, a term at
a time, from each of the eight precincts.

"He has large ideas, Dray! He owns much land, dwabur
after dwabur, and wishes to develop. If my old business head
will aid me now, he and I will strike a pretty bargain or two!"

"May Opaz shine on you, Dorval, my friend."

"And but for you, Dray Prescot, I should be bait for the
Manhounds of Antares!"

"Don't think of such things, Dorval. They are of the past."
A commotion began outside, with the sound of zorca hooves,
the tinkle of bells, and the soft silver sound of trumpets.
These were not the famous silver trumpets of Loh, but they
made a brave welcoming sound. Aymlo darted outside to
greet his guest by the light of flaring torches.

I strolled after.

The conviction grew on me that I should not push myself
forward here. This was business—and, Zair knew, I had done
enough of business during my time as Strom of Valka, and
later as Prince Majister of Vallia, when I had worked hard
with the Companies of Friends—and my instincts were that
Aymlo would want to prosecute his plans to his own fashioning. So I wandered out to stand in the shadows of the
entranceway as the Vad of Tungar alighted from his zorca.

He made an impressive sight.

Clad all in crimson silk, with a lavish display of gold and
jewels about his person, the straight sword of Havilfar they
call a thraxter swinging at his side on a silken baldric heavily
embellished with jewels and gold thread, he ran up the steps,
hand outstretched, calling: "Lahal, Dorval! Lahal! Your
happy return brings joy to my heart."

It was Aymlo's business, but this man was a Vad, a rank
below that of a Kov, though a high rank, nonetheless. I
felt an itch of apprehension, and then every other thought
was banished from my head as I saw Tulema move forward

into the torchlight. Tom Dorand moved, a vague shadow, at her back. Tulema looked radiant. She wore a sheer gown all of white silk, with crimson embroidery at throat and hem, cunningly slit so that her long legs showed in a gleam of warm flesh. The baths of nine and much scented oils and costly perfumes had transformed Tulema, the one-time dancing girl from a dopa den. Now she was the great lady.

I saw her face. She stared at the Vad of Tungar as risslaca stare at a loloo's egg.

And—he halted in his impetuous greeting of Aymlo, and stared up at Tulema there in the torchlight, and his business was done for him.

So they stared at each other, and I looked at them, and a hateful croaking voice sounded in my ears, coming from no earthbound denizen of Kregen.

"Truly, Dray Prescot, you are a prince of onkers!"

And the blue radiance took me, and swirled me up, and twisted me, and so departed . . . . I felt stinking rock beneath my naked body and the stench of slaves in my nostrils and I knew I had been thrust brutally back once again into the barred slave pens of the Manhunters of Faol.

Chapter Thirteen

Concerning the purposes of the Star Lords

I didn't believe it.

I couldn't believe it. I didn't want to believe it.

How could I, again, have brought out the wrong person from under the slavering fangs of the Manhounds of Antares?

It was all a cruel jest of the Star Lords, to punish me for being a prince of onkers.

Surely, after taking Tulema safely out, and spending so much time in her company, after she was safe, in Ordsmot, she had to be the right one! I lay there in the stink and gloom of the barred caves and I confess I came as near as I ever allow myself to despair.

Then I roused myself.

There had to be an explanation, and I was too stupid to see what must so clearly be dangling in front of my nose.

Princess Lilah. The Pallan Golan. Latimer the voller magnate. And Tulema the dancing girl.

Well, none of these four was the one I had been sent here to seek.

Then an awful thought struck me.

Tulema had said, distinctly, that she was the last of those who had been with me in the cave when I arrived.

There was no one left for me to rescue—apart, that was, from a milling mass of a hundred or more filthy, unwashed, clamoring slaves.

So that must be the answer. I was to release them all.

I pondered on this carefully, for as I have indicated, the rash freeing of slaves, no matter how desirable that may be, is not wisely undertaken without much forethought. If these miserable creatures were released they would rush screaming into the jungle, and the Manhounds of Antares would lope after them, red tongues lolling in human imitation of hunting dogs, and devour them all. They would perish in the jungle.

They would die on the plains. How many, if any at all, would reach safety?

I had vowed with my Delia to end the abomination of slavery on Kregen, thinking that a part of what the Savanti wished. But how would that vow help me now?

"By Hito the Hunter!" said a voice in my ear, a startled voice. "I thought you were dead for sure!"

I looked up from the floor and there was Nath the Guide, bending over me, wearing a mightily puzzled frown. Of course he could recognize me, for I had gone through the baths of the nine, and had my hair and beard trimmed, and so looked something like the Dray Prescot who had first arrived here. And, also, something else I should have observed much earlier then struck me. These so-called guides who claimed to guide people out to safety would hardly swear by the name of a mighty hunter. No, I should have seen that earlier.

"And I thought you dead, also, Nath."

I refrained from immediately leaping up and dealing with him as he had left us to be dealt with by the great Jikai. It was through no help of his that Princess Lilah and I had escaped. "You disappeared, and we feared a leem had taken you."

He cobbled a story together swiftly, and, truth to tell, he was more concerned with his lies than he was to find fault with my story of running and walking until strange beastmen had taken me and so, eventually, sold me back here.

Nath talked on, very volubly, about his concern for the slaves and how he sorrowed that he had been snatched away by wild beasts, and fought them, and so won free. In truth, there in the barred caves cut into the rocks, we had a high old time swapping lies, and this brought me back to something of a better humor.

"I would like to go out again, Nath, and this time escape clear away."

"Of course! A party is due tomorrow. You must be with us." Then, meaningfully, he added: "There are three Khamorros among us, and they are very fierce men."

"So be it."

There was no doubt in my mind why I needed to go out with a hunted party of fugitives. I would take their treacherous flier from them, as I had done before. I had to take care not to betray any knowledge of what had transpired here after my Jikai with Nath, and nothing of the disappearance of Inachos the Guide passed my lips. But I guessed Nath and his fellows, and Nalgre, may Makki-Grodno rot his liver, were mightily perplexed.

If I make keeping my fingers off Nath the Guide's throat sound easy—believe me, it was not.

Wild plans scurried through my head, and I slept fitfully, awaking with the others to rush at the stentors' call to the feeding cave. In the morning we would be taken out and prepared in the slave barracks. Fantastic and unworkable schemes flitted into and out of my imagination, as a flick-flick shoots its tendrils out to gobble flies.

Many of the slaves had been beaten into submission and could not respond to the meal call, and the usual Kregan custom of six or even eight square meals a day did not always impel them to answer the stentors' summons. I noticed a little Och with a chin fuzz and skinny arms and legs who, so Nath told me, was due to go out with us in the morning. Then this Och, a man named Glypta, pulled back as an ancient, yelling female Och rushed into the chamber beating her broom wildly behind her. Screeching like one of those devil-bats from the hell-caves of Karsk, the old Miglish crone rattled into the chamber, thwacking her broom at the Och woman, raising a great dust and commotion, catching the Och woman cunningly around the head, then switching to trip her legs and so tumble her sprawling into our filth.

"Keep off! Keep off, Mog!"

"I'll see Migshaanu the Ever-Vengeful tears out your liver and your tripes and strips your skin off!" The Migla was stuttering in fury, thwacking with her broom, a very witch in truth, from her mass of tangled hair to her bare and filthy feet. "You don't trick Mog and regret the day you dropped into this world!" And *thwack!* went the broom and the little Och shrieked and tried to spring up and run, and *thwack!* down came Mog's broom again in a gigantic rustling and swishing of twigs.

Bedlam broke out with scufflings and dust flying. Then the Och managed to scuttle out. Mog leaned on her broom and the liquid sheen of her eyes as she leered after the Och sent a shiver up my spine, as I remembered Tulema's avowed declaration that this Miglish crone was in very truth a witch.

"She'll think on!" said this Mog the Migla, in a shrill cackling tone of satisfaction. "Ar!"

There was no Tulema to pull me away.

I stared at Mog.

And the thought dawned. The thought I felt a deep reluctance to face. The thought that must be a true thought. "Now, may Zair take my ib for a harpstring!" I said, but to myself. And so I continued to stare at this old harpy, this filthy harridan with the rat-tail hair, crooked nose, and nutcracker jaws, and I thought that I had taken four people out of here and all of them wrong and this—this monstrosity of a halfling witch—had to be the right one.

She had been here when I arrived. Tulema had said so. And she was still here.

Mog the Witch!

Incredible!

What could the Star Lords be about, to want this object restored to the outside world of Havilfar?

However much I did not wish to believe what I had so belatedly discovered, I had to believe. And if I freed all the slaves and did not set Mog at liberty, I had the nastiest of suspicions that I would be hurled back here yet once more.

I set myself to talk with the witch, and she beat at me with her broom, and spat, drawing her filthy old blanket up around her shoulders as though I assaulted her, and bade me clear off or, by Migshaanu the Mighty-Slayer, I'd be sorry!

"But, Mog," I said, "I can get you out of here."

She cackled at that.

"Get me out!" she mocked. "Onker! Nulsh! And you'd take me out for the manhounds to gnaw on!"

"Not so, Mog."

"Yes, yes, you great ninny!"

"But, Mog—" I said, breathing hard and gripping both my fists together lest they do harm I would feel sorry for after. "The guides!" I repeated what the deluded slaves believed. "The guides will take us through to safety."

She leered at me, mocking, spitting, drool running down that promontory of a chin, the black hairs in her nose quivering. "Onker! Idiot! Nulsh! The guides are—" She swung a bright beady eye to where Nath was deep in conversation with a fair-haired girl, and she cackled like any loloo laying a square egg, and drew a corner of her gray blanket up over her face. "May Migshaanu the All-Glorious turn your belly to porridge and your back to paste!" And she scuttled from the chamber. I lost her in the gloom of the maze of passageways.

There was only one way to settle her hash for her.

I tried to get some sleep and vowed that if there was a bigger fool than me on Kregen he belonged to the Star Lords.

I had been blowharding a lot just recently. Mind you, I felt fully justified, but it was enough unlike me to make me take stock. Old Mog called me a nulsh and I knew that was as foul a term of abuse as most on Kregen. The rast, which is a six-legged rodent infesting dunghills, is often contemptuously referred to as a disgusting creature, and the term of abuse is likewise powerfully disgusted; but a rast is only one of the creatures set down on Kregen like us all and must act out its duties in its own nature. This old Migla crone was only acting as her nature impelled her. Surely, the circumstances in which she found herself were enough to make anyone scream, and the fact she had become a tame slave to sweep and cook meant only that she had a slightly less precarious grip on life than the rest.

Anyway, she was coming out with me the next morning and that was all there was to that.

I awoke to Nath's ungentle toe in my ribs and I yawned and sat up with much play of knuckling my eyes and stretching. Although the air was foul, I came alert and ready for action the instant I awoke, the result of long years at sea being called in the dark of the middle watch to face crises of all imaginable horrors . . . but I had the idea of putting Nath off guard.

All went as before. Again, and to my distaste, the Notor leading the brave band of hunters was this Trelth. His doughy face gleamed under the morning suns.

The band of runners lined up for Nalgre's inspection. As was customary we all cringed back—even I, for I had no wish to start something that, in finishing, might end up disadvantageously for the Star Lords—and, as you may guess, I was not thinking of them when I wished no foul-ups to occur.

The thin old Och, Glypta, did not cringe.

He simply stood, upright, a distant lost look on his face, and I knew I watched a man who had already given himself up for lost and who put no stock by Nath the Guide's encouraging words.

"Why do you not bow to me, Och?" demanded Nalgre. He was interested. He was accustomed to the instant servility of slaves. His whip twitched in his thick fingers.

"I have reached the bottom, the end. There is nothing more you can do to me. I have no more fear, for I am finished."

Nalgre laughed.

"Aye! I have heard political prisoners speak like that, Och. They imagine—oh, they imagine many things, the degradation, the hollowness, the utter irrationality of imprisonment. They believe that in negation they overcome." He laughed, and the sound chilled the blood. "I tell you, Och, you have no conception of the hell that can be yours if I wish." He flicked his whip and the female manhound gamboled out. "I have no need, even, to cause you suffering from my manhounds you do not as yet comprehend. The whip, ol' snake, will quickly teach you that you have not reached the end of suffering. I can make you fear again, Och—as many political prisoners have found before."

I knew he spoke the sober truth.

I was thankful to see that Glypta, too, through the miasma of his suffering, had been jerked back from that self-congratulatory abyss of suffering so many politicals, believing themselves beyond fear, indulge in. He cringed and Nalgre laughed.

What the slave-master might have done next for his amusement remained thankfully unknown, for Notor Trelth with a thick impatient rasp to his voice said: "Have done with the rast, Nalgre. If a slave will not bow the neck, have his head cut off and thus make him bow for good and all."

A woman with Trelth, with pearls in her hair and a plump and well-fed figure she had somehow crammed into tight hunting leathers, so that she bulged, tinkled a laugh. "Let him run for our sport, Ranal! I shall joy to tickle him!" And the fat fool had the effrontery to finger the thraxter at her side.

Ranal Trelth chuckled. "He shall be all yours, Lavia, yours for yourself, my precious."

I did not miss the tip of her scarlet tongue as it licked her rich lips, shining in the radiance of the twin Suns of Scorpio.

As we trudged off to the slave barracks, I heard the slave-master Nalgre have the last word.

"Ah, but, Notor Trelth, if you take off the head of an impudent slave, he does not suffer!"

There would be no chance whatsoever of convincing my fellow slaves that Nath the Guide, the one man to whom they looked for deliverance, was a traitor. I did not stand in the same danger vis-à-vis him as I had done with Inachos, for I had told Nath nothing, as I had blabbed to Inachos. I had to wait my time, and then strike, and trust in my own skill and strength to bring me through. Of one thing I was absolutely, irrevocably sure. I could expect no help from the Star Lords beyond an insulting jibe from their spy and messenger.

Up in the first floor above the hard-packed earth of the slave barracks we found two other parties waiting to go out, and a third joined us later on, when Nalgre had attended to them. There were sixteen in our party, of whom nine were halflings. The three Khamorros did not appear to me, at first glance, to be friendly to one another, and there were two human girls, the fair-haired one and one with very short dark hair, who by that token had been slave for a very short time. The girls were frightened of the Khamorros, and everyone else was, too. Nath himself trod warily, and I remembered the brave futile fight of Lart on that very dirt below us.

Glypta the Och, with the return of fear, also needed the return of reassurance, and Nath spent some time with him. I welcomed that. I took myself off to the darkest corner and ate my food alone and attended to what it was necessary to do without crossing any of the others. The Khamorros kept up an argument, but I made no attempt to follow its ramifications. There were two of them against the third. I did gather that they were khams of different training disciplines, different syples, but that the point of dissension was not, as might have been expected, the relative superiority of their own syple.

A certain amount of luck was with me, for when the suns went down I knew I would have two burs at the outside when only a couple of the lesser moons were in the sky. I waited with what patience I could muster.

When all was dark I carefully felt my way down the wooden ladder. Below, the guards were thrown into black relief by the glare of torches becketed into the walls alongside the door with its lenken beam. Lart had had difficulty in lifting that beam.

Like a wild leem of the plains, I crept up behind the first guard, silenced him, snaked across to the second, and served him likewise. I looked about for more, guessing they would be well on the alert for fear of the deadly men so well versed in the art of unarmed combat.

There was time for me to slip into the leaf-green tunic of a guard whose shoulders were almost the equal of my own, and to don his helmet. I extinguished one of the torches and cursed, a good Hito-the-Hunter oath.

The Deldar walked in from the guardroom, cursing in his turn. They all carried crossbows, ready spanned. Him, I tapped on the nape of the neck and dragged into the shadows. Two more I served in the same way so that there were six unconscious guards, sprawled on the hard dirt of the slave barracks. Then I lifted up the lenken beam and went out.

Getting into the barred caves was easy. No guard challenged me, for I was dressed as a guard and therefore above suspicion. And, too, no one had escaped from the caves of the Manhunters of Faol for many many seasons.

Inside the barred opening I ripped off the leaf-green uniform. Guards came in here in search of pleasure, and some, at least, never returned. I padded on towards the feeding area. Mog the Migla lay asleep on her filthy pallet in her den, surrounded by discarded bones and cracked and rimed platters—and her great bristly broom stood against the wall. I lapped a length of her foul blanket about her mouth and seized her and lifted her upon my shoulder and so, without a cry or a struggle, carried her swiftly outside.

A guard lowered the point of his spear as I stepped through the unlocked gate. Its bars were barely visible in the faint filtered light of the tiny hurtling moons.

"Now, by Foul Fernal himself! What is this?"

Had he talked less and used his spear more, he might have discovered what this Foul Fernal, whatever demon he might be, would now never tell him, for I stepped inside his spear and with my one free hand gripped him and cross-buttocked him with such force that his spine snapped. But he did have time to scream, whereat I let out a low Makki-Grodno oath.

I took his sword and spear and left him where he fell. I gathered up the leaf-green uniform and helmet, and carrying all in an awkward bundle, raced into the darkness.

Some distance along the trail the fugitives took to leave the compound I found a nice comfortable spot partway up a tree bole, and with movements very rapid and barely seen in the gloom, lashed Mog safely to the trunk. Her tattered blanket provided gag and bindings. Her eyes glared at me and I saw no terror in them, only a mindless and shaking sense of outrage and feral hatred. I slammed in a palisade of thorns that, although skimpy, would serve, and then dashed back. If you ask why I did not at once flee with Mog through the night jungle, you have not yet rightly understood me.

I knew the fliers were kept nowhere near the caves. Where they were kept I did not know. The Jikai villas were some way off and would be guarded. If I aroused the compound now there scarcely would be a hunt the next day. I had left

"I seized her and lifted her upon my shoulder."

the barred cage door open. The dead guard lay sprawled just outside. That would cause commotion enough.

Back in the slave barracks I flung the uniform back on the guard, kicked the Deldar, who was moaning, and scampered up the stairs. Up there all was quiet. I crept to my corner and lay down. A shadow moved. A man eased gently up to me.

A voice said: "You tried to escape, dom. You came back. Why?"

I recognized the voice of the third Khamorro, a light, pleasant voice, to come from such a deadly kind of man.

"If you wish to know," I said, "go down and see."

He chuckled. "I am going to escape tomorrow. I would not wish anyone to spoil that for me. I hope you have not done so."

"Go to sleep."

I was perfectly ready in case he leaped on me. But he did not. I heard him ease himself back to his pallet. His voice trickled through the darkness. "You are a strange man. Tomorrow, we will see."

With the morning there would be the final nonsense with Nalgre, and his female manhound, and then we would set off through the jungle. I hoped this Khamorro would welcome what he then discovered.

All followed exactly as before.

The only difference that a dead guard had made, and an open cage door, was a strong body of guards marching into the slave caves and beating about, aimlessly, and then marching out having found nothing and accomplished nothing. The slaves ready for the run today were counted, and then counted again. The Deldar, who had awoken first, must have said nothing of the inexplicable sleep he and his men had indulged in. But, as none of the slaves had escaped, there was no harm done. If anyone noticed the absence of old Mog, they would scarcely credit that she had slain a guard and taken off into the jungle, witch or no witch.

The Khamorro who had spoken to me, whose name was Turko, gave me a meaningful glance. I ignored him. Strange, how to look back on that day I can so clearly recall how I wished this Turko the Khamorro to hell and gone! Strange, indeed, is the way of fate.

With which not particularly original reflection we all began our march into the jungle, hunted men and women and halflings, sport for the great Jikai.

Nath the Guide led off very smartly, acting his part as the guide and mentor of this little band of fugitives. He had decided we should strike north, and his words were the self-same words that Inachos had used. They learned their duplicity by parts, these treacherous guides!

When we came to where I had left Mog I sprinted ahead, and with the dead guard's thraxter cut her down.

She came all asprawl into my arms and I caught her odor and I gagged.

"You nulsh! Migshaanu the All-Glorious will fry your brains and frizzle your eyeballs and rip out your tongue and—"

I said: "If you do not still that wagging tongue of yours, Mog, I will probably rip it out, instead of Migshaanu." I was bending forward, glaring at her, mightily wroth. She looked up with those bright agate eyes, and saw my face, and she stopped talking. I have noticed that effect I have on people. It is not something I am proud of. But it is, nevertheless, mightily useful at times!

Nath shouldered up, flustered, shouting: "What is this! What is she doing here? Mog—Dray Prescot—what—?"

One of the Khamorros, the largest of the three and a thumping, ugly great fellow, bellowed out in anger:

"The old crone cannot march! She cannot come with us—you must leave her, cramph."

"I will carry her, if need be."

For I had felt a surprising strength in that thin figure when she had tumbled out of the tree upon me.

"We shall not wait—"

Turko walked up with a lithe swing, his dark hair tumbled about his face, his features bronzed and clear, and, as I noticed for the first time, a look about him at once reckless and contained. With all this his build, all muscle and sliding roped power, advertised his enormous physical development, and, if that were not enough, he was damned handsome too, into the bargain.

"Leave it, Chimche," he said. "This nul Dray Prescot will carry the crone, as he says, or be left behind."

The bulky form of Chimche started to quiver and Nath said quickly: "We had best press on. There are shoes and food and wine ahead—and knives."

I had to keep my fingers still. I knew that wine.

So we hurried on along the trail, with Chimche turning often to give me a glare. But I had given him no further cause of offense, and I was carefully watching Mog. Having seen how matters stood, and at her first immediate rush back down the trail being firmly stopped by me, she screeched and waved her arms but trudged along. Every now and then I had to give her a push. I watched her, as I say, very carefully; the impression had formed that she playacted rather more than she cared folk to perceive. And her walk, once the shuffling scuttle she habitually adopted in the caves proved troublesome swinging along the trail, changed imperceptibly into a much firmer and longer tread. She would not be the first woman to make herself look old and hideous in captivity.

Still, she was a halfling and, by Zair, she was hideous in reality!

When we reached the cache of food and clothing Mog was more than happy to rest. We donned the gray tattered tunics and took the knives and put on the shoes, and all this petty finery was designed to make us feel we had outwitted the manhunters, to give us hope, to make us run!

Mog wouldn't wear the shoes Nath offered.

Toward the end of the march I had to carry her, slung over a shoulder, and every now and then a filthy dangling leg would give me a sly kick, just to remind me.

When we made our camp up a tree, erecting a palisade of thorns, and Nath prepared his lower aerie, I knew the time approached. Nath hefted up the wine bottles, their leather bulging. I was looking at Mog. She was tied in place. I knew she had the willpower and the courage to march back through the jungle. Now, as Nath offered her the wine, she cowered back, trembling.

"No, no, Nath. I do not want the wine."

Chimche bellowed at this, his dark florid face flushed.

"Then give it here, you crone!"

"Why will you not drink the wine?" persisted Nath. He upended the spout over Mog's mouth, trying to force her, letting the wine drop through in that frugal way Kregans have.

"No!" She was terrified now. "No, the wine is drugged! We will all sleep and the monsters of the forests will eat us!"

Turko laughed at this, but Nath backhanded Mog across her rubbery lips. "Drugged!" he shouted, in a fury. "You lie, old crone! You lie!" And he hit her again.

I took Nath the Guide's arm and bent it back.

"She does not lie, Nath. The wine is drugged so that you

may creep off in the night, and leave us prey to the man-hounds."

He stared at me, his arm bent back, and a sickly smile distorted that frank and manly face. We all saw. We all saw the guilt that glazed on that face.

"By the Muscle!" bellowed Chimche, shoving forward. "It is true!"

The other Khamorro, Janich, elbowed up, pushing me out of the way, reaching for Nath the Guide.

"The wine is drugged and the guides are false!" screeched Mog. Her agate eyes glared up in the terror of the moment.

Janich's hefty push and Nath's convulsive effort broke my hold on his arm and he scuttled back up the tree branch. He stared down on us, and saw the murder in our eyes, and he screamed at us.

"It is true! It is true! The wine is drugged and you creeping yetches will be dead tomorrow when the Manhounds of Faol tear your limbs apart and splash your blood into the jungle."

Shouts and calls broke out as the slaves tried to get up the tree at Nath. He lifted his knife. I think, then, he knew he was doomed, for the Khamorros are frightful fighters, and he with all his forest experience knew he would not elude them among the trees. But he would make the effort. You could feel sorry for him, as you might feel sorry for a risslaca—about to kill and eat a dainty lople—being suddenly caught in a snare and feathered with barbed arrows.

"You are all doomed!" Nath the Guide screeched it down at us. "And the witch shall die first!"

The whole reason I was here, in this hideous situation, was to rescue Mog the Migla and take her to safety. And now, with the speed of a striking leem, Nath hurled his knife at the old Miglish crone.

The knife flew, a darting sliver of steel in the forest gloom, full at Mog's unprotected throat.

Chapter Fourteen

Turko the Khamorro

Straight for that stringy defenseless throat the knife flashed. The movement of the knife struck everything else into a paralysis, a stasis wherein Nath's throwing arm remained outflung, Mog recoiled against the bonds, Turko and the other Khamorros stood caught in the passions of the moment, the halflings below stilled in their clamor.

The sword I had taken from the guard rasped as it cleared the scabbard.

That old Krozair trick of striking away flying arrows with the superb Krozair longsword must serve me now—and before I had time to finish the thought, everything happening so fast events blurred, the thraxter flicked out and the knife struck the blade with a high ringing pinging and spun away into the gloom of the forest.

Nath the Guide galvanized into motion, screaming, clawing back up the tree.

From below a Rapa—one I had noted as of that fierce, predatory, arrogant kind that meant he had once been a mercenary—threw his own knife. It flew true. Nath the Guide stood, arms spread, transfixed, his face twisted with the defiant fear—and he fell. Nath the Guide, son of treachery, fell full-length down the tree and so into the greenery to smash face-first into the mud and detritus of the jungle floor.

"Let his foul Hito the Hunter aid him now!" quoth the Rapa, and went down very agilely to retrieve his knife.

This Rapa was one Rapechak, and I remember that he must have been less offensive to smell than most, or I was growing accustomed to the typical Rapa stink. Those Rapas who had fought with me in Dorval Aymlo's courtyard, too, I recalled, had been in nowise as offensive as other Rapas I had known.

"Now what do we do?" demanded the big Khamorro, Chimche.

Mog remained petrified and dumb. The halflings were raising a great hullabaloo. Janich was yelling at them to cease their noise or, by the Muscle, he'd break their bones to powder.

Turko said: "This nul Dray Prescot knew the guide was false. So did the old witch. What is fitting that we should do with them, khamsters?"

"Did you know, witch?" shouted Chimche, thrusting his nose at Mog. She cowered back, blinking.

"Only stories!" Her shrill voice poured words out in a torrent. "May Migshaanu the Ever-Radiant stand as my witness! Rumors—we heard stories—the wine was a sleep potion—the shoes were baited—the tame slaves were frightened. Enil was found dead in his den, and Yolan went for water and never returned." She shook as she screamed. "We dare not speak! The guides murdered us! By Magoshno and Sidraarga, I swear it!"

Janich went to strike her, so wrought up was he; but Turko took his arm, saying: "Leave the old nul, Janich. She is harmless and in fear for her life."

"Aye." Janich looked down at Turko's hand on his arm. "She should be. And so should you be, nul-syple!"

Turko took his hand away.

He removed that hand from Janich's arm neither too quickly nor yet too slowly. I admired that coolness. I could guess what had transmogrified the situation. The syples were the different kinds of Khamorro training and belief, and a nul, clearly, was anyone not a Khamorro. So that for Janich to call Turko a nul-syple was a great insult. Yet Turko did not instantly retaliate. He had put his hand on a man who was not a syple-brother. The answer must be given.

I said: "If you wish to yammer and quarrel here all night, you may do so. As for me, I am going to take a flier off these Makki-Grodno guides."

I still held the thraxter naked in my fist. I reached across to Mog, and with my left hand wrenched her bindings free, lifted her up, and slung her over my shoulder. She screamed and then tried to bite me, whereat I thwacked her narrow bottom with the flat of the blade. The thraxter is a medium-long straight sword, with a blade heavier and wider than a rapier, a vertical blade, and it smacked with a satisfactory smack. Mog yelped.

Down the tree I went, slipping and sliding most of the way. At the bottom the Rapa, Rapechak, straightened up with his knife freshly cleaned on Nath's breechclout. "You mentioned a flier."

"Aye. This way. And keep silent."

So I set off with the halfling Mog draped over my shoulder and a rout of halflings following me through the forest. I found the clearing and thumped Mog down and said: "Stay there, old witch. If you try to run I'll draw your guts out for a knitted vest."

Without knowledge of any signal the flier up there might be awaiting I could only wait patiently for him to descend. Inachos had stood out and waved; I could not do that. The Twins were up, the two second moons of Kregen eternally revolving one about the other, casting down a pinkish sheen of light in which details stood out clearly. A rustle on the back trail heralded the three Khamorros.

"You, Turko," I said. "If you stand in the clearing and wave up, and then scamper back here, and look lively about it, we might see the flier this Zair-forsaken night."

Again Turko favored me with that long, almost quizzical look. I turned away and went to stand by Mog.

Turko walked into the clearing, looked up, waved his arms, and then walked back. As a performance it would not have done for Drury Lane, but it worked.

The flier ghosted down, shimmering in the pink moonlight, drifting gently to the clearing's mass of rotting vegetation, fallen trees, and creeping shoots. A guide looked out and shouted something about Hito the Hunter and the stupid yetches of slaves to be run in the morning and needing a drink . . . and Rapechak the Rapa's knife buried itself in his neck so that he pitched over the lenken side of the flier, choking and writhing in convulsions, before Chimche reached him and twisted his head in a single savage crunching action.

I was working with fearsome allies, now, but they did not have the unwanted responsibility of Mog the Migla on their hands.

Janich said with great satisfaction, "I can fly a voller."

I said, "We will have to squeeze everyone in most carefully. There is not too much room—"

But Chimche and Janich both stared at me, as though I were mad, and then they laughed, and Chimche said: "You? A stinking nul? We do not take you aboard our voller."

And Janich chuckled and added: "But we will take the two shishis. They will make brave sport!"

The two girls, the fair and the dark, screamed at this and cowered back from the forefront of the group of halflings. Truth to tell, I had taken no notice of the girls, for I had had Mog to concern myself with. Now Turko said in a quiet, even, leaden voice: "And me?"

"You?" Janich threw back his head and laughed aloud. "You nul-syple! You will be left with these others, for the yetches of manhounds to gobble up! I am only sorry I cannot be here to see it."

I moved forward. The sword glimmered pinkly in my hand.

"I do not think you will take off and leave us, Janich. The airboat belongs to us all. We are all slaves together."

If I had expected an argument from a Khamorro I was a fool.

All I had heard about these fearsome men flashed through my mind. Tulema came from the same land, from Herrelldrin. She knew. "Terrible in their cunning, Dray! They practice devilish arts that let them crush a man's bones as a straw in summer in their hands! They do not fear the sword or the spear, for they know arts to outwit swordsmen. Come away, Dray, from a Khamorro, if you value your life!" And, I had seen Lart the Khamorro die and so I knew that all Tulema said was true—at least, the results of her observation if not the causes of the Khamorros' skills.

Janich rushed across the tangled floor of the jungle clearing.

He came at me with the intention of taking me in a grip that would snap my neck. I was familiar with the trick from long training and discipline with the Krozairs of Zy, of whom these Khamorros would never have heard.

I sidestepped and at the same time slid into an instinctive avoidance routine. Also, I slashed the thraxter down Janich's side. He slipped most of the blow and elbowed away the flat of the sword. He roared in enjoyment.

"See, Chimche! The stupid nul believes himself a man with a sword!"

"I seldom slay unarmed men, Janich."

At this Turko called out: "A Khamorro is never unarmed, Dray Prescot."

If it was a warning it could not help; if it indicated Turko would not interfere, it was useful. I did not know how deeply ran the animosities between syple and syple in Herrelldrin.

Janich circled, like a leem. In the clear pinkish light of the Twins I could see the shadowy interplay of his muscles. Beautifully built are the men of the Khamorro! He circled me and he was not in the least afraid of the sword, and I saw with great sorrow that this could only end one way— I would be forced to slay this Janich the Khamorro.

As we circled I saw Turko standing immediately to the rear of Rapechak. The Rapa's arm was twisted up and there was no knife stuck down his breechclout.

Then I had to concentrate on Janich. I admit my sorrow at what followed, for all that Janich had proved himself a mean-spirited man, but, as Turko had said, he was not unarmed.

He taunted me.

"I shall break your arm off, Prescot, and drive your own fingernails into your eyes! I shall twist your head so you may view your shoulder blades! A Khamorro cannot be mastered."

Why I said what I did, I do not know for sure; perhaps I was sick of the whole stupid affair already. We should be flying to safety in the voller instead of brawling!

"Unarmed combat, Janich, is very wonderful and brave. But people who develop it are slaves and without liberty, men kept down by a superior people who have weapons, real weapons, of their own. A man fights with his hands, or a stick, if he is subservient and not allowed a steel weapon."

By this time Janich was really annoyed and yet he did not lose his temper. He came in, weaving and ducking, very quickly, to take me in another grip I recognized. I eluded him and again I found that reluctance in my sword arm to plunge the blade home.

"You are done for, Dray Prescot," shouted Turko.

Well, it is all a long time ago, now, and Turko's voice spurred me in a way I did not then understand.

Janich kept on taunting me, and I replied once more.

"A man with a sword is not to be bested, Janich, even by so marvelous a hand-fighter as you. I would not slay you—"

He let loose a torrent of invective, foul words and many of them incomprehensible to me then, although I grew well-enough acquainted with them in later days. I could see he was puzzled and annoyed that he had not slipped my blade and taken me and gripped me and so broken my neck or my back. He bored in again, and he used a trick the Krozairs of Zy would never practice on one another—although only too happy to employ against an overload of Magdag—and he nearly got me so that I had to furiously twist aside and let his iron-hard toes go whistling past. My body did what it has been trained to do, released at last from compunction of my reason, and the blade slashed down. Janich the Khamorro staggered back with a ruined face and blood everywhere, ghastly in that streaming pink radiance. Then Turko yelled and I went flying as Chimche smashed into me from the side.

Somehow I clung onto the thraxter and shoved up and saw Chimche and Turko locked, and Turko flipped into the air to land with a smash. Chimche glanced at Janich, who was dead, and at me, and he roared mightily.

"Stinking nul of a sworder! You will die now!"

He rushed. I staggered up, for a fallen branch had not rotted enough and a jagged splinter of wood had sorely bruised me and taken my wind. I circled the blade, sliced at his wrist, drew blood, and made him stagger back, roaring.

"You have not learned, Chimche," I got out. "A sword will settle for you, you cramph." And I started after him.

Turko leaned up on an elbow, gasping, his face drawn with pain. I circled the thraxter again and then, and I suppose for the first time, Chimche got a clear look at my face.

He turned, bolted for the voller, clambered in, and the next instant the flier rose above the treetops, fleeing into the pink moonlight flooding down over Kregen.

I admit, then, I shouted a few uncomplimentary things after Chimche the Khamorro, comprehensively anatomizing his ancestry and his lineage and his personal habits and his eventual fate and where I would like to see him. Oh, yes, I was annoyed!

I had handled the whole affair like a green onker straight out of nursery school!

Where, I said to myself, is the Dray Prescot of the Clansmen of Felschraung, of the bravo-fighters of Zenicce, of the Krozairs of Zy, not to mention that puffed-up Drak of Valka? Had the Star Lords and their bedeviling demands completely addled my brain?

I swung back to Turko and helped him get up, for he had been thrown heavily and had been struck a shrewd blow.

"And don't prate to me, Turko, about not laying hands on a Khamorro. You have seen how I deal with Khamorros. And now, by Makki-Grodno's diseased left armpit, we have to deal with the manhounds and those perfumed idiots who think they are on a great Jikai. We're all in this together, now."

Turko stared at me, his eyes half-closed, rubbing his bruised side.

"We march with the moons!" I shouted to the beast-men. "We take the trail away from the slave pens. And, first—" And here, at the mouth of the trail we must take, I cut a long stake and pointed it and thrust it at an angle into the ground, camouflaging it with leaves. "May a manhound degut himself on that, to the glory of Opaz!"

Then, with Mog the Migla witch slung over my shoulder and my other arm around Turko supporting him and helping him along and followed by a jabbering crowd of halflings and two pretty girls, I, Dray Prescot, set off to outrun the Manhounds of Antares.

Chapter Fifteen

Of mantraps and medicine

Along the jungle trail we left a fine old collection of traps.

There was no time I would spare to dig pits, but whenever we came across a natural hole that a few murs of labor might turn into a mantrap we happily spent that time, barbing the bottom with spikes, laying thin branches and many leaves across the top and sprinkling about the stinking detritus of the rain forest to camouflage the trap.

We constructed deadfalls, of a variety of patterns to make their discernment less easy. Rapechak entered into this work with great gusto. Turko had been badly knocked by the fall and although I had prodded his ribs, to his silent suffering, and found nothing broken, I was not happy that he did not have a broken bone in that magnificent body of his somewhere. I would not listen when he wanted to help with the trap-making, and snarled at him to lie down and rest. "If you must show how brave and noble a Khamorro you are, Turko, keep your eyes on Mog. I don't want her to run off."

She had moaned and shrieked, but now she was silent, except to say, now and then: "No one escapes the manhounds, Dray Prescot, you nulsh. We are all dead."

Whereat I shouted across: "Keep the old witch quiet, Turko, or, by thunder, I'll gag her in her own foul breech-clout!"

We left many pointed and cunningly positioned stakes along the trail. I hoped a manhound, loping after us, sniffing the scent from our baited shoes, would leap full onto the sharp point of the stake and so wriggle with the dark blood dropping down until he died.

I'd far rather see, I own, one of the hunters in that position, but I knew them. They used the manhounds to track and corral the quarry; then they stepped in with their beautiful and expensive crossbows, their swords and their spears.

Once, Mog shrieked at me, "You ninny, Dray Prescot! The shoes the guides give us are baited. The manhounds can pick up the scent a dwabur off! Why do you not kick off the shoes?"

"Quiet, you old crone!"

Rapechak took his shoes off and was about to hurl them into the jungle when I stopped him. His fierce beaked face swung down to look at me, and his eyes glared, ready for an instant quarrel. I had suffered much from Rapas in the past. But I was prepared to explain to this Rapechak.

"Later. Later we will dispose of the shoes. Not now."

He would have argued, but I swung away, shouting about a tree trunk the halflings were trying to angle as a deadfall, and threatening to crush their own stupid brains out in the process. Rapechak put his shoes back on.

We could march for some distance yet. There was plenty of light from the Twins and later from She of the Veils; the enemy would be fatigue. Already, as seemed to be their custom, a Fristle man carried a Fristle woman. I didn't want to have to help the two human girls, for I had Mog to worry about and, to a different degree, Turko. He was in great pain, but not a murmur of complaint passed his lips. And, to me a strange fact, he still looked handsome. Suffering sometimes ennobles and makes one look radiant; not often.

When I calculated that we would exhaust our strength without adequate return by pressing on, I told everyone to take off their shoes. We found a great tree and climbed into its lower branches and there with the rammed-in thorns formed our palisade and made camp. We ate the rest of the food, and water was found in a nearby stream. I looked at this bedraggled band.

"Rapechak," I said. And, to a Brokelsh, "You, too, Gynor. Are you done yet, or are you for a little sport?"

They didn't understand. When I explained both Rapa and Brokelsh gave expressions of pleasure in their respective halfling ways.

We three, then, struck off along the trail where it turned along by a river. We had prepared stakes which we used to make of that trail a death trap, unless one went cautiously, and inspected every fold of leaf. Presently, after a bur or so, we came to a gorge into which the stream fell. We threw the shoes down, having rubbed them well along the brink.

"May all the manhounds go the the Ice Floes of Sicce!"

said Gynor, the Brokelsh. He was strong and his black body-
bristles sprouted fiercely.

We went back to the camp and Turko looked up and said,
"Mog is still here, Dray Prescot," to which I replied, "Good,"
and so we all rested. We set watches, for that was prudent,
here in the rain forests of Northern Faol.

In the morning, by first light, a mingling of opaline radiance, we set off again along the small trail leading off from
the other side of the tree. Here we set no traps but pressed
on as far and as fast as we might. Those of the slaves whose
feet were in the worst condition had rags wrapped about them,
and we all struggled and slipped through terrible country,
half-naked, gleaming with sweat, for it was very hot, panting
and plunging on. We looked very much like fugitives then.

At a resting place, when it was time to move on, for I
would not stop to catch food and eat, Turko looked up as I
lifted him.

"Leave me, Dray Prescot. I cannot go farther. I am done
for."

I ignored him and got him on my back.

Mog cackled as Rapechak, who understood I meant what
I said, prodded her on.

"He is a fool, that Khamorro!" The old witch spat out the
words. "Migshaanu the Pitiless witnessed it! He attacked the
great kham Chimche when Chimche would have broken you
like a reed, Prescot! And now look at him, his guts caved in."

I said to Turko: "I believe you attacked Chimche, Turko,
and for this I thank you. Now do not prattle like a baby
onker. I will not leave you for the manhounds."

"So be it, Dray Prescot."

I could not tell him that great kham or not, Chimche would
have been a dead man if he had fought me, without Turko's
assistance which, truth to tell, had thrown me off balance. A
fighting-man, used to the melee as it is known among my
fighting clansmen, keeps the eyes in the back of his head well
open all the time. As witness poor Alex Hunter, back there
on a beach in Valka. And that seemed a long time ago, by
Zair!

That day we hurried on rapidly, and turn and turn about
the stronger helped the weaker. I noticed the two girls, who
claimed to be rich merchant's daughters, kept close to me.
Beyond learning that their names were Saenda—the fair
one—and Quaesa—the dark one—and that they came from
different parts of Havilfar and already were putting on airs,

one claiming superiority over the other, only to have some other remarkable fact brought to life in opposition, I took no notice of them except to see they kept up with the party.

My plans had gone disastrously wrong, all because of those fool Khamorros, although Turko was a Khamorro and was proving a tough and reliable companion.

Although, as you will instantly see, I have forged ahead in this story; for at this time Turko was badly injured, in great pain, and a liability on our onward progress. Once he saw that I did not mean to abandon him he remained quiet and did not suggest I leave him again. Mog, however, mentioned the idea more than once, having discovered how much more pleasant travel was across my shoulder than struggling and stumbling through the gloomy aisles of the forest.

And perhaps, if you guess I did this to spite the Star Lords—you would not be wrong.

We were attacked by a species of risslaca, all squamous and hissing and tongue-flicking and claw-clicking; but I was able to slide the thraxter into an eye, and then into the thing's scale-white belly, and so dispatch it. Turko stared up at the fight from where I had dumped him beside the almost-invisible trail. When it was all over, he grunted as I lifted him, whereat I said: "I would not cause you pain, Turko. For the sake of Opaz, man, tell me!"

All he would say was: "It is better than lying on the ground and rotting and being eaten by ants or snapped up by a risslaca such as you have just slain."

Oh, yes, he was tough, was Turko!

After a time, he said, "You have handled a sword before."

"Yes."

"The trick with the knife, when Nath sought to slay the old witch. That was clever."

Truth to tell, I had looked back at that old Krozair trick and knew it to be not at all bad. I had not been using the great Krozair longsword which, with its two-handed grip, is suitable for the quick subtle twitchings and flickings necessary, and I had been aiming for a flashing sliver of a knife and not a clothyard shaft. Yes, that had been something of a little Jikai. I said, "A knack, Turko. Now, rest as best you may."

Presently Rapechak, prodding Mog, pressed up to my side.

"I will carry Turko the Khamorro, if he will allow, Dray Prescot, if you will take charge of this—this—" Rapechak rubbed his thin shanks and glared at Mog. "She is a devil from the Ice Floes of Sicce, by Rhapaporgolam the Reaver of Souls!"*

I did not chuckle, although I believe my lips ricked up.

"And what do you say, Turko?"

He faced a struggle, then, did Turko the Khamorro. Only later when I learned more about the Khamorros and the awful power their belief in their khamster sanctity has over them could I realize that for a Rapa to touch a Khamorro was far worse than, for instance, the touch from an Untouchable of old India.

Not understanding all this at the time, I said, "Rapechak has shins that are black and blue from the old witch. I shall not allow her so to maltreat me. Let Rapechak carry you for a space, Turko, my friend."

Turko yielded. He said something under his breath, and I caught the trailing words: ". . . Morro the Muscle's recompense and atonement."

We pressed on, for by this time the Manhounds of Antares lolloped on our back trail, and the traps would only hold them up for as long as they were stupid enough not to do the obvious. When I caught a glimpse through a gap in the overhead cover of a skein of fluttrells winging past, and ordered instant stillness until the magnificent flying beasts and their armed riders had passed, I suspected that they must be a part of the manhunters' search.

"Fluttrells and vollers," cackled Mog. "They will catch us, you nulsh, Dray Prescot, and rip our throats out and feather us with barbs for their sport."

"Maybe," I said, making it a casual statement. "But they will be sorry they found us, that I promise you."

So, with many rests that grew more frequent and of longer duration, we pressed on. I caught one of the little jungle palies, similar to the plains species but with zebra-striped hindquarters, and we all ate. By the time Far and Havil sank and the Twins appeared and we made camp we were pretty well done for. A complete night's rest was imperative.

At this camp I took the opportunity of making a bow. Oh, it was a poor thing, vine-strung, and of a pitiful throw; but with the fire-hardened points of the arrows, quickly fletched

---

* Prescot has used this oath of the Rapas before and I have deleted it; here it sounds absolutely right. He spells it out and pronounces it with a clearing-of-the-throat sound.   A.B.A.

with feathers from a bird brought down by a flung stone, I fancied it would give us just that little edge of time. We might have to buy the time we needed dearly.

"Weapons," said Turko. He lifted his hands, and turned them about in the screened fire-glow in its crook of tree-trunk, for the trees hereabouts were powerful and large of bole. "I have been taught all my life that a man's hands—and his feet and head—are more potent than artificial weapons."

"Sometimes, Turko. What I told Janich is true. I know you boast you can dodge and deflect arrows; and certainly you may outwit a swordsman if he is not reasonably good with his blade, but—"

"Aye, Dray Prescot. *But.*"

"Now sleep, friend Turko. Tomorrow we will show these Opaz-forsaken cramphs of manhunters the error of their ways."

"Tomorrow?"

"They will find us tomorrow."

There was no answer to that, and with watches set, we slept.

Turko had a bad night. He awoke with a groan he could not still and I fetched water and bathed his forehead, which felt feverish, and gave him a little to sip, for I feared internal injuries. Mog woke up and swore at me. By this time she must have realized there was some special interest in her for me, and she would have been thinking very carefully on what her future would be. She could have no knowledge of the Star Lords, or so I believed. That I looked out for her was clear—the other halflings looked out for themselves, and the two girls, Saenda and Quaesa, had already shown signs of anger at my concern over old Mog—and so she must be racking her evil old brains for the explanation. That she could never find one that would make sense was obvious. I had no idea why the Star Lords should bedevil me with the old witch.

Now she swore at me, vilely. "Get your rest, you great nulsh, Dray Prescot! Why waste your strength on the Khamorro? He will die tomorrow. I can see that, for I have great powers in healing, and he is done for."

Turko looked at me and I saw his lips rick down. The hand holding the roughly fashioned leaf-cup shook. That was from weakness and pain, I guessed, never from fear.

With Turko looking at me I went down to old Mog.

I took her by the neck and I glared into her eyes.

"You say Turko will die tomorrow? You are sure?"

I let her breathe and she gobbled: "I know!"

"You have skill in medicine?"

She started off to boast of her secrets and her mysteries, and of how Migshaanu the Great Healer would aid her—and then she stopped, aghast, glaring at me, a hand to her mouth. She saw, at last, what the situation was.

I nodded. I have given orders in my life that I dreaded to give. One demand must be measured against another, and there is no certainty when it comes to command. Hesitation is a sin the fates punish by destruction.

"You will be able to gather plants from the forest, herbs, leaves, fungi—you will be able to fashion needles from the thorns—you will cure my friend Turko. If you do not, Mog the Migla, I shall certainly leave you for the manhounds."

She tried, shrewd enough to have read much of my intentions, for, after all, they were very patent.

"You took me from the slave pens, Dray Prescot. You saved me for some great purpose of your own—or your masters. You will not kill me or leave me to the monsters."

"Cure Turko, or you will be turned off into the jungle."

By this time for her to return to the caves was beyond her strength, wiry and whipcordlike though it might be. She gibbered and mewed, but I remained adamant. Just why I did this I can see quite clearly, now, was to make the Star Lords pay. Oh, poor old Mog was the instrument to suffer— although she had had an easy ride compared with the others— but the Star Lords would, I hoped, suffer a little along with her.

With many imprecations and mutterings Mog gathered what she would need and soon was concocting potions. She stuck thorns into Turko, and watching her, I saw the sureness with which her gnarled fingers worked, and knew she had the skill of Doctor Nath the Needle, back in Vallia. She felt him all over and pronounced nothing irremediably broken, and gave him the draft to drink. He lost his pain the moment the last needle had been inserted, so powerfully beneficent is the art and science of acupuncture upon Kregen. Presently he slept and Mog crept back to her place, pronouncing him as well as could be expected, that she had done all she could, and now it all lay in the merciful hands of Migshaanu the Great Healer.

A grain of Earthly comfort I took was that Turko had not bled from his nose or mouth or ears.

He had tried to save me, charging Chimche, who must be

of a higher kham and thus almost certain to defeat Turko. He had sustained these injuries trying to help me. I could do nothing less than use every effort I could to save his life.

From the time when I had flown over the jungle escaping with Tulema and Dorval Aymlo and the others, I could only estimate the distances to be traversed to the coast. Once there I had no doubt we would steal a boat well enough. Had Turko not been injured we might have made it, and he realized this and said nothing, and looked at me speculatively.

We were, in truth, a sorry-looking bunch. When we creaked our way down out of our tree in the morning, and shivered, and stretched, and looked about on the dim vastness of the jungle, pressing us in to a narrow circle of hostile greenery all about, I realized we could not go on. The two girls' feet were lacerated and torn despite the muffling clumsy rags they wore. Some of the halflings were in worse case, although many were holding up reasonably well; but with that stupid prickly pride, I had, without any conscious volition on my part, decided we would all get out together. By this time I was heartily sick of the jungle. I know we spent a weary time in the green fastness, and I contrasted it with others of my marches upon the hostile, terrifying, beautiful face of Kregen, but it was a chore laid on me and it was something I had to do.

I said, with that harsh intolerant rasp in my voice, "Stay here. I will return."

Most of them simply sank down, thankful not to have once more to plunge into that steaming hell. I left them and walked carefully along what was left of the trail. All about me, almost unheard, rustled the vicious life of the forest. Soon I came to a clearing—not large—but I fancied it would do. To bring everyone there and safely sheltered up trees, with palisades, took a frightening long time. But, at last, we were ready.

Turko opened his eyes and stared at me and I could have sworn amusement curved his pallid lips as I spoke to cheer him.

"Now, friend Turko! Let the manhounds come! We'll make 'em sorry they sniffed us out!"

"Yes, Dray Prescot. I really think you will."

Chapter Sixteen

The fight for the voller

Almost immediately half a dozen fluttrells bearing armed warriors passed in a skein over the clearing. I remained still. I hungered for a voller.

As the morning wore on and Far and Havil crawled across the sky and the temperature rose and we sweated and steamed, more fluttrells pirouetted above us until I began to think we would have to decoy them down, enough for all fourteen of us, for we had lost three and gained one. In the end I saw what must be the truth of the matter and cursed; but having deliberately walked all this way through jungle in order to decoy a suitably proud hunting party, the loss of a few more burs hardly counted. When the next skein of fluttrells was sighted I stepped out into the clearing and waved.

"Have a care, Dray Prescot," called Turko. "Remember, they will have real steel weapons, also."

His light voice sounded stronger, which cheered me, and I did not miss that underlying mockery. Truly, he counted me a nul, never a true khamster, and this was inevitable and right.

The fluttrells slanted down. There were five of them, and they looked bright and brave against the glow of the suns.

This was just another of those occasions on Kregen when I faced odds. I hoped the fluttrells would wing away after an inspection to report to the manhunters that they had discovered our whereabouts. The mighty hunters on the great Jikai were almost certainly sitting with their feet up, sipping the best wines of Havilfar—or possibly, if they could afford it, a fine Jholaix—and waiting until a sighting report had been brought back by their aerial scouts.

My hope was vain.

The first four fluttrells continued their descent; the fifth winged up in a flash of velvety green over the beige-white, his streamlined head-vane turning. He disappeared over the jungle roof before his comrades alighted. The men astride the fluttrells although new to me then were of a type, if not a nation, with which I was perfectly familiar. I had seen their like strutting the boulevards and enclaves of Zenicce, lording it over the slaves in the warrens of Magdag, supervising the Emperor's haulers along the canals of Vallia. Hard, tough, professional, man-managers and slave-masters they were, like the aragorn I had bested in Valka. They jumped down with cheerful cries, one to another. They unstrapped their clerketers, and their weapons clicked up into position, the crossbows spanned, the moment their feet hit the tangled ground of the clearing.

They wore flying leathers, and braided cloaks cunningly fashioned from the velvet-green feathers of the fluttrells themselves. Their feathered flying caps fitted closely to their mahogany-brown faces, and streamed a clotted and flaring mass of multicolored ribbons, very brave to see in the slipstream of their passage across the sky. They advanced without any caution whatsoever.

My bow felt the ill-made thing it was in my fist. I could have no hesitation here. The Star Lords' commands impelled me.

The first arrow took the first flyer in the throat. The second arrow, a fraction too late, struck the second flyer in the face as he ducked to the side. I had read his ducking and his direction but the clumsy arrow loosed not as accurately as a clothyard shaft fletched with the brilliant blue feathers of the king korf of Erthyrdrin would have done. By the time the third arrow was on its way crossbow bolts were thunking about me.

They had difficulty in seeing me against the gloom of the jungle and the third arrow pitched into the third flyer's throat above the leather flying tunic. The fourth flyer looked dazedly at his companions, at what must have seemed to him to be a deadly wall of jungle sprouting arrows—and he turned and ran for his fluttrell.

Much as I dislike shooting men in the back this was a thing very necessary to be done.

When it was all over Mog crackled out: "A great Jikai, Dray Prescot! You shoot well from ambush. Hai, Jikai!"

Which displeased me most savagely, so that I cursed the old witch in the name of the putrescent right eyeball of Makki-Grodno.

"They are flutsmen, Dray Prescot," Rapechak called. He

walked across, carefully cut out the arrow from the nearest
body, turned it over with his foot, and bending lithely, took
up the man's thraxter. "I have served with them, in the long
ago. They are good soldiers, although avaricious and without
mercy. Because they ride their fluttrells through the windy
wastes of the sky they consider themselves far better than the
ordinary footman. They are disliked. But they earn their pay."
He waved the thraxter about a little, and I saw the feelings
strong upon him as he once more grasped a weapon in his
Rapa fist.

The flutsmen, so I gathered, were not in any sense a race
or a nation. Rather, they recruited from strong, fierce, vicious
young men of similar natures to themselves, forming a kind
of freemasonry of the skies, owing allegiance to no one unless
paid and paid well. True mercenaries, they were, giving their
first thought to their own band, then to the flutsmen, and,
after that, to their current paymaster. Men from all over
Havilfar, aye, and from over the seas, served in their winged
ranks.

Gynor the Brokelsh approached. He looked determined.
"There are four fluttrells, Dray Prescot. Will you four apims
take them and fly away and leave us halflings?"

Apim, as you know, is the slang and somewhat contemptuous term used by halflings for ordinary human beings—for,
of course, to any halfling *he* is ordinary and the apims are
strange.

"You have put an idea into my head, Gynor, for, by Vox,
I hadn't thought of it."

He eyed me again. "You may speak truth. You are a
strange man, Dray Prescot. If not that, then what?"

"We must capture a voller—" I began, but with a rush of
long naked legs and a hysterical series of screams, the two
girls were upon me, panting, breathing in gulps, their hair
all over their faces—very distracting and pretty, no doubt,
but quite out of place in the serious work to hand.

"You must take us, Dray!" they both wailed. "Fly with us
to safety in Havilfar!"

I pushed them aside, and they clung to me, sobbing, pleading to be taken away instantly from this horrible jungle.

"I want to get out of this Opaz-forsaken jungle more than
you do!" I blared at them, outraged. "Now for the sweet
sake of Blessed Mother Zinzu—shut up!"

They had no idea who Mother Zinzu the Blessed was—of
course, the patron saint of the drinking classes of Sanurkazz—

but everyone swore by their own gods, and so everyone was used to outlandish names in the way of oaths. They recoiled from my face.

"Look!" I said, pointing to a couple of Lamnias and the Fristle couple, all of whom were far gone. I marched over. "You, Doriclish," I said to the Lamnia, who was making an effort to smooth his laypom-yellow fur down. "Can you ride a fluttrell?"

"I have not done so since my youth, when the sport was a passion—"

"Then you can. And you? And you?" to the others.

It turned out that when it came to it, most everyone in Havilfar was quite at home in the air, whether aboard a voller or astride a fluttrell or other flying saddle bird or animal, and so I could shovel out another load of responsibility. "Very well. You may take the four fluttrells and make a flight for it."

If I had expected argument from the other halflings, I did not receive it. Only Saenda and Quaesa reacted, and they had to be told, pretty sharply, to behave themselves.

"Your feet are well enough," I said. "And there will be a voller before long."

"I shan't forget this, Dray Prescot!" shouted Saenda.

"You'll be sorry, Dray Prescot!" screeched Quaesa.

I saw the four halflings safely strapped into their clerketers, the straps buckled up tightly, and then with a final word of caution, sent the four great birds into the air. They flew over the jungle, going strongly, until they were out of sight. I thought they had a very good chance, for no other fluttrell patrols came by until, sometime later, the voller arrived. No doubt the mighty hunters had stopped for a final drink before setting off.

Between us we now disposed of four crossbows and five thraxters. I was disappointed there were no aerial spears, like the toonons used by the Ullars, but Rapechak snorted and said the flutsmen were kitted out for light patrol, not for battle. Then, he said, they were flying armories. Some people have talked and even written of aerial combat with short-swords from the backs of flying birds; it is doubtful if they have ever tried it. But, as is the way of Kregen no less than that of Earth, there are to be found people who believe non-sense of this sort. I looked at the crossbows. They were beautifully made instruments of death. Not as shiny or as flamboyant as the hunters' bows, they were weapons of professionals. I felt very satisfied with them. I changed the guard's thraxter for one of the flutsmen's swords; the one I chose was nicely balanced, firm in the grip, with a blade very reminiscent of the cutlass blade of my youth, although not quite as broad and strengthened with a single groove. The grip, of red-dyed fish-skin, and the guard, reasonably elaborate of a kind of open half-basket pattern, pleased me well enough. Oh, the sword was no great Krozair longsword or that superb Savanti weapon, but I would use it to good purpose in the service of the Star Lords, for my sins.

The flutsmen employed a novel form of goat's-foot lever to span their cross-bows, and although I knew it was perfectly possible to span an arbalest with cranequin or windlass when flying by use of adapted equipment and if one was skilled, I appreciated this goat's-foot lever of the flutsmen.

Gynor said he could handle a crossbow. Rapechak, of course, was an old mercenary. Two other halflings came forward saying they wished for nothing better than to sink a bolt into the guts of the manhunters. So we waited, rather like leems, I confess, as the voller came in.

Instead of an eager hunting party of untrained and amateurish nobles jumping down from the voller to slaughter, there leaped with vicious howls four couples of manhounds.

The change in our fortunes rattled in so subtly, so quickly, so disastrously.

"Do not miss, my friends!" I called in a voice I made firm, driving, intolerant. I do not think that was necessary, now, looking back, but *then* I felt the precipice edge of disaster at my feet.

The jiklos picked up our scent at once and with fearsome howls bounded toward us. They looked their hideous selves. If any nobility exists in beasts, as I believe it does, then these men-beasts had lost all. Jagged teeth glinting in the suns-light streaming into the clearing, leaping fallen trees and tangled undergrowth, blood-crazy, they bounded for us.

Four crossbow bolts sped true, driven by brains and eyes trained in hatred and loathing. My bow loosed, and loosed again. That was six down and the seventh took a shaft along his flank and was on me.

My thraxter rasped as it drew from the scabbard and I went over backward with the manhound all bloody and messy upon me, screeching, his teeth clicking together in rage and pain, seeking my throat. The sword was deeply buried in him somewhere low, and my left hand gripped his neck and forced those clashing jaws away. Blood and spittle fouled me. His mad blood-crazed eyes glared on me, and his thin lips worked, his tongue lolled out, and then to my infinite relief the light of intelligence faded in those crazed eyes and he slumped. I stood up carefully, throwing the carcass away so that my right hand could drag the thraxter free.

Men were yelling over by the voller.

Gynor and Rapechak and the other two halflings with swords left off plunging their blades into the mangled body of the eighth manhound. This one had been a female, and, sickened, I turned away to stare with hatred at the hunters.

They had heard the shrieks and the muffled howlings, and, too, they had seen some of their manhounds fall, stricken in mid-leap.

"Span your bows!" I spoke as I used to speak in the smoke and thunder of the broadsides, when the old wooden walls drifted down to bloody battle, and I must see my battery of thirty-two-pounders kept on firing until only myself, perhaps, was left to sponge, load, ram, and pull the lock string.

The people from the voller were uncertain. One called in a loud, hectoring voice: "Gumchee! Tulishi!" That would be the female manhound, I guessed. "Colicoli! Hapang!" They could call until the Ice Floes of Sicce went up in steam but they'd get no answer from those four couples of manhounds.

Rapechak said, "We are ready, Dray Prescot. May your Opaz go with you."

Turko shouted. He spoke loudly, angry, raging, shoving up from his bed of leaves. His face lost its look of pain and took on the semblance of superior anger more habitual to it.

"And is no one of you stinking half-men going with Dray?"

Of the nine halflings who had started with the party, only five were left now, and four were ready to do damage with the crossbows. The last, a little Xaffer, would be of no help in a fight.

Mog started to cackle something and the two girls were sobbing, clutching each other. I shouted back: "I will have to go alone. Now, *cover me!*"

Even then Turko tried to get up, to stand and to rush out with me, but his legs buckled and gave way and he fell. Then I waited for no more but started a mad dash for the voller.

I say mad dash, for I was mad, clean through, and I dashed, for the mighty hunters of the great Jikai had their crossbows ready.

I lived only because they were such lousy shots.

The only one from whom I expected real danger would be their guide, a man similar to the one I had snatched from his zorca on the plain with the Pallan Golan. Rapechak knew this, also. By the time I reached the voller three of the hunters lay with bolts skewering them. I had dodged and weaved in the last few yards. Up there and peering over the voller's side the guide looked down. His face showed contempt and rage and only a tinge of fear—and I fancied that was for his dead clients. He lifted himself to get a good shot at me—and the last crossbow quarrel, loosed by Rapechak the Rapa, penetrated his face and knocked him back.

The hunters drew their thraxters to face me. There were five of them and I must draw a veil, as they say, over what followed. I did not kill them all. Three of them were unarmed and then my halflings had reached me, and before there was anything further I could do, there were no hunters left alive. Truth to tell, apart from not really being able to blame the fugitives for their ready justice, I could only have left the hunters there in the jungle. That would have been a more prolonged end, if they were not picked up in time.

This time I said to Rapechak: "Keep an eye on the voller, good Rapechak. We are all comrades, now, in adversity, and this flier is our means of escape."

He took my meaning clearly enough.

Before I went back for Turko and Mog I respanned the bow, the most handsome of them all, I took from the dead hunter who lay so messily among the rotting detritus of the clearing.

With Mog, Turko, the two girls, and the Xaffer I returned to the airboat. We went some time stripping the dead and cleaning their clothes and putting them on. I could not find a tunic to fit and so had to content myself with fashioning a breechclout out of the only scarlet length of material there, and of slinging a short scarlet cape over my left shoulder. Then we all climbed in and, with a feeling of some relief, I sent the voller up into the clean blue sky of Kregen, where the twin Suns of Scorpio blazed down with a light so much more genial than before.

Chapter Seventeen

Of Havilfar,
volleem—and stuxes

"You are a get-onker, Dray Prescot! You're a fool, you nulsh! I wouldn't go back to Yaman for all the ivory in Chem!"

So spoke Mog, the Migla witch, as we flew out over the sea from the manhunters' island of Faol.

This voller was a larger and more handsome craft than that in which I had escaped before, and in the comfortable cabin aft Turko could lie on a settee and drink the wine we found aboard and make sarcastic remarks about Mog. The girls had recovered, and chattered about what stories they would tell at all the marvelous parties to which they would be invited on the strength of their marvelous adventures.

When they heard Mog shriek at me that she would never set foot in her city of Yaman again, the girls looked up.

"We are agreed, Dray Prescot," said Saenda, somewhat sharply. "Quaesa and I are going to Dap-Tentyrasmot, my own city, where she will be received with all ceremony. Then the halflings may return to their homes, if they wish."

The effrontery of the girl was amazing only because she had recovered so rapidly from being slave; and was sad because these halflings were her comrades of captivity.

I said, "We go to Mog's city, Saenda."

Quaesa said, with a flirting sideways glance from her dark eyes, "If you wish, Dray Prescot, we shall fly to my homeland of Methydria, the land of Havil-Faril, where my father owns many kools of rich grazing and where you will be most welcome."

By Havil-Faril she meant beloved of Havil, that is, beloved of the green sun. That was not, in those days, calculated to make me, a Krozair of Zy, amenable to her suggestion.

"Yaman," I said. "Let there be no more argument."

141

Of course, I was being selfish. I recognized that. I could have taken all these people home and then gone to Yaman. But I was tired of Mog the witch, and I wanted to get to my home, which was in Valka, or Vallia, depending on where Delia might be, and the quickest way to do that was to dump Mog where the Everoinye wished her. We could drop off a number of the halflings on our way, as we had planned to do before. Turko said, flatly, that he could not return to Herrelldrin. I did not press him. This might be because he had broken some of his syple vows with the slaves, or he might be a wanted man there. A more likely explanation, however, lay in the argument I had had when I had pointed out that a people learned unarmed combat when they were subject to another, and could not afford or were not allowed real weapons. Tulema had not wished to return home, either. I would find out soon enough; now I had to find out what the hell was up with Mog.

"My people have been enslaved, you nulsh," she said.

I spoke quietly. "I do not believe I am a nulsh, Mog. I do not call you rast or cramph—or not very often. I own I am an onker—a get-onker, as you will. But watch your tongue or I'll see what your Migshaanu the Odoriferous can do about it."

Turko laughed. He was much better, and that was a relief.

Mog took a deep breath. She still wore her stinking slave breechclout hanging down, and she smelled. I promised myself to give her a damned good wash at the first opportunity. Now she explained, remarkably lucidly, all things considered, and with a refreshing absence of insults, just what was wrong with her city of Yaman in the land of Migla.

Her story interested me only to the extent that I was always eager to learn about Kregen, my adopted planet. There was much I knew already, but I have not as yet related it for it does not fit in with my narrative. I hope I am managing to keep unentangled all the various skeins of fate and destiny that both manipulated me and which I, in my own way, attempted to manipulate, to the confounding of the Star Lords.

The Miglas had been a quiet, contemplative, peaceful race, much given to religion. Mog said she was the high priestess of the Miglish religion, using many strange expressions I will tell you of when necessary. But they had been overthrown and subjugated by a fierce and warlike race who invaded from the island of Canopdrin in the Shrouded Sea in Havilfar where terrifying earthquakes had destroyed cities and flooded fertile valleys and laid the land waste.

"They were few, the bloody Canops, but they were clever. They destroyed my religion. They took me and chained me and defamed me before the eyes of my people. They slaughtered all the royal family. But it was our religion, our love of Migshaanu the All-Glorious through which they enslaved us." She looked shrunken and miserable, and my feelings toward Mog the witch were forced to undergo a change. "My people believed their lies. They worshiped their false images. They made sacrifices, where we of Migla have not sacrificed for a thousand seasons—more! They made of Migshaanu a mockery. And if I return, Dray Prescot, they will surely slay me before all the people of Yaman."

So, I said to myself, what of the Star Lords' orders now?

"Not sacrifice, Mog?" I said. "But you are continually threatening me with what this Migshaanu will do to me."

She stared up, her bright agate eyes hard on me, her witch's face slobbered with tears, her hooked nose running. She looked a horrible object, but she also looked pathetic, and I suppose, for the first time, I really thought of Mog the witch as a person.

"Migshaanu the All-Glorious is peaceful and calm and gentle, and her love shines upon all, twin rays from the suns, in glory and beauty! It is the foul nulshes of Canops who do the things I threaten! I merely put them in my mouth as from my Migshaanu the Ever-Virtuous to—to—"

She had no need to go on.

"I have heard that no religion can be crushed utterly. There will be people who would welcome you back, the high priestess?"

"Yes. There are a few. Scattered, weak, feeble, hiding their adherence to the true beliefs under a mask, bowing to the bloody Canops in the full incline with despair in their hearts."

"Well, it is settled. I will take you to your friends."

All the fight seemed to have been knocked out of her. She just squatted down in the aft cabin, and presently she started rocking back and forth and crooning. Saenda shouted at her crossly to keep quiet, but the old crone hardly heard and went on rocking and crooning. I heard her say, between a clear change of musical pattern in the crooning dirge: "Oh, Mag, Mag! Where are you now?" And then she went on with her crooning and her rocking, and Saenda cursed her and came up to sit by me at the controls.

The girl started in at once, chatting gaily about how wonderful it was that we were free, and flying to Havilfar, and she tried her arts and wiles, but I took little notice. Old Mog worried me. I'd said that, by Zim-Zair, I'd rescue her and take her back, and that was what I was doing. She hadn't wanted to come. I'd put that down to fear, and, as was afterward proved, her suspicions of the treacherous guides. But the truth lay deeper. As a high priestess she had been defamed and sold into slavery, for she had said that the Canops, with all their vicious pride, had quailed from having her killed. Now, if she returned, they would not hesitate to do what they should have done in the first place.

The impression grew on me as we flew over the first scatterings of tiny islets fringing this part of the coast of Havilfar that this Mog the high priestess of the Miglas had many more surprises in store for me. Certainly the little Xaffer, when he discovered just who Mog was, reacted in a way that left me in no doubt that the powers of the priesthood of Migla had reached his ears.

Calling Rapechak, I asked him if he would care to fly the voller for a space. I phrased it like that, carefully, and in the doing of that apparently simple thing surprised myself. I realized I had been relying on Rapechak rather too much as a loyal lieutenant; he was a Rapa, fierce, predatory, one of a race of beast-men who had given me much grief in my time. He twisted his beaked face in that grimacing way Rapas have and said, "I recall when we flew down on Harop Mending's castle, Dray Prescot. I flew a voller then that had been half shot away by a varter and with a shaft through my shoulder."

"You are still a mighty warrior, Rapechak, for all that you were a slave with the manhunters. You were on the losing side in a battle, I take it?"

"Surely. It is over and done with, now. I think I might venture to look at my home, a Rapa island to the south and west of Havilfar. I have not seen it for nigh on sixty years."

If I noticed then that he did not give me the name of his home I made no comment. His business would be Rapa business and I wasn't interested in halflings—with the exception of Gloag, always, of course. We flew on with Rapechak at the controls and I went aft to talk seriously to the Khamorro, Turko.

I found him being fed a potion by Mog, mixed with wine. She had given over her crooning, and she glanced up at me the moment I ducked my head to enter the cabin, her old hooked nose and chin fairly snapping at me, like a crab's claws.

"I've decided to go to Yaman, to find my friends, and to keep out of trouble, Dray Prescot. By Migshaanu, if you insist on taking me home, I'll go, although I won't thank you."

I brightened. This was more like the Mog I knew.

"Very good, Mog. That is settled." She rose and left Turko, with a final quick wipe of a clean cloth to his lips, in a gesture that, I realized, moved me. Turko leaned back on the settee, his overly handsome face eased of pain, staring at me with rather too much mocking knowing in his eyes. "Now, Turko, we must decide what to do with you."

"What would amuse me, Dray Prescot, is to take you to Herrelldrin and there see how you fared against a Khamorro or two—without edged weapons in your hand."

Oho! I thought to myself. So that is what itches the good Turko. He might get his wish yet, if the Star Lords willed it, but I doubted it, although, of course, not being in any way privy to their devious schemes.

"Perhaps we may meet a khamster or two—" I began. He pushed up, frowning, and yet relaxing, as it were, all in a movement. I knew what had goaded him. Khamster was the name used by Khamorros of themselves between themselves. I started over, amazed at my softness. "Perhaps you Khamorros travel Havilfar. We might yet amuse you."

"As to that, we are not allowed—that is, yes, we do travel, as guards and servants. I was indentured to the King of Sava. The caravan was attacked and with a crossbow bolt aimed at my guts I was taken to Faol. Iron chains may not easily be broken, even with syple disciplines."

"I know," I said, remembering.

The shape of Havilfar is interesting, looking something like a rounded rectangle that has been badly bitten and hacked about. Gouging into the southeastern corner is the Gulf of Wracks, which leads to the great inland sea called the Shrouded Sea. To the northeast of this sea lie many kingdoms and princedoms and Kovnates. To the west lie wilder lands, although the coastline contains many ancient kingdoms, for philosophers say that it was here, along the coasts surrounding the Shrouded Sea, that men first settled Havilfar. The whole northeastern corner of the continent consists of the puissant land of Hamal. Hyrklana, a large island, although not counted as one of the nine islands of Kregen, juts wedgelike from the eastern central coast in temperate and pleasant climate. Far to the west and just below a great beaknosed promontory that extends southward of Loh lies Herrelldrin, with Pellow tucked into a great bay.

"If not Herrelldrin, Turko, then where?"

"You fly to Mog's Migla, do you not? That will do."

He amazed me.

Migla, situated at the western point of the Shrouded Sea, consisted of three large promontories running out northeastward and a tract of country inland. The Shrouded Sea is thus named for volcanic activity, which must be fairly frequent, as much as for the mystery it posed to the first inhabitants of Havilfar.

I ought to mention that the northern coastline of Havilfar extends upward past the latitude of southern Loh, almost reaching the equator. Ordsmot and the Orange River lie north of Ng'groga in Loh. And Loh, as you know, has the shape of a Paleolithic hand-ax, with the point northward— and that point is Erthyrdrin.

"Then we shall go to Migla by the Shrouded Sea and I will leave you with Mog and her friends."

"If Morro the Muscle so wills, Dray Prescot."

He had shouted so passionately at the halflings when I had been about to attack the voller, and then he had called me Dray.

The two girls called me Dray all the time, of course, and I wondered when I'd shout at them to address me as Horter Prescot. My name is Prescot. I try to allow friends only to call me Dray, although friendship is a rare and precious thing to me. Maybe that is part of the reason. To digress; there was once a man—an apim—called Rester who familiarly called me Dray while insulting me and what I was doing in his sneering insufferable way, and when he staggered up with a smashed nose crying and vomiting, I could find little pity in me, for he had considered himself so superior and knowing and all the time he had been acting, as I well knew from other sources, out of spite, cliquishness, and a petty denial of human dignity to a fellow human.

When he had been carried off I broke into laughter. I, Dray Prescot, laughed. But I was not laughing at the pitiful rast Rester. I was laughing at myself, at my folly, at my arrogant puffed-up and foolish pride.

We flew due south after a space to avoid Faol, and the voller sped through the air levels with her firm steady movement so unlike the pitching and rolling of a ship at sea. Turko explained what had itched the redheaded youth who called himself Nath of Thothangir when we flew inland on that previous flight. Somewhere among the forests of central northwest Havilfar lay a region over which vollers would not fly for fear of what—they knew not. But it was an area to be avoided. We drove on southerly down the coast, and we would swing southeast when we were opposite Ng'groga, although Turko identified the place by reference to Havilfar, and so strike across the narrow neck of the continent here to reach Migla.

To the west of Hamal and extending north and south ran a range of mountains that, so I gathered, might rival The Stratemsk. There was much to learn of Havilfar, the fourth and last continent of this grouping on Kregen.

We had a long distance to travel and, accustomed as I was to employing the free winds to blow my vessels along, or the oar when occasion was right, I could afford to think with some scorn of the clumsy steamships appearing on Earth's oceans and their dependence on limited supplies of coal. The vollers, by reason of that mechanism of the two silver boxes, needed no refueling and would fly as long as was necessary. For food and wine we would have to descend sometime, and I counted us fortunate that the mighty hunters after their fashion had a goodly quantity of golden deldys among their clothing. These coins were of various mintings, from a variety of Havilfarese countries, but as a rule the golden unit of coinage in Havilfar is the deldy.

Gold and silver, with bronze also, seem always to be the noble metals for coinage; men and halflings alike hewed to the style. I have come across other systems of monetary exchange on Kregen and these all will be told in their time.

There occurred one fright that made us realize we were not on some holiday jaunt with picnic baskets and thoughts of pleasure.

Emerging from a low-lying cloud bank the voller soared on into the suns-shine and I saw a cloud of what at first I took to be birds winging up from a broad-leaved and brilliant forest below. By this time Turko was able to walk about without discomfort, although still fragile, and it was he who shouted the alarm.

"Volleem! Volleem!"

"Volleem! Volleem!"

He needed to say no more. Shrieks arose from the girls and curses from the men. The leems, those feral beasts of Kregen, eight-legged, furred, feline, and vicious, with wedge-shaped heads armed with fangs that can strike through lenk, are to be found all over the planet in a variety of forms and all suitably camouflaged. There are sea-leem, snow-leem, marsh-leem, desert, and mountain-leem. These specimens were volleem.

They flew on wide membraneous wings extending from their second and third pairs of legs, very conveniently, and like the flying foxes they could really fly. Their colors were not the velvety green I might have expected, seeing that their camouflage might seek to ape the fluttrell; they were all a startling crimson as to back, toning to a brick-red underbelly. The wings shone in the light, the elongated fingerlike claws black webs against the gleam.

"Inside the cabin!" yelled Turko, and bundling the old Xaffer before him, he pushed us into safety.

Turko might know these parts and be aware of the vicious nature of the volleem, but skulking in a cabin was not my style. I know I am headstrong and foolish, but also I feared lest the volleem damage the airboat.

"Their fangs will rip us to pieces," I said.

"We are on a rising course," said Turko. "They will not follow us far from their forest treetops."

He was proved right.

Even then, as I looked at this superbly muscled Khamorro, I wondered why I had listened to him instead of doing what I had felt right, of rushing out, sword in hand, to battle the volleem. One reason for his action was clear: unarmed combat against a leem usually results in a verdict of suicide.

Because of this the Xaffer and the other two halflings decided they would get off at the next stop. I had to quell my reaction, thinking that, once again, I was doing nothing more than running a coach or an omnibus line. Gynor the Brokelsh said he would alight, also, so we divided up the remaining deldys fairly, not without some rancorous comment from Saenda and Quaesa, and we bid Remberee to our departing comrades.

Rapechak looked thoughtful when the voller swung to the southeast, over the land toward the Shrouded Sea.

"My home is down there, Dray Prescot, not over far from Turko's Herrell. It is cold, but I think of it often."

"I will be pleased to visit, Rapechak," I said. "After Mog is unhung from around our necks."

"Perhaps." He said that the southernmost part of the continent was called Thothangir. I thought of the redheaded Nath, and was more than ever sure that he had never come from Thothangir.

So we sped on southeastward across the neck of Havilfar and after a lapse of time, for the voller was swift, we saw the clouds rising ahead and then the intermittent gleam of water. The temperate regions were very welcome after the heat and sweat of Faol. Mog roused herself and gave her instructions. I was reminded of that arrival with Tulema at Dorval Aymlo's home. Well, this time we would land among friends.

"You must go in at the darkest portion of the night, you great onker. The bloody Canops have patrols and soldiers and guards and mercenaries and spies everywhere."

"We will do that, Mog, and we will keep a watch."

Yaman was situated a little inland up from the broad sluggish river that ran down to the second of the large bays separating the three promontories. We waited until Far and Havil had sunk and only She of the Veils rode the sky, for this night she would be joined later by the Maiden with the Many Smiles and by the Twins and then it would be almost as light as a misty day in the Northern parts of Earth, although the shifting pinkish radiance from the moons always created that eerie hushed feeling of mystery inseparable from shadowed moonlight.

Mog insisted we hide the voller in a grove of trees on the outskirts. She said the trees were sacred to Sidraarga. Then, hitching our clothing and weapons about us, we set off for the home of one Planath the Wine, who owned a tavern that one might take a newly wedded bride to, as Mog put it with a cackle. Coming home had brightened and invigorated her. If we ran across a Canop patrol I felt she would not be the one to run screaming in fear.

Once again I trod the streets of a strange city in a continent of Kregen new to me. The houses reared to either hand, strange shapes against the starshot darkness, with She of the Veils riding low in the clouds, and very few lighted windows there were to see, and only a few hurrying pedestrians who avoided us with as much fervor as we avoided them. An air of mystery, of an eerie horror no one would mention aloud, hung over the city of Yaman.

As we hurried along in so strange a fashion I could feel

the excitement rising and rising in me. Only a few short steps to go and then Mog the Migla witch would be in the hands of her friends, and I would be free! By this time I felt convinced Mog must be the one whom the Star Lords had sent me to Faol to rescue. I had felt this about Tulema, and been proved a fool. That could not happen again, by Vox, no!

But, all the time, I kept expecting at any moment to see that hated blue radiance and the enormous insubstantial shape of a scorpion dropping upon me from the pink-lit shadows.

The cobbled streets of Yaman passed by, and the darkened fronts of houses and shops, the ghostly emptiness of squares and plazas. I saw the moon-sheen upon the sluggish waters of the River Magan and the black blots of islands riding like stranded whales, the fretting of river boats against stone quays and wharves. In my ears the night sounds of a city ghosted in thinly. We pressed on and Mog led us down past the narrow entrances to alleyways, past wide flights of steps leading to the quays, down and through even narrower alleyways, and across slimed steps where, below, barges sucked in the mud.

At last we reached the tavern of Planath the Wine.

This was, I thought, a strange place to find a remnant of an outlawed and proscribed religion.

A gnarled tree hung over the crazy roof of the tavern. All the windows leered at us, dark ovals pallidly reflecting a pink sheen of moonlight. Around to the rear padded Mog, with many a cunning glance about, and so she rapped upon the door, a complicated series of rhythms, like a drum-dance.

The door was snatched open and a hoarse breathy voice whispered: "Get in! Get in, in the name of Migshaanu the Virtuous, before we are all taken!"

In we all bundled, with Mog cursing away at barking her skinny shins against the jamb, and so came into a dark, breathing space where I knew people stood about waiting for the door to close so they might turn up the lamp.

And now, to give you who listen to this tape an understanding of what then happened, there in the back room of *The Loyal Canoptic* as a concealed taper relit the samphron-oil lamp, it is necessary to tell you a number of things all at the same time.

The first thing I noticed, something I had been wondering about ever since my interest in Mog had been so brutally forced on me, was the physical appearance of these halfling Miglas.

They were not apim.

The people gathered here, about a score, sitting on benches along the walls so that the central floor area of polished lenk remained clear, all possessed two arms and two legs, and one head with features. But those features could never be mistaken for human features—always bearing in mind what I have said about that prickly word, "human." The old women looked a little like Mog, although nowhere so bent or vicious or cunning. The old men looked like nothing so much as those thick-legged, thick-armed, stumpy-bodied, and idiot-headed plastic toys the children on Earth nowadays play with. Gnomes, if you like, thick-heads, bodies as squat as boilers, dummies, grinners, with ears that swung like batwing doors, they all stared at Mog with looks of reverence and shock and holy awe—and vast surprise.

The younger men and girls, although far more prepossessing in the manner of bodily proportions, all wore that idiot grin, that flap-eared dog-hanging look of bumbling good humor that masks a cranial cavity filled with vacuum.

They all wore ankle-length smocks with scooped-out necks and no sleeves. The color was a uniform rusty crimson, as though the dye used, probably from a local berry or earth, had not taken properly in the coarsely weaved stuff. Their hair was dark and vivid and cropped, even the girls'. I stood behind Saenda and Quaesa as the lamp flared up and Mog stepped forward. Turko moved at my side, and Rapechak moved out from the other side.

Insane shrieks burst from the Miglas. The women clawed the children to them, the girls flying to crowd around the old folk at the far end of the room. The noise burst inside my head with the unexpected force of a magazine explosion. The Migla men rummaged frantically behind the benches.

They swung around to face us, pushing past Mog, who yelled at them.

"Do you not know who I am? I am Mog, your high priestess!" She used a number of those special words and phrases that meant a great deal in the religion.

The men—eight of them—stood resolutely before us, their womenfolk and children screaming behind them.

The eight looked highly comical, their flap-eared faces slobbering with fury and fear. They held the spears they had snatched up from behind the benches in grips that—I guessed

Rapechak would have seen and Turko never failed to miss—were amateur in the extreme.

"Do you not hear, migladorn? These are my friends. They are the friends of the high priestess of Migshaanu!"

The heftiest man, with a fuzz of side-whiskers, spat out: "You are the Mighty Mog! But these cannot be your friends! They have tricked you! Two are apim warriors, one is a Rapa warrior, and two are shishis! They must all die!"

From the lighting of the lamp to the utterance of that word—"die!"—scarce a handful of heartbeats had passed.

The eight spear points leveled. Then, with sudden and astonishing speed, a ferociously lethal and completely un-expected reaction, the front three Migla men hurled their spears.

And—there was nothing amateurish about that spear-throwing. With terrifying accuracy the deadly shafts flew toward us.

Chapter Eighteen

Saenda and Quaesa
exert themselves

Three spears flashed toward us.

We were: one, a Rapa mercenary; two, a Khamorro; and three, an Earthman who had made Kregen his home.

We reacted in three different ways.

With a fluid litheness of movement so fast no untrained eye could follow him, Turko slid the spear and it thunked solidly into the lenken door.

With the least amount of physical effort, Rapechak let his body lean to the side, and as a precaution, thrust up his forearm, so that the spear hissed past, to thunk into the door alongside the other.

I, Dray Prescot, had to show off—and yet, in truth, my way had been proved in the past and was to prove in the future by far the superior—and I had not needed the Krozairs of Zy to teach me this. I took the spear out of the air, my hand closing around the shaft with that familiar solid soft chunking of wood against flesh, and so I reversed it and hefted it and said, "I will let you have your spear back, if you wish."

Over the women's screaming Mog lifted her voice and there in that bedlam in the back room of *The Loyal Canoptic,* I heard for the first time the high priestess.

"Put down your spears! I am Mog the Mighty, high priestess of Migshaanu! Put down your stuxes or risk my certain wrath! These apim and this Rapa have aided me and brought me here."

Then old Mog the witch glared at me as she ducked her head as the spears went down. And I knew! Oh, I knew! She was saying to me: "Well, Dray Prescot. You brought me here, why I know not, so now what to do, hey, onker?" And also: "And you put your spear down, too, idiot, or they'll cast for sure and spit you like a paly!"

154

I lowered the spear.

A moment of natural tension was heightened as both Rapechak and Turko turned and jerked the spears from the lenk. Even then, I had time to say, just so that they could hear: "What, friend Turko? A spear?"

To which Turko the Khamorro replied: "I thought you might need another if your first missed."

I chuckled. Oh, yes, that seemed a worthwhile moment to chuckle.

After that, with Mog the witch acting very much as Mog the Mighty—by Makki-Grodno's worm-eaten liver! Old Mog, called Mog the Mighty! Incredible and laughable and hugely enjoyable!—after that, as I say, we all sat down to eat and drink and for Mog to tell her news and to catch up on what had been happening in Yaman in the land of Migla in her absence.

Somehow or other Saenda had seated herself on one side and Quaesa on the other, and they were both holding my arms and snuggling up against me, pouting their lips and trying to claim all my attention, and I couldn't be too hard on them. By Vox! But they'd had a scare!

Even then, Saenda said to Quaesa, "Did you hear what that awful one with the ridiculous side-whiskers said?"

"That's Planath the Wine—"

"He called me a shishi! I'll give it to him when I get a chance. Nobody calls me a shishi and gets away with it."

"Nor me!"

"What will you give him, Saenda?" I hoped I was stirring things up.

"Humph!" she said, with her nose in the air, and so disposed of my question.

I didn't care. Mog was home with her people. These Migla were gathered in secret to celebrate a rite of Migshaanu and so the news of the high priestess' return would that more quickly spread over the city. I had done my work. Now I would go home.

Yes, I had decided. There would be time in the future to find out about the airboats and to question the scarlet-roped Todalpheme on the whereabouts of Aphrasöe. Do not think I had dismissed the importance of either of these projects, but I hungered to see Delia again, and to hold little Drak and little Lela in my arms, and tell Delia of my undying love.

Momentarily, I shuddered at the prospect of that blue radiance dropping about me with the great presentation of a scorpion, but I thought I knew, now, that I had done the Star Lords' bidding. The two girls prattled on, one in each ear. Although only half listening to them, being far more interested in what Mog and Planath were saying of conditions in Migla, I could not fail to become aware that the girls' intentions were becoming far more serious by the mur. Each wished me to take her to her own home, the idea that one should go to the other's as an honored guest having, apparently, been abandoned. They waxed warm.

"My father's totrixes are renowned over all southeast Havilfar."

"My father's merchant house has agencies far beyond southeast Havilfar."

"The Migshaanu-cursed Canops took Mackili, only last week, and impaled him over by the ruins of the temple."

"The ruins are infested by rasts."

"Methydrin is a wonderful country, with riches to spare!"

"In Dap-Tentyra we could be so happy. It is more of a city these days than a smot."

"We starve if we do not work and work is only given to those who worship Lem, the silver leem."

"And, dear Dray, you would not find me unappreciative."

"And, my Dray, I would be kind to you."

"It is death, slow and horrible and certain, to be found on the streets with a weapon."

I leaned forward, to ask a question about the spears, which had been restowed beneath the benches. These spears were ash-shafted, with heads wide yet short, exceedingly sharp, and fairly heavy in the hand so that a cast from them would spit a target with most ferocious thoroughness. So I leaned forward and the soft breathy whispers in my ears sharpened.

"Dray! You're not listening!"

"Dray! You haven't heard a word I've said!"

"On the contrary, appreciation and kindness are fine. But they are not for me. I am not going your way."

Their soft bodies, pressed so suggestively close to me, stiffened, and moved away, and bright color mantled their cheeks. Their competition remained as fervent as ever; for neither would give an inch and almost immediately I felt them approach to engage yet again in this allurement for their own ends.

Standing up, I left them whispering sweet nothings to each other across six inches of empty air, and went across to Planath the Wine. He cocked his eyes up at me, somewhat apprehensively, I thought, so I sat down and did what I could about making my face less the unholy figure-head lump exposed to wind and weather it is.

"Tell me, Horter Planath. These spears of yours. You may not carry them openly on the streets?"

Turko butted in, mockingly. "They would be difficult, by the Muscle, to carry concealed."

I ignored him.

"That is so, Horter Prescot. The casting spear, the stux, is our weapon—for we are a peaceful people and know little of swords and bows—and hitherto we have kept ourselves to ourselves. We hunt the vosk with the stux, for they roam in their millions among the back hills and forests."

"A goodly weapon. And the Canops?"

Mog worked herself up into a denunciation, to which all the Miglas listened with profound attention. When she had finished, Planath the Wine said with grave politeness, "They are fierce and vicious and horrendous. They crushed us with ease. But we would have fought, despite that we would certainly have lost, but for—" Here he paused, in some distress, until Mog jumped up, swinging her arms, and finished for him.

"Aye! But for the degradation of your religion and the profanation of Migshaanu's shrine and the defamation of your high priestess! Aye, they were reasons enough."

They all began talking then, as Mog sat on the floor and drew up a crimson covering they had given her. I thought of the stux, the usual name for the heavy throwing spear of Havilfar and of how they would have fronted these deadly Canops and all hurled, with their deadly aim, and then the arrows would have whistled in and the sword-wielding mercenaries would have cut and thrust them to pieces. Maybe they were better off, now; at least, they lived.

With only a little more conversation, in which the name of Mag was mentioned—I did not pick up the reference and so pushed it away to be dealt with later—the Miglas rose and took their leave. They did not take their spears, however, and these remained secreted in the cavities beneath the benches. Even so, the adherents of Migshaanu took their lives in their hands as they made their way home under the lights of the moons.

We were quartered in a garrett room under the crazy roof, and, as we had during the nights of our escape, we all slept

more or less together. Mog, alone of us, was conducted else-
where. Tomorrow, I told myself, before going to sleep, tomorrow I would start for home.

In the night both Quaesa—first, and very prettily—and
Saenda—second and most urgently—came to my pallet. I
turned them both out, and I did not scruple to kick Saenda's
remarkable rear to help her on her way to her own pallet. In
the morning neither girl referred to the night's pantomime,
but I knew they were storing everything up against me.

Discovering that the busy and highly populated country
over on the eastern shores of the Shrouded Sea contained the
homes of both girls, I could afford to forget them. That part
of Havilfar, extending from the river border of Hamal in the
north, the coast opposite Hyrklana in the east, and open
ocean in the southeast, to the river running from the southern
end of the mountain chain into the top of the Shrouded Sea
on the west, had been settled for thousands of years. Kingdoms and princedoms and Kovnates riddled it with boundaries and capitals and petty rivalries. All the girls had to do
was hire a passage aboard a voller or a ship and cross the
Shrouded Sea and they would be home.

Planath the Wine looked at my scarlet breechclout and my
scarlet cape and clicked his teeth. He was not a human being
of Homo sapiens stock, but he was a man.

"Crimson is the color of Migshaanu the Blessed. We wear
it only on high occasions, for it is proscribed." Truly, this
morning he wore a brown smock with winestains upon it.
"I think, Horter Prescot, if you will pardon, that the Canops
will resent that brave scarlet."

I pondered. As you know, previously I would have made
some uncouth remark, involving a diseased portion of Makki-
Grodno's anatomy, and said that, by Zim-Zair, scarlet was
the color of Strombor, my color, and the color of Zair. No
monkey-faced Canops would tell me to strip it off. But I pondered, as I said, and thought of Delia and the twins, and so
changed into a dull and offensive brown sack Planath called
a robe.

But I kept the breechclout even as I unstrapped the sword.

Rapechak surprised me—but only for a moment.

"I am a mercenary. I could take service with these Canops.
If they paid enough."

"You could, Rapechak." I eyed him.

"I do not think I am old enough to return home. Anyway,
it is too cold down there. I have grown used to warmth."

"Very sensible."

"And I have not made my fortune—so far."

"It distresses me to hear it."

Turko stood by, listening, that mocking half-smile on his damned handsome face. Rapechak cocked his beaked head at the Khamorro.

"Turko has nowhere to go." He rubbed that beak of a face of his, that Rapa face of which so many have been beakless and no longer faces when I got through with them. "You have not as yet said where you are going, Dray Prescot."

"That is true. I have not said."

There hung a silence in the back room of *The Loyal Canoptic*.

Both girls started in presently claiming that I was taking them home, and may Opaz rot the idea of going anywhere else.

"There are deldys enough to pay your passages," I said. "And you may have all mine, except a handful for food and wine. I am not going your way."

"Well, then! Which way do you go?"

"That is my affair. Come. I will see you to the voller offices—or the shipping agents, if you prefer."

Backward though Migla might be, and relatively poor if compared with many of the nations of Havilfar, nevertheless I knew there would be passenger services operating.

Migla was a case of a mild and overly religious country being taken over and subjugated by a smaller but infinitely more ferocious group of people. The other nations around the Shrouded Sea would not help; probably they had all been relieved when after the earthquakes that destroyed their island home the Canops had gone to Migla.

From all that I heard of them, these Canops were a very nasty bunch indeed.

The halfling Miglas went in deadly fear of them, the beast-men convulsed by terror at the thought of acting in any way that would bring down the sadistic and destructive retribution of the Canops. The tiny handful who still met to worship Migshaanu did so with terror in their hearts and, as I was the first to say, with high courage and selfless devotion to their own ways and religion. I am not an overly religious man, as you know, but I know what I know, Zair knows!

Into the back room of the tavern from the stairway entrance walked a halfling woman clad all in crimson, with heavy gold lace and embroidery, with jeweled rings upon her fingers, and a massive golden, silver, and ruby crown upon her head. Her face shone. Her lips were rubbery-thin the Migla way, and her hooked beak nose and toe-cap chin jutted arrogantly. She carried a great staff of plated gold in one hand—the likeness of the head of that staff I shall not say, at this time—and jewels flashed and coruscated from every part of her crimson and golden person.

Hovering with a mixture of awe and pride Planath the Wine and his wife, Ploy, followed this gorgeous halfling creature into the room.

Saenda and Quaesa ceased their silly babbling. Turko flexed his muscles, and was still. Rapechak twisted his great beak of a face, and hissed beneath his breath, and was silent.

"All hail!" called Planath, a little huskily. He wore his crimson robe, but now across it had been slung a glittering gold cloth baldric, and in his hand he carried a small silver replica of the staff of power in the Migla woman's hand. "All hail!" Planath said again, and his voice grew and the quaver vanished. "All hail the high priestess of Migshaanu the Glorious!"

No one said a thing. I didn't care much, one way or another, for all my selfish thoughts were set on Delia and Valka, but I felt that those gathered there looked to me. For the sake of Mother Zinzu the Blessed I cannot say why, but, not then wishing to spoil the effect, I lifted up my voice and said loudly: "All hail the Mighty Mog!"

Which, I thought, was a suitably ironic comment, when all was said and done.

The old witch caught my meaning at once.

"You may mock me, Dray Prescot! But I am what I am. One day, Migshaanu willing, I shall return to a rebuilt temple and once more the people of Yaman shall worship their true god."

You couldn't say fairer than that.

"I devoutly hope it will be so, Mog," I said.

With that, as though she had achieved what she had set out to do, Mog swept her stiffly brocaded garments about and swept out—in the sense that a loose scrap of straw caught in her skirts swept away with her. I did not smile. Truth to tell, I already knew there was more to Mog the witch than appeared. The Star Lords did not fool with worthless people.

"Well!" said Saenda. "Such airs! Anyone would think she was a queen."

I admit to a relief that Planath had gone, also.

I said, "With regard to Mog, Saenda—and you, too, Quaesa—you will oblige me by keeping a civil tongue in your head. Otherwise I shall not hesitate to show my displeasure."

"If you were in my father's hacienda!" began Quaesa, very hotly, her dark eyes regarding me with fury.

"If my father ever found out about you, Dray Prescot!" began Saenda, interrupting. The girls started another of their arguments. For a moment they forgot me in their quarrel, which suited me fine. Neither of the little idiots had much idea of how they had become slaves. They might live in different countries, but the way of their taking sounded suspiciously alike to me. They had gone to a party and had thereafter remembered nothing until they were en route for Faol. I thought that the Kov of Faol paid hired kidnappers to procure pretty girls and handsome men for him to run as quarry for his customers. There was still, in my mind, the idea that I might pay a call on this Kov of Faol one day.

On our way through the suns-lit streets of Yaman with the Miglas hurrying about their work and not looking too happy about it, I pondered on what had so far befallen me in Havilfar. I knew that nothing I did for the Star Lords was without a reason. Ergo; if I had rescued four people the Star Lords did not require they would hardly have let me rescue them and return them to safety. Of them all, Lilah, the first, had been in the most peril at the end, and I was in two minds to go and visit Hyrklana, to make sure. The Star Lords guided me; what I did today might be of use twenty seasons into the future. That this was true you shall hear, and the wonderfully cunning way of it too, into the bargain.

Miglas ahead of us on the street began running.

These houses were strange spiky houses, tall and narrow, with crazily pitched roofs and toppling tall chimneys and roosts jutting up at geometrically alarming angles. Many of the roosts gave resting places to fluttrells and other saddle birds. The idea of this, with my experience of the Hostile Territories, affronted me. But then I saw that here in Havilfar everyone was accustomed to saddle birds and flying animals; therefore they were merely a part of the armaments of each country, and thus deployable in war as any other force. Given that Havilfar was in many respects further advanced than Segesthes or Turismond, they were not faced with the implacable barbarian winged horde.

"What is happening?" demanded Saenda, in her imperious, petulant voice.

"Protect me, Dray!" screamed Quaesa, clutching my arm. The little onker clutched my sword arm. Granted I had no sword—but: "If you trap my sword arm, Quaesa, I shall not be able to help myself, let alone you."

"Oh! You're impossible!"

With Miglas running every which way around us I hauled the girls into the shelter of an awning-draped store where a few amphorae stood in sardine-rows against the wall and an old Migla who looked like a washed-out edition of Mog shrieked and fled indoors and slammed her shutters. We had seen a few apims, human beings of Homo sapiens stock, walking about and we had attracted little attention, even Rapechak. We had seen a couple of Ochs, a Brokelsh, and a few Xaffers chewing their eternal cham; we had seen no Chuliks. So it wasn't us that caused this commotion.

Down the center of the street came a body of men. They marched in step. They wore armor, scaled and gleaming in the light of the suns. They carried thraxters belted to their waists, and crossbows all slanted at one angle across their bodies. Their sandals had been solidly soled, and the clicking crack of iron studs on the cobbles sounded loudly, harsh and dominating. Their helmets were tall, crested with the peacock-bright feathers of the whistling faerling—which is the Kregan peacock—and they looked hard, confident, and extraordinarily professional.

At their head marched four men with brazen trumpets, but they had no need to sound these. Following the trumpeters strode the standard bearer. He was gorgeously attired. The standard consisted of a tall glittering pole, wrapped around with silver wires, a multicolored banner flaring, and atop that and arranged most ferociously, the silver representation of a leaping leem.

Strange, I thought at once, that men should take the leem as their symbol!

Then I saw the men's faces as they marched with machine-like step in their quadruple ranks. Harsh, domineering, in-tolerant, yes, all these things. But I have seen many men's faces with those characteristics and, as you know, I admit to my shame that my face bears those betraying marks. There was about this something more, something yet more horrific.

The halfling Miglas were running now and scurrying out of sight. The old Migla put her head out of a crack in the shutter and called to us: "Bow your heads! Bow your heads or you will be sorry!" and, smack, down came the shutter fully.

Rapechak, the old mercenary, understood at once.

I suppose I did, in a weird way I would not tolerate or believe. Turko came from an enslaved people and so he, too, bowed his head as the silver leem, the symbol of Lem, went by.

The officer—he was a Hikdar—strutting at the head of the main body, with his armor splashed with silver and golden medallions, turned his head. He saw the girls, and under the visor of the helmet, thrust upward and hooked, his dark eyes betrayed all the thoughts I could understand so well.

Turko reached out with both hands and, with his supple khamster skills, bent the heads of the girls down. He couldn't reach me, and, anyway, even then I doubted if he'd try.

The Hikdar looked down his nose at me and yelled.

"Nulsh! Bow to the Glorious Lem."

I did not bow.

Me, Dray Prescot! Bow to a stinking leem! Even if it was only a silver toy called Lem.

The Hikdar rapped out a command and every right foot bashed down perfectly alongside a left and the column halted.

The Hikdar strode over. He swaggered. He drew his thraxter as he came and there was on his dark face that look of enjoyment that has always baffled me.

"You bow, nulsh, before it is too late."

I said, "You are Canops?"

He reared back as though I had struck him.

"Filthy nul! Of course we are Canops! I am Hikdar Markman ti Coyton of the Third Regiment of Canoptic Foot. And you are a dead nulsh!"

The horror of it almost made me slow. The horrendous, the vile, the vicious, the despicable Canops—were human men like me! I felt the sick revulsion strong upon me. I saw the thraxter jerk back for a lethal thrust.

I said, "So you are Canops! I do not like you, Hikdar Markman, and I detest your race of kleeshes."

And I kicked the Canoptic Hikdar in the guts.

Chapter Nineteen

I visit Turko and Rapechak in Mungul Sidrath

I say I kicked him in the guts. I had not forgotten he wore armor, and so my kick went in lower and at an angle and it did the business I intended well enough.

Before he had time to spew all over me, although he was turning green in the face already, I yanked him forward, took away his thraxter, clouted him over the nose with the hilt, and said to Turko, Rapechak, and the girls: *"Run!"*

To our rear lay a maze of alleyways and hovels and I fancied the smartly disciplined men of the Third Regiment of Foot would not welcome breaking ranks and chasing about in there. I knew, also, that in the next few seconds the crossbow bolts would come tearing into our bodies. Turko did not hesitate, and neither did Rapechak. They grabbed a girl each—Saenda fell to Rapechak and she squealed—and they vanished into the mouth of the alleyway where the crazy houses hung their upper stories over the cobblestones.

As you may well imagine, I was furiously angry.

Angry with myself.

What an utter onker! Here I'd been, all nicely set to take off for Valka, and this stupid imbroglio had burst about my ears. I had been too stupid for simple cussing.

Mind you, the shock of discovering that these detestable Canops were apims, men like myself, had been severe.

I recognized their breed, all right. They were not the mercenaries to which I had grown accustomed in the other parts of Kregen I had up to then visited. These were men of a national army. Their discipline would be superb. They had a far more sheerly professional look about them than had had the rather unhappy army of Hiclantung. These men were trained killers, and they fought and killed and, no doubt, died not for cold cash but for hot love of country.

164

They would present a problem far graver than I had anticipated.

The Deldar leaped out from the leading rank and began yelling and the lines of crossbows twitched up.

If I hung about any longer it would be pincushion time.

The mouth of the alleyway struck cold across my shoulders.

I dodged against the near wall and ran—oh, yes, I ran!— and the bolts went *chink, chink, chinkaroom,* against the far wall. Maybe these soldiers would have been trained to penetrate alleyways, to leap up and down steps covered by fire from their files. This cashbahlike maze might hold no terrors for them. I ran. I had been running a lot lately, and that, I assume, was the reason I hadn't bowed to the silver leem. I just do not like running, although it can be, as I had demonstrated on the jungle trail back in Faol with underhand and cunningly vicious traps, an absorbingly interesting pastime.

There was no sign of the others and I guessed they had pelted hell-for-leather as far and as fast as they could.

Following them, as I thought, I rounded corners, leaped offensive drainage ditches, hared through archways, and roared down the flights of narrow steps, flight after flight. I saw no one, but, of course, many eyes watched me as I ran, and, no doubt, as well as marveling consigned me to Sicce as the greatest onker ever spawned.

By the time I reached the last alleyway and debouched onto the wide steps leading down to the quays, I knew I'd missed Turko, Rapechak, and the girls.

For the first time in a very long time, I was on my own.

That could not, however much I welcomed it, be allowed to continue. Through my stupid action the others had been put in danger of their lives. I had, if for no other reason than my stupid stiff-necked pride—which I detest—to ensure that they were safe.

A disguise would seem appropriate.

I was not a Migla and I would need a rubber mask even to approach the look of one. I was a human and must therefore disguise myself as another sort of human. I found the man I wanted in a low-ceilinged taproom with the smell of mud and stale wine everywhere, and the acrid tang coming off the flat and sluggish waters of the River Magan.

He was a wherryman—I knew about those—and he willingly parted with the dark-blue jersey of his trade, together with the flat leather cap that went with it, for a silver coin that bore the likeness of a man-king of some country somewhere in Havilfar. His eyes opened wide at sight of the thraxter, which I had carried beneath the old brown robe.

"Those Opaz-forsaken Canops see you with that, man, you're dead."

"They might be dead first, though. You get along with them?"

"Huh!" He had sized me up—as he thought—and without questioning my motives, was ready to talk. "I had a nice little line going here before they came. Worse'n eight-armed devils from Rhasabad, they are! Can't abide 'em. It's all regulations, regulations, regulations now. I'm thinking of moving on. No family; sell me wherry. There's plenty of openings across the other side." He meant on the other shore of the Shrouded Sea, and I learned a little more. "I got along real fine with the Miglas. Now—why they can't abide the sight of me. Remind 'em of the Canops! Me—who took their kids on outings when it was Migshaanu's special days!"

Sympathizing with him seemed in order, and we had a jar together. The wine was a thin stuff, palely red and nothing like the rich color of a rosé, and was shipped in from a country over the Shrouded Sea that must be making a fortune from fourth and fifth pressings.

He told me there had been a brisk trade in the old days before the Canops came. The Miglas exported vosk-hide, which they knew how to cure to a suppleness of surprising strength and beauty by a secret process, and colored earths. But most of that had stopped now and the Canops were trying to develop a quite different economy. "Bloody fools!" said the wherryman, who was called Danel, and looked about him in sudden remembering fear.

Bidding Danel Remberee I took myself off with the thraxter rolled in the old brown robe to *The Loyal Canoptic.* I had not missed the irony of that name for a tavern where gathered a remnant of those loyal to Migshaanu. My traveling companions had not arrived back. Planath told me, with a quiver, that the city buzzed with the news. A Hikdar of the Canoptic Army had been struck. He had been kicked! Patrols were everywhere seeking the madman responsible. I upended a blackjack of a wine little better than that I'd drunk in the taproom with Danel, and waited, and fretted, and the suns passed across the heavens. In the end I had to admit that Turko and Rapechak and Saenda and Quaesa were not returning to *The Loyal Canoptic.*

When She of the Veils sank into the back hills of Migla and the sky was filled with the shifting light of the Twins, Planath brought me the news I quailed to hear, had known I must hear, and which distressed me greatly.

"They were taken, Horter Prescot. Taken by a patrol and now they languish in the dungeons of Mungul Sidrath."

I sat there, on the settle, the blackjack in my hand, and I could have broken into curses that would have frizzled this comical worried ugly little halfling's ears off.

Mungul Sidrath, I was told, was well-nigh impossible to break into. The citadel stood on a solid bed of rock jutting into the River Magan and it dominated the city. In the old days the royal family had lived there with their hired mercenary guards, and they had smiled on the city of Yaman and on the daily worship to Migshaanu, and the suns had shone. Now the city commandant lived there, controlling the city by terror. He had many regiments under his hand as well as mercenary troops, very wild and vicious, quite unlike the old king's mercenaries, who had served him all their lives and grown fat and happy with their job, which consisted, in the main, of providing honor guards and rows of guardsmen with resplendent uniforms and golden-headed stuxes. Well, I had to break into Mungul Sidrath.

There was no need for me to do this foolhardy thing.

The Star Lords had commanded me to bring out Mog, and I had done so, and she was safe. After that, I was free to return home. There would be no blue radiance and no scorpion this time. I felt sure of that, now, now when it was too late. Of course I could fetch the airboat from the sacred grove of Sidraarga and fly north-northwest and so come to Valka.

I could.

There was nothing to stop me.

Turko and Rapechak and the girls were hanging in chains in the dungeons of the Canops in Mungul Sidrath, but they were no concern of mine. My concerns were all with Delia and little Drak and little Lela, and Vallia and Valka, with Strombor and my clansmen. What was this local petty matter to me?

It was no good cursing. All the Voxes and Zairs and Makki-Grodno oaths would not change one iota of this mess.

I stood up.

"I have to go to Mungul Sidrath, Horter Planath. Would

you give me food and drink?" I took out the golden deldys.

Planath bristled. He thrust the money away.

"Ploy!" he shouted. "Hurry, woman, and prepare food. Horter Prescot is hungry!"

After I had eaten and drunk I wiped my lips and laid down the cloth and looked at these Miglas. Old Mog had silently walked in. Now she said, "You are a fool, Dray Prescot." Her voice had lost all its stridency. "A get-onker. But you are a man, and, I now know, beloved of Migshaanu. She will go with you on this desperate venture."

"That is good—" I was about to say, just her name, Mog. But I paused, and then said: "I shall be glad of the help of Migshaanu the Glorious, Mighty Mog."

Her hard agate eyes appraised me and her nutcracker jaws clamped, then she relaxed. I think, even then, she realized I had given over mocking her—for a space, at least.

Wearing the wherryman's old blue jersey with its rips and stains and with the flat leather cap pulled down over my forehead I went up against the citadel of Yaman. I went without weapons in my hands. I kept to the shadows and as I went I bent over and shambled. And so I came to the outer stone wall of the fortress where it reared, pink in the moonlight, rising against the stars of Kregen.

The place was old, for there is much that is ancient in Havilfar, and although well-built in olden time was much crumbled and fallen away in parts. An arm of the Magan encircled the fortress like a moat and the bridges were guarded by smart and well-drilled infantrymen of the Army of Canopdrin.

As I skulked in the shadows from the towers, where the Twins threw down their roseate-pink light, I saw something I had never seen before on all of Kregen.

I stared, for a moment letting the urgency of my mission slide, staring at the soldiers who guarded this massive pile.

These foot soldiers wore armor, like the men of the Third Regiment of Foot I had earlier seen. They wore bronze helmets with tall plumes, weird under the streaming moonslight, and their greaves gleamed in that light. They carried the stux, and at their waists were belted thraxters. They did not carry crossbows. I stared at what made them, as far as I was concerned, unique in all of Kregen—if you did not count my old slave phalanx from the warrens of Magdag, and they must now be scattered and slain or slaving once more on the monolithic buildings of the overlords. Not even the Ochs counted here.

For these soldiers carried shields.

The shields were oval, like the windows in *The Loyal Canoptic*, of a goodly size, much decorated and embossed, with a broad silvery rim. The men handled the shields as though they knew what shields were for. In Segesthes, in Turismond, I had never come across the shield as an article of warlike equipment, the men of those continents regarding the shield as the coward's weapon, behind which he might cower.

That I knew different—and, perhaps, gloated a little in my so-called superior knowledge—meant now that I had just been my usual foolish self.

I went around the angle of a bastion—for the towers were square-angled and not rounded—and prowled on, brought back to my senses by the hurtling passage of a lesser moon across the heavens. I found the man I sought leaning on his stux and opening a packet made from soft leaves to get at the wad of cham inside. I hit him cleanly on the back of the neck, below the neck-guard, and he pitched to the stones.

Dragging him back into the shadows of a wall and stripping him took little time. I had been careful, the man I wanted not being the first sentry I had seen, and his equipment fitted—but only just.

Dressed and accoutered as a soldier of the Army of Canopdrin I stepped out, leaving the man bound and gagged, and marched boldly for the bridge.

While it is true to say that the necessary demands of discipline and organization make one army very much like another, and the better an army is the nearer it approaches to an unattainable ideal, there must of necessity be many differences between army and army, details that are unique to any fighting force. I felt confident I could bluff to a great extent; after that, I would just have to take my chances, for there was precious little chance of finding another way into the fortress as quickly as this.

Common sense had dictated that I find a bridge as far from the one the sentry's comrades would be guarding as I could. On my shield, below the embossed image of the leaping leem, there had been painted in white the stylized representation of a fluttrell, with the figures for six and five. By their relative sizes I judged this would be the sixth regiment and the fifth subdivision of that regiment, called what I did not know as yet, for Planath had no knowledge of military organization. The men guarding the bridge I chose, besides having a different color arrangement of the streamers over their shoulder armor, carried on their shields the silver leem and, below it, a blue-painted zorca with the figures for eight and two.

I marched in boldly and, as I had seen the men do on the bridge, brought the stux up and across in a salute. Without breaking step I strode on. An ob-Deldar looked across and called: "It's your guts, is it, soldier?"

An ob-Deldar is the lowest one can get—as any ranker will say—and so I answered hoarsely: "Too true, Deldar. They pain something awful."

The ob-Deldar laughed with great malice and so I passed on into the dark shadows of Mungul Sidrath.

Observation that had helped me thus far could no longer give me a guide on the behavior patterns of the men of this army.

Down in the dungeons, Planath the Wine had said, shaking his head. Therefore, I must go down, and to descend I had to find a stairway of some kind. I had ideas on the proper situation of stairways in fortresses, and I found that whoever in the ancient times had designed Mungul Sidrath had come a long way along the path of fortress construction. The stairway was exceedingly narrow, and spiraled the wrong way—that is, it had been designed so that a man going down, as I was, had the advantage of the curve. This could only mean the designer had recognized the possibility of entrance below and had decided on the main-gate level as his central stand-area. He had ruled out any idea of defenders running below against a successful entrance by attackers through the gate. Going up into the towers the curve would be against a man.

The stones were surprisingly dry, considering the Magan flowed nearby, and only occasional runnels of water trickled across the stones. Where they did so they stained darkly and lichens grew. The air grew unpleasant but breathable.

At the bottom the stair curled in on itself, so that a man might stand and loose against men running up the passageway. The ceiling here was low and I took off the tall helmet. Farther along the way widened and two guards, their stuxes leaning against the wall, were crouched over tossing dice. They looked up suddenly as I approached, saw I was a mere ranker, and pulled back to get out of the way. Farther along there might be a single sentry; so leaving these two to a mercy they had no idea had touched them, I went on.

They had not spoken. The language used by the ob-Deldar had varied only minutely from the universal Kregish, and I guessed it was Canoptish, the local language of Canopdrin. The sound of rushing water ahead and a marked cooling and freshening of the air made me lengthen my stride.

In a man-made cavern carved from an original bubble in the rock water poured through from a black cleft high in one wall, dropped in a great weltering and rushing of foam and spume, sped sheeningly through a wide conduit, and passed in another broad shining curve of water down and out of sight beyond an arched opening in the opposite wall. The passageway opened onto nothingness and the path was carried on a narrow wooden bridge across the pelting water. Steps led to a neat contraption after the fashion of a waterwheel by which water could be lifted from the stream and raised, level by level, until it was carried out of sight into the mouth of a shaft. Buckets hung from the shaft mouth. Here guards cracked their whips and slaves of all kinds turned the great waterwheels, level by level, and lifted the fluid up and into the fortress so that, no doubt, the great men of the Canops might drink and wash and waste the water that had cost so much effort.

The noise blattered unceasingly. Water splashed and hissed. Whips cracked. Men screamed and guards yelled obscene orders to work faster, faster, and smash went the whips, and around and around hauled the slaves, all filthy and naked and hairy, and in fountains of silvery leaping spillings the water lifted high. The name on Kregen for water fitted that scene.

Passing on, with a salute for the Deldar in command, I came into an area of gloom, for the torches guttered low and there were no fireglass panels above, as there had been in the cavern of the waterwheels.

The sight of these hair naked devils writhing and struggling and hauling, the spouts of water slopping everywhere, the insufferable noises, affected me profoundly. Truly, there was a foretaste of the Ice Floes of Sicce, here!

"In the name of Lem! Who are you?"

From a side passage barred by an iron door, now open, a Hikdar stepped out. He carried a shield like my own, except that the fluttrell and the numerals six and five were raised from the surface and colored silver. He glared at me with his hard, mahogany-tough face filled with a surprise that swiftly changed to suspicion and then to certainty as he spoke.

"I know every man of the eighty in the Fifth Pastang! You

are not one of my men—there is no desertion from—by the Great and Bone-Crushing Lem himself! You are Dray Prescot!"

And his thraxter whipped out and his shield came around with a thump and he charged straight for me.

Even as I responded in kind I had to fight the nausea of knowing that these devils of Canops had forced information from my friends; this Hikdar could never otherwise have known my name. He came in very expertly, shouting the while to summon more men. He had to be dealt with quickly. Using a shield like this, with a sword, came strangely at first, but I had not forgotten what I had taught my old vosk-helmets of the warrens. Thraxters clashed against shields, and I bashed him low, against the swell of the lorica over his belly, and then slipped a nasty little thrust in that finished him. The thraxters were suited for this work, being not too long yet long enough to make swordplay of some value, coupled with a shield used as an offensive weapon. The sound of iron nails on the stone blattered echoing along between the walls.

There was just the one way to go and that was the way I took. Around me now barred openings revealed cells. Hairy bewhiskered faces pressed up against the bars and a dolorous chorus of catcalls and shrieks echoed through the dimly lighted way. Many prisoners, there were, and yet they were all probably segregated, there on punishment detail, military prisoners serving sentences. Those I sought would be lower, in the dungeons. A crossbow bolt hissed past and a voice lifted, ringing between the stone walls.

"Do not kill him, nulsh! He is to be taken and questioned."

That, I feel sure, had little bearing on the bolt that bounced off my head. It is doubtful if even the tall bronze helmet would have done much. I felt the blow, saw a blinding stream of sparks flaring across my eyes, and then I fell into darkness.

Unconsciousness could not have lasted long. The blow had been a glancing one and when I opened my eyes I could feel the wet stickiness of blood down my face. Hands were placing a rough bandage around my head, tucking the ends in, most painfully. I tried to kick the offender, but he avoided the blow, and a voice said: "The nul is conscious."

They used the word nul as the Khamorros did, did these Canops, to mean a person who was not one of themselves.

They had stripped off the armor and the white tunic beneath and the short white kiltlike garment that was all they considered a shield-carrying man would need there in the way of defense. I was clad only in the old scarlet breech-clout. They dragged me along by my hair, whereat I turned, sluggishly, I know, and tried to bite the wrists of the hands that dragged me, and was beaten back for my pains.

The broad-flagged stone chamber into which they dragged me was clearly a guardroom. There were seven Canop soldiers and a Hikdar. Also there was a Khamorro. I knew this lithely muscled man must be a khamster from every lineament of him. That he wore a green breechclout meant nothing. Around his head a broad risslaca-leather strap had been cinctured tightly and from it dangled an assortment of objects that, at the time, meant nothing to me. He was obsequious to the soldiers, and ready to do their bidding, and I guessed he stood in their employment as Turko had suggested the Khamorros would be employed—not as slaves but as special and highly prized body servants.

The Hikdar had already sent word of my capture up through the underground ways to the nobles above, and they would soon want me dragged before them, if they did not save the trouble and come down here themselves to witness my punishment. I guessed Hikdar Markman ti Coyton would be in their forefront. I just hoped his guts still hurt.

Unlike the guards of Prince Glycas of Magdag, these Canops had not heard of me. They tied me up with thongs and bundled me into a corner to await the chaining and the questioning when the city commandant and his retinue arrived. So there was time.

The thongs came free with a series of wrist movements and a final bursting surge. I stood up. The soldiers turned, gaping, and I knew they might all die but that the Khamorro, without a weapon in his fist, must be the man I must consider most. So after I kicked the first guard and broke the neck of the second, the thraxter I snatched up and flung took the Khamorro between the ribs. The second thraxter I scooped up did not last much longer, breaking as it wrenched free of the fourth guard. The Hikdar was raving, swirling his sword, urging his men on to attack me and at the same time yelling for them to span a bow and shoot me in the legs. By the time he had sorted out his priorities he had run out of men. The seven of them and the Khamorro lay where they had dropped.

But this Hikdar of Canopdrin was not without courage and he came at me with his thraxter held most neatly—but he fought without a shield, for there had been no time for him to snatch one up from the arms racks along the wall. This was a tremendous disadvantage for him, and he went down, still trying to fight. Now I would have to hurry. No time, therefore, then, to feel sorry for these Canops—vile reavers though they were.

I took two crossbows and two thraxters, the finest I could find. I did not stop for shields or armor but padded out and very quickly ran across a guard party marching back off guard duty. The three soldiers went down with ruthless speed. The dwa-Deldar I showed the point of a thraxter and then jammed it into his throat just enough to draw blood.

"Where are the prisoners, kleesh? The Khamorro, the Rapa, and the two apim girls?"

He told me. I hit him over the head, for that had been our unspoken compact, and ran off down the tunnelway indicated. The dungeon was barred by an iron grille. The guard there was most happy to open it for me. Beyond that lay another grille and this guard—large, surly, and evidently in a foul temper for rating this duty, wanted to contest it with me. I cut him up—I had to—and passed on. Inside the dungeon only my four companions waited to greet me.

They had been stripped stark naked and hung against the wall in chains.

The two girls glared at me with mad eyes, not believing this half-naked apparition with the scarlet breechclout and the red blood splashed all over him could be me, the Dray Prescot they had been trying to cozen.

Rapechak said, "You are welcome, Dray Prescot."

I placed the crossbows and the quivers of bolts down and turned my face up to look at Turko. He looked in bad shape, clearly he had not fully recovered from that experience in the jungle of Faol. He looked at me and then his eyes flicked in a sharp gaze over my head.

"Lahal, Dray Prescot," he said. "Yes, you are most welcome. But you will have need of your weapons, I think."

I turned swiftly.

Ten paces from me stood two Khamorros. Both were large, superbly muscled, fit and tough, and both stood with hands on hips regarding me as they might a plate of palines.

Around their heads both wore wide bands of soft risslaca-leather and again a mixed assortment of objects hung down.

"They are only Khamorros, Turko," I said, prodding. I wanted to get his spirit back.

"The reed-syples," said Turko, in a strangled voice. "The headbands," he added, for my benefit. "These are great khams, both. Without your weapons, Dray Prescot, you are a doomed man."

Perhaps there was no mocking taunt in his voice. Perhaps I read into his words what my own guilty conscience put there. I do not know, but I acted as the most callow and vainglorious onker of a boaster could act.

"Great khams, Turko? I do not believe I need mere steel weapons to deal with them."

And I pitched the two swords onto the stone floor, where they rang like tocsin bells, and swung to face and two Khamorros, my hands empty.

Chapter Twenty

The Hai Hikai
creates a shield

"You great nurdling fool!"

Turko's anguished cry racked up from the foundations of his being. Now he gave himself up for lost.

Rapechak the Rapa shouted: "Now by Rhapaporgolam the Reaver of Souls! You are a dead man, Dray Prescot!"

Saenda screamed almost incoherently: "You horrible onker, Dray! I'll never forgive you for this!"

And Quaesa simply burst into a long howling shriek.

The two Khamorros stared as though they could not believe their eyes. One of them, the slightly smaller of the two, even went through a quick routine of flexing his muscles and rippling his strength at me. He looked up at the naked bodies of the girls and, again letting that stupid bravado overwhelm me, I clapped my hands.

"Excellent, nulsh," I said. "A great performance. I hope you do as well when your head rolls into the north corner and your body rolls into the south."

Oh, yes. It shames me now when I look back at that long-gone day, and seeing the whole scene as though brightly lit upon a stage, recognize my own youthful headstrong passions and my own stupidity! I was a bit of a maniac in my younger days, and here I'd been boasting to myself that I had been conquering that hasty arrogance of mine, that harsh intolerance, that desperate desire to kick and smash anyone and anything that smacked of authority and sadism and attempts to put me down. I had bowed the knee and kowtowed and done the full-incline—and here it had all ended with as foolhardy an act of onkerishness as any two worlds witnessed.

For these were great khams. They had reached enormously elevated heights in the heirarchy of the Khamorros, their khams sky-high. They were of a different syple from Turko—had

they been of his own syple they might have rescued him—
and they were as contemptuous of him as of me.

They thought to make of it a sport, and, not without a
certain charming politeness, debated one with the other who
should have first crack at me. Remembering the sage counsel
of old Zinki during those painful sessions of combat on the
island of Zy in the Eye of the World, I was content to let
them come to me.

The shorter, the one who had gone through the quick
exercise drill, stepped forward. He had yielded because he
was that much fractionally the lesser of the two, as he admitted. "I am Boro, and I am a great kham." He went on
then to describe himself and his renown, his attainments and
his exploits. At each word poor Turko moaned, and I heard
him say: "By the Muscle! You have picked the wrong men to
demonstrate to me, Dray! They are masters! Great khams!"

When this Boro had finished he stood waiting.

So, to humor him, and because if I did not end this farce
soon guards with real weapons would burst in, I said, "I am
Dray Prescot, Krozair of Zy."

If he didn't understand, as I didn't understand all his
titles and accomplishments, that was his loss.

Then, very swift and deadly, he was upon me.

I did what I had planned to do . . . almost . . .

He was quick, and he was strong and he was very, very
good. I felt his blows. I could feel it when he hit me. I slid
his rush, for, of course, it was no blind-chunkrah rush, and
he laid a hand on my arm and I had to do a quick double-
twist and near break his fingers before he would let go. He
stepped back and a great pleased smile lit his face.

"So you know the arts, Dray Prescot! I shall enjoy this!"

This time I managed to deflect his attack, and for a short
space we twisted, body to body, doing all the things I had no
desire to do. Everything he did I matched, but I was in
defense all the time except for a single opportunity and that
ended with Boro going up in the air and landing on his
shoulder blades. He roared as I jumped on him, and rolled
away, so that I missed and gouged the stone floor instead.
Like a leem he was on his feet, and now his face was dark
and congested with anger, which proved that his kham was
a trifle shaky.

"I shall tear your limbs off and—" he started.

"Save it, Boro the Boaster! There's no time!"

We set to again, and again he used all his skill and avoided the grips and blows that would have flattened a lesser man. I could feel my anger at his strong obstinacy boiling up and I had to keep it down. I'd gone into this childish exhibition and now I had to pay the reckoning.

He circled, came in from the side, and I bent and took him and he took me. We rolled on the floor and he tried to break my arm, as he had threatened, and I cross-checked him so that he cried out, shocked at the sudden pain, and managed to break and leap clear. My parting blow hissed past his ear.

His comrade, the bigger Khamorro, said, "It seems, Boro, that he bests you." At which Boro roared his anger. "I am Morgo. I am a greater kham than Boro. You will not escape so easily from me."

I circled them both, warily, for they were both after me now. I shouted up to Turko, high: "Are all these Khamorros such braggart boasters and such spineless fighters?"

Turko said something, I know not what, and Boro and Morgo charged. I backed swiftly and in a succession of flurries of dodges and weavings, of arm blocks and of kicks, I won free. This could not be allowed to go on. The next time I would have to do something drastic. Old Zinki had laughed, one time, telling us of what Pur Zenkiren had done to a couple of Magdaggian overlords. I had a great affection for the austere Pur Zenkiren, who was Archbold-Elect. If I could pay him the compliment of imitating him, I would do so.

Boro and Morgo split me between them and came in from both sides. I backed again, circling, and my foot hit against a sword where I had tossed it down so contemptuously.

"Pick up your sword, Dray! For the sake of the Muscle, man! Use the weapon you understand! They have only been playing with you!"

If that was true, of course, life would become exceedingly complicated and remarkably interesting in the next mur.

Deliberately, I kicked the sword aside.

Turko moaned.

The two Khamorros flexed their muscles. The sweat stood out on their skins like liquid gold. Working as a team they rushed me again and in a flurry of chops and grips that failed and hooks that barely missed, Boro wrenched away the bandage around my head so that blood flowed down over my face and left eye. I blinked and cursed.

"By the Black Chunkrah! You fight foul!"

They did not answer; they were both panting, their magnificent chests heaving and glistening with sweat.

This time, I saw, they meant to finish it. Boro came in a little ahead of Morgo, and he designed, I saw instantly, to feint an attack and then roll under me so that I would fall into the arms of Morgo. When Boro rushed I sidestepped. He came with me and our forearms smashed together and I stepped back.

For an instant he had an opportunity, for the distance I had gone seemed to him to be overlarge, giving him the chance of taking two skipping steps and putting in the jagger. This is that blow delivered by the feet with the body wholly off the ground. He chose the double jagger, with both feet. He did it superbly well, and for any ordinary wrestler it would have been the end, for those iron-hard soles of his would have crushed into the chest and knocked all the wind out and smashed the fellow over, to be gripped and thrust facedown into the dirt, finished, if his ribs weren't all cracked to Kingdom Come.

Turko's scream ripped into the stink of the dungeon.

Morgo's bellow of "Hai Hikai!" passed unheeded.

Everything happened in a fluidity of motion beautiful to behold, making me wish I'd been there when Pur Zenkiren did this to those overlords of Magdag. I took Boro's ankles in both fists and I leaned back, as a hammer-thrower leans in the circle, and spun. He carried all that forward momentum into a sideways rotation, with my body leaning back, muscles ridged, acting as the hub. Around me he spun, parallel to the ground. I lifted a little higher as his head flew around and aimed him, and, as though wielding a great Krozair longsword, I laid his head smack alongside Morgo's head.

I let go.

Both Khamorros collapsed. Blood and brains gushed from their nostrils and their ears.

"By the Muscle!" I heard Turko whisper.

Quaesa wouldn't stop screaming. Saenda had done things she afterward would never remember. Rapechak said, "I believe the correct term is Hai Hikai, Dray Prescot! Hai Hikai!"

He was right. The unarmed combat masters, like the Khamorros, like old Zinki, do not used the swordsman's great Hai Jikai—instead, they say: "Hai Hikai."

Turko the Khamorro looked at me. His face held a frozen look of horror. Then he spoke, in a husky whisper.

"Hai Hikai, Dray Prescot! Hai Hikai!"

Freeing the four prisoners was simple enough, for the keys had been in the keeping of Morgo the Khamorro, who was now no doubt practicing his art somewhere under the alert eye of Morro the Muscle himself. They were stiff and sore and the two girls collapsed, moaning, for Quaesa had stopped screaming the instant she felt my hands on her, unlocking the chains. Turko picked up the blood-soaked bandage and rewound it around my head. He looked at it, his dark eyes filled with a pain he did not believe.

"As a reed-syple, Dray Prescot, that bloody bandage is extraordinarily fitting."

As you know I make it a rule never to apologize; I would have apologized to Turko, then, for acting in such a stupid way, when Rapechak, picking up a crossbow and quiver of bolts, said with an evil chuckle: "I think we may fight our way out now, Dray Prescot."

I handed him one of the swords. I made up my mind. I said, "Turko, you called me Dray, back there. I would—like—it if you and Rapechak dropped the Prescot."

This was no trifle.

We said no more, but I know Rapechak, the Rapa, at least, was pleased. At the iron grilles we took clothes from the guards and sketchily gave the girls a breechclout each and a few rags for the men. Turko stopped. He looked down at the guard's thraxter, still in his fist. The shield lay to one side. Turko's face was completely expressionless.

I watched him. He bent and picked up the sword. He held it for a space, the guard's open hand like some mute testament below. Then he tossed the sword down. I started to turn away and then halted. Turko picked up the shield. He hefted it, looked at the straps inside, turned it around, slid it up his left arm, swung it about. Then, turning to face me, holding the shield up, he said, "I am ready to follow you, Dray."

"Good, Turko. We march now to freedom."

But we both knew we meant much more than merely escaping from this fortress-prison of Mungul Sidrath.

With both crossbows spanned and ready, with Turko at my back with his shield, and the girls following on, we padded on away from the dungeon and on toward the cavern of the waters.

Halfway across the bridge I halted. In the noise and confusion of water spouting, great wheels creaking, and slaves screaming as whips whistled down, we could not fail to attract attention. But the danger lay ahead. On the far side of the bridge a body of men appeared and instantly they were revealed as the nobles and officers come down to question their prisoners, and, perhaps, to have a little sport with them.

In the forefront, as I had cynically expected, stood Hikdar Markman ti Coyton.

He screamed and pointed and dragged out his sword, his words unheard in the din of rushing water, creaking wood, and other screams so much more brutally dragged forth.

At Markman's side stood a man who blazed with the stiff regalia of pride and authority. This Canop had to be the commandant of Yaman. For good measure I put the first shaft into him. I saw his mouth open as he fell, but did not hear his dying scream. Rapechak let fly and slew a Chuktar directly to Markman's rear. Markman turned and tried to push back through the officers. Being officers and having come on a sporting occasion they had no bowmen handy, but very quickly bowmen could be deployed and then we'd be skewered, there on the open bridge with the roaring water beneath.

I put my face close to Turko's ear.

"Over with you, Turko! And breathe deeply!"

I said the same to Rapechak.

They both wanted to argue and Rapechak, bending his great beaked face close to mine, barely avoided the quarrel that sizzled past to thunk into the wooden railing in a showering of yellow chips. They were arguing about the girls. There was no time to reload. Turko moved forward, and in a twinkling crossbow bolts stood in his shield like angry bristles. He screened us. I was not sure of the Rapa's capabilities as a swimmer, and Turko was in no real condition to look after anyone but himself.

I pushed them both over and grabbed the girls about their waists and leaped. Half a dozen crossbow bolts ripped the wood of the bridge as we hurtled down. We hit the water in a fountain that vanished almost instantly in that smooth, heavy flow and the current swept us frighteningly fast down and into the arched opening leading onto darkness.

Sword and crossbow had gone and I now had armfuls only of wet and terrified girls. I lunged up, my head above the surface, and dragged them up. There was no sign of the others. "Breathe!" I yelled, and then took a frantic quick breath, as deeply as I could in the time left, and then we were over and falling in the midst of the cascade, with only darkness, and water, and noise all about us.

Accounted a superb swimmer and able to dive for long periods I may be, but that gulp of air had not been enough. I felt the pains in my chest, the flecks of fire before my eyes that were wide open and staring blindly into the roaring darkness. On and on we were tumbled, turning and twisting like chips in a drainage ditch. I felt then that for a surety I was done for. This was the end. This was where they tossed the broken and bleeding corpses of the dead slaves after they had worked until they died, this was where they disposed of the prisoners they had questioned beyond the limits of toler- ance. Down and down we went and on and on and then I knew I had finished and there was nothing else to do but end this agonizing pain and open my mouth.

But, being Dray Prescot, a stupid onker, I kept my mouth shut and I fought the pain and we swirled along like refuse. I felt a sudden rising shock as lights stung my dazzled eyes, and cool night air laved my face and we were afloat on the surface of the River Magan.

Turko waved an arm and yelled. I did not see Rapechak.

We swam into the bank and on the oozing mud a severe session of arm-pumping and kissing brought the girls around. They were shattered by their experiences and unable fully to comprehend that we had escaped. I felt that we would have little time. Finding a boat was easy enough and I selected a craft typical of river work, with sharply flared bows and a broad beam, shallow-drafted and with a sail and awning. At the oars—at the oars! How eerie and strange a feeling that was to be sure!—we pulled around in circles, calling as loudly as we dared for Rapechak. But we did not find the Rapa. I would not think of that. At last, and with regret, I set the bows downriver and pulled steadily away in the dying light of the Maiden with the Many Smiles.

By dawn we were well down the river. We had a few scraps of clothing, no weapons, and no money. But we had our lives.

"I can sail this boat well enough," I said. Hell! If I, Dray Prescot, couldn't sail a boat the end of two worlds was in sight! I felt relieved, light-headed, and yet let-down. This was the end of this adventure, for there was food and wine in the boat and fishing lines and bait, with a breaker of water, and so all this evidence pointed to a fishing party this day. We might be pursued. If the boat had belonged to a

Migla, I did not think the halfling would report its loss to the Canoptic authorities.

Turko said, "The girls ought to know this country, Dray. If we can sail out of the country of Migla we can find friends. If what Saenda says is true . . . and what Quaesa boasts of is so."

The girls shivered in the dawn as the mists rose from the sluggish river and a little breeze got up. We could set some canvas very shortly, for the wind blew fair.

"My father—" began Saenda. She swallowed. "If we could reach Cnarveyl, on the coast to the north, or Tyriadrin, the country to the south, we would find agencies of my father's. Or we might try one of the islands—but they are infested with renders."

"Take your pick," I said with a cheerful note in my voice. "The wind is fair for either."

Quaesa spoke up then. Both girls had drunk a little wine and pulled their fingers through their hair—a sovereign remedy, that, for miserable feelings—and they fell to arguing which country would be the better, having a mind to their father's vast interests and agencies. Turko looked at me and raised his eyebrows, and smiled.

Turko, who had taken half a dozen crossbow bolts into and through the shield, arguing with me there on the bridge, before I pushed him over. I would not think of Rapechak. He must have swum clear and been taken in a different direction by the sluggish current. He had to.

Well, whether it was to Cnarveyl to the north or Tyriadrin to the south, we would equip ourselves with clothes and money and the girls would go home aboard one of their father's ships or vollers, and I—I would go home, too, to Valka. And Turko would go with me. He wanted that, I knew. And, now, I wanted him with me. He did not know what a Krozair of Zy was, but he had seen what their unarmed combat techniques could do, and he was prepared to grant me all the khams he cared to.

The banks lightened under the suns and I considered. They were well wooded, with many muddy creeks, and again I cocked my eyes at Zim and Genodras just glowing through the mists, turning them into a chiaroscuro of emerald and ruby, and I considered, and then turned the boat toward the opposite bank.

"We lie up for the day," I said. No one thought to argue with me or question the decision.

That day, hidden beneath overhanging missals, we saw the
boats passing down the river, long lean craft propelled by
a single bank of oars, twenty to a bank, and I could guess
the Miglas were rowing there, under the lash of the Canops.

From time to time fluttrell patrols passed overhead, swinging in their ordered skeins across the pale sky. Vollers, too,
searched for us. They could not see us through the screen
of leaves, the oared boats did not push far enough in up the
creek, and the land patrols riding totrixes or zorcas could
not approach the banks here by reason of the mudflats, which
were very treacherous. So we waited the day out, eating and
drinking frugally, and the girls calmed down completely and
fell to arguing over me, and trying their wiles on me, whereat
Turko harrumphed and took himself off.

Just before I was ready to push off I, too, went up the
bank. I stared up at the sky and thought that very soon I
would see my Delia again, my Delia of the Blue Mountains,
my Delia of Delphond! And, too, I would hold in my arms
those two tiny morsels of humanity we had called Drak and
Lela. Oh, yes, I yearned to return home. I had done what
the Star Lords commanded. No blue radiance had dropped
about me. No hideous Scorpion had lowered on me to transit
me back to the Earth of my birth four hundred light-years
away, the planet that, I admitted with joy, I could no longer
call home.

In the last of the light, in that streaming mingled radiance
of the Suns of Scorpio, I turned to go down to the boat and
push out into midstream and so ghost down to the mouth and
sail away from this miserable land of Migla.

I turned, one foot was in the air—and a beat of wings
above my head, a flash of scarlet and gold, and a hated voice
screeched down on me from above.

I looked up.

The Gdoinye circled there, low, terrible of form, glorious
and shining and altogether hateful.

"A fool, Dray Prescot! Nothing less!"

"Go away!" I shouted up. My passion broke out then in
foul words. I shook my fist, for I had no other weapons of
steel now, and yet I had proved that a man's hands are more
terrible than the sword.

"You think you obey the Star Lords? You who do not
understand a tenth, no, a millionth part of their purpose? You
are an onker, Dray Prescot! Why did you bring the Mighty

Mog here to her home in Migla which is cursed by the Canops?"

When I heard him refer to the Migla witch, old Mog, as Mog the Mighty, I knew. I knew! The agony of it struck in shrewdly and almost I fell to my knees and begged the Gdoinye to let me be. But I knew the penalty of refusal. I knew I must do what the Star Lords commanded, or I would be banished to Earth four hundred light-years away, and might languish there for years as my twins, my Drak and my Lela, grew up into wonderful children, and my Delia pined for me as I hungered for her.

"What is it the Star Lords command, bird of ill omen?"

"That is better, Dray Prescot! You should know you have not completed your task. Not until the land of Migla is cleansed of the Canops and Migshaanu is returned to her rightful place—for a time only!—will your work be done."

"I am almost naked, I have no weapons, no money, two girls depend on me, the whole country is up in arms against me. You are hard taskmasters—"

"You have been naked before, Dray Prescot, and weaponless. You will do this thing."

With a loud and harshly triumphant squawk, a cry of triumphant rage, the raptor winged away into the fading suns-glow. Zim and Genodras, which hereabouts I should call with all hatred Far and Havil, sank in a smoldering angry blaze of jade and ruby, firing bloodily into a savage crimson glow dropping down over the horizon. Darkness closed over the land of Migla upon the continent of Havilfar on Kregen.

Stunned at the enormity of the sentence passed upon me I went down to the boat.

In the darkness, before any of the seven moons of Kregen rose, I pushed off and in silence took the looms of the oars into my hands.

What I must do I must do.

Oh, my little Drak, my little Lela!

And—my Delia, my Delia of Delphond—when would I see her again and hold her dear form in my arms?